PRAISE FOR
THE THIRTEENTH CHANCE

"With fast-pitched dialogue and romantic chemistry worthy of a World Series pennant, *The Thirteenth Chance* is yet another home run in Amy Matayo's winning collection of stories."

—Nicole Deese, author of *A Season to Love*,
A Cliché Christmas, and the Letting Go series

"Amy Matayo knocks it out of the park with this sweet, opposites-attract romance. You'll be cheering for Olivia and Will with every page."

—Jenny B. Jones, award-winning author of *I'll Be Yours* and
Can't Let You Go

THE
Thirteenth
CHANCE

ALSO BY AMY MATAYO

THE
Thirteenth
CHANCE

AMY MATAYO

Waterfall
PRESS

This is a work of fiction. Names, characters, organizations, places, events, and incidents are either products of the author's imagination or are used fictitiously.

Published by Waterfall Press, Grand Haven, MI
www.brilliancepublishing.com

Amazon, the Amazon logo, and Waterfall Press are trademarks of Amazon.com, Inc., or its affiliates.

ISBN-13: 9781503935778
ISBN-10: 1503935779

Cover design by Jason Blackburn

Printed in the United States of America

*This book is dedicated to anyone afraid of trying
something different.
Go ahead and try it. Different is good. It might lead
you to your calling. It might lead you to discovering
your passion.
It might even lead you to write a book about baseball.
#batterup*

Chapter 1

Olivia

I am a fourth-grade teacher, but on days like today I'm not entirely sure why. I remember having a dream about being a teacher when I was a small girl—maybe eight, maybe nine—but I also remember dreaming of being a ballerina, so I'm not sure why this particular dream stuck. I'm five feet nine and fairly thin, so being a dancer wouldn't have been entirely out of the realm of possibility.

I look at my hands. As usual, they're sticky, some kind of brown ick on my fingertips. There are a lot of germs involved in being a teacher. For the dozenth time today, I walk to the sink to wash off a few million and imagine them screaming in fear as they slide down the drain.

Morbid maybe, but they're germs. They benefit nothing, and no one likes them anyway.

The bell rang an hour ago, and since then I've been wiping down desks, straightening them into the standard ninety-degree angles that some children refuse to keep in place because of kicking and fidgeting and general restlessness that sometimes send me over the edge. Today one child was so rambunctious that I actually bit a fingernail down to the skin. I never bite my fingernails; manicures are a must every Thursday afternoon. It's been on my regular schedule for years: manicure at four o'clock, right after driving through Sonic for lime-infused water and right before picking up Taco Hut enchiladas for dinner. Three: one bean, one chicken, one cheese. The chicken is topped with white sauce; the other two with red because I like a little spice and adventure in my life, and I've found this to be the perfect way to get them.

I look around the room and sigh.

I've heard a dancer's life is rigid and structured. I would have fit right in.

"You're still here? I thought you'd be long gone by now." My friend Kelly pokes her head into my classroom.

Kelly is perfect in a way that makes most women jealous. With her big brown eyes and wide smile, she's quietly confident, like Anne Hathaway in that office movie with Robert De Niro, the one where she was a working mom with a cheater husband and a killer wardrobe. Except Kelly isn't a mom. Or a wife. But her wardrobe rocks, which makes me hate her. A worn Prada bag hangs from her shoulder, and cute sunglasses are perched on top of her short brown hair. She teaches art in the classroom next door, the reason for the persistent smear of paint that is usually somewhere above her neckline. There's a one-inch pink stripe on the right side of her jaw as we speak. One might think it a scratch if one—meaning me and all the other teachers who work here—didn't know better. On Kelly, it somehow adds to her glamour. Now I want to stab her.

"No, I'm still here. I will forever be here with the mess these kids make. I mean, look at this room." I sigh and run a hand across my forehead, not missing the way Kelly looks around with a slight frown on her face. I know what she's going to say even before she opens her mouth.

"There's no mess in here at all, Olivia. My class could eat dinner off your floor, the place is so spotless."

Everyone—and I mean everyone—says this.

I glance around and pretend to agree with her. But I know better. My mother would run a white glove over this room and demand I start over.

"I guess you're right. A few more minutes and I'll leave."

I'll be here at least another hour. Two, more likely.

"Okay, as long as you promise to get out of here and enjoy your Friday night. You need to have a little fun, let your hair down a little."

Without thinking, I let my hand find the nape of my neck . . . the spot where the black elastic holds my blonde hair in place in a perfectly aligned ponytail. "I will, I promise. Maybe I'll even—"

"Why don't you come out with me? A few of us are going out for drinks later tonight. Around nine thirty? Want to join us? It will be fun."

By a few of us, she means fellow teachers. I know this because Kelly asks me every weekend. I want to say that I'm planning to watch a movie on Netflix right after I treat myself to a nice dinner of grilled vegetables, steak, and potatoes. I bought the groceries yesterday, and I've been looking forward to the meal all day. But that sounds lame, and I know what they think of me. Olivia Pratt: twenty-nine, a bit neurotic, can't get a date, and has a cat for a best friend. I rush for a better-sounding explanation. Normally I have one ready, but I've run out of nice excuses. My mind goes blank for a second, and before I know it, I say an incredibly stupid thing.

"I can't. I have a date."

I have a date?

"You have a date?"

Wait. Is it really that unbelievable?

I swallow around the lie and repeat it. "Yes, I have a date. A guy I met at . . . the gym. He asked me out over the ten-pound free weights, and I said yes. We're going to a movie."

Two things about this: One, I don't do free weights. Too many chances to drop one on my foot and break a bone—been there, done that, no thanks. So I stick with the treadmill for half an hour and then move on to the bench press; it's much safer as long as you remember to push straight up. Pressing backward—even slightly—nearly doubles your chance of a strained neck muscle, and no one wants to deal with that.

And two, with the movie mention I've just eliminated any chance of Kelly running into me later and discovering I'm there by myself. She's the only person I've ever met who hates movie theaters. I mean, I understand the fear of germs touching your backside from those nasty, unsanitary seats, but what about the popcorn? I do not understand the meaning behind a life without regular movie-theater popcorn, extra butter, and nacho-flavored salt. It's one of my greatest pleasures . . . after spicy red sauce.

Not that I eat only junk food. During the week it's a regular diet of detox tea, multivitamins, kale, spinach, beets, and the occasional onion—a woman can't go too crazy. But I've found that if you follow a strict eating plan eighty percent of the time, letting a bit loose during the other twenty can't hurt too much. Not if you're diligent, like me.

Again, why am I not a ballerina? Other than the vomiting on demand (which I've heard is definitely a way of life), I'm pretty sure I could have had that career in the bag.

I realize this makes no sense, but it's the way my mind works. It's also the bed I've made. Now I need to lie down, roll over, and drool on a pillow.

Kelly just looks at me for a second, an odd mix of emotion on her face like she can't decide whether to congratulate me or demand I fess up to my obvious untruth. Finally, and much to my relief, she grins.

"Well, look at you. Miss 'Happily Single' is finally coming out of her shell. I'd really like to meet the guy sometime. I'd venture to guess we all would."

Of this, I have no doubt. For all intents and purposes, I am very happily single. This fact drives my coworkers insane with an incessant desire to match make me. Now, with my convenient little white lie, I've eliminated the need. For now. If the established pattern stays in effect, the matchmaking should resume by next Friday. Maybe even Wednesday, because everyone needs something to escape the midweek slump. My fellow teachers are no exception.

"Let me see how it goes first. Who knows? Maybe someday soon you'll all be helping me plan a wedding." I add a tiny smile for effect.

But the lies. They keep piling up. Between them and the bitten fingernail, I barely recognize myself today.

Kelly slips on her sunglasses and pats the doorway. "Maybe so. You'll be the most beautiful bride ever, that's for sure. And I call dibs on maid of honor, just so you know. See you Monday." She waves two fingers at me and walks out. After I hear the sound of the door closing, I sit down in a student's chair and let my head fall to the table, counting on the coolness of the laminate to calm my nerves a bit.

A date?

Maid of honor?

If I keep this up, next she'll ask to be godmother.

I allow another minute of feeling sorry for myself, and then I stand up. Push in the chair. Align it with the permanent circle imprints in the carpet. Stand back and survey the room with a sigh. And do a little pirouette because no one's here to watch me.

I'm midspin when I spot Avery's backpack still hanging on the hook by the door.

My heart sinks. He forgot it again. I walk over and unzip it, peering at the contents. A box of granola bars, two apples, a package of pretzel twists, and a can of Coke—his favorite. I have a soft spot for that kid, the one who is always overlooked when group projects are assigned and classroom partners are chosen. He's also very poor and somewhat malnourished. At nine, he has the body of a six-year-old. If the school knew I slipped food inside his backpack to tide him over through the weekend, I would probably get fired. But rules like that are stupid, and I don't let them stop me. Human compassion is worth more than a job, especially when a child is involved.

There's nothing worse than hurt and neglect, especially when all you really want is for someone to care, even for a moment.

Will

We're losing, and it's a trend I'm getting more than a little sick of. In the six weeks that I've been with the Rangers, we've had one long winning streak, followed by a spotty three weeks of the weirdest combination of wins and losses—three straight wins followed by two losses, then repeat four times in that exact order, the worst of which were on my watch—and now it's been six straight losses, heading for a seventh. Everyone knows I'm treading in the magic-number zone. One more, two more, three more losses and someone goes down, and by down I mean back to Triple-A. In this particular case, that someone will be me. Me. Will freaking Vandergriff. And I'm sorry, but my skill level surpassed Triple-A a long time ago, even if none of these stupid southern fans think so.

Not that it matters. If there's any finger-pointing going on right now, all the middle ones in the stands would point directly toward me—the Yankee trade who's as foreign as he is unwelcome, even now. I hear the jeers. I hear the taunts.

I'm sucking up this game just like the last five I've played.

This has to stop, and it needs to stop today.

With a growing knot in my gut, I have a feeling it just did.

My coach steps onto the field, and everything inside me begins to itch. My throat. My chest. My brain. I've only been pulled once since I was traded to the Rangers, and that was during my last game. I'm heading toward number two, and no one gets yanked two games in a row unless everyone has had enough. Judging by the look on his face, the skipper finally has.

He stops and meets me eye to eye. "You're out. Ricky is taking your place."

A protest is on its way up, but I swallow it down. I know better than to be that stupid. I grind my back teeth together and look toward the stands. Ricky. I could say so much about him—he's new to the game, he doesn't have as much experience as me, he's green. But he's a teammate, not an enemy. If anyone's my enemy, it's me. My own worst one. Besides, I'm the one who just overthrew to third and caused the latest home run. I'm the one who failed to prevent a steal to second in the last inning, which also resulted in a score. This game was mine at the beginning of the night. Since then, I've wrapped it up in a freaking bow and handed it to the Dodgers.

The Dodgers. They've sucked for years, and somehow I'm single-handedly making them look good.

"Yes, sir. I'll do better in the next game." But I can't guarantee that, and we both know it. We're losing by five. The entire debacle is shameful and currently being broadcast on ESPN. I can almost hear the announcers: *Vandergriff yanked again? Think his days in the major leagues are numbered?*

"You can try again next time," my manager says. "But something's got to change. Figure out the problem and fix it."

I nod and stomp off toward my teammates as the crowd cheers and whistles in a unified cry that practically calls for my televised hanging. My hat comes off before I make it to the steps, and once inside I fling it toward the wall. It slams against wood and slides to the pavement. No one around me even flinches. The dugout is dead silent when I take the walk of shame down into it. The tension is palpable; my teammates won't even look at me. I thrust a paper cup under the Gatorade cooler and take a long drink, then wipe my mouth with the back of my hand and turn to face the game. The view from here is a lot more bitter than it is sweet.

By this time tomorrow, I might be on a bus headed straight back to the minor leagues.

Chapter 2

Olivia

No one saw me at Avery's house, including Avery himself—exactly the way I hoped it would be. They've spotted me once before, his brothers. What ensued was an endless round of *Who are you?* and *What do you want with our little brother?* that resulted in both older boys opening his backpack and emptying it of the apples, crackers, and miniature boxes of Cheerios that I had carefully tucked inside. They opened the cereal right in front of me and ate it by the fistful while I stood by and tried really hard to keep from yelling at them. It isn't that I have anything against those boys and their obvious shared hunger; it's that I know they're old enough to hold jobs, and I've seen the way Avery talks about them. With fear. With caution. Definitely like he has something to be afraid of. Not saying his brothers are the cause—more than likely it's their alcoholic father and strung-out mother, neither of whom I've ever met and, honestly, I have no concrete proof that they drink or use drugs. But I've heard rumors and, statistically speaking, it's a strong possibility.

Someone once spread a rumor that I'm a germophobic freak, something I cried about for exactly a day and a half. Misery loves company. Maybe I need to remember that when passing off secondhand information as fact, even in my own mind.

Thankfully, this time no one witnessed me sliding his pack inside the secret spot under his front porch, the one that he told me about earlier this year and that I know he'll check after the sun goes down. A few seconds later I was back in my car, pulling away from my spot down the road.

Now that I'm home, I've never been happier to see a weekend in my life. Especially one as beautiful as this one. With the car door propped open, I reach for my phone and snap a picture of the cloudless sky. I like to remember things, and who knows when a day will be this clear again.

Tossing the phone in my purse, I grab the bag of groceries that I just picked up at Walmart and climb out of the car. When I close the door with my hip, I see them—spots. Spots on the hood and back door, likely caused by the obnoxious sweet gum tree over my parking space at the edge of the school parking lot. I usually don't use it, preferring to park farther back from other vehicles and definitely away from trees.

And now my car is covered in spots, and there's only one way to remedy it.

After setting my bag on the ground, I open the door again and reach for the tube of Armor All wipes, then yank one out and get to work. I'm not sure this brand works any better than Lysol, but I've bought into the commercials like everyone else in America. Besides, this car is my baby, the first major purchase I made after becoming a teacher, and I would hate to see the paint chip or even dull. Dulled paint is as much an eyesore as spots are.

I've owned the car for five years now, but I've kept the miles down and the condition up. The white Camry is as practical as it is useful, although a far cry from the red Mustang I had been eyeing for a few months. Red is sporty and fun and what I'd dreamed of since earning my license at seventeen, but red is expensive to insure. It's also a target among the law enforcement crowd—namely the police. And though I would never dream of speeding on either back roads or highways, I didn't want to chance anything and felt an all-too-familiar need to blend in.

Let your brother have his moment, Olivia.

Fade into the background, that's my life's philosophy. It always has been. At least since I was seven and my mother shut down any dreams I'd had to dance professionally. My dance lessons didn't align with his baseball practice, and something had to give.

Anyway, I went with the white car and I've never been sorry.

I'm scrubbing away the last spot when something catches the corner of my eye. Looking up, I feel my eyes go wide at the same time my heart stops. The sun is shining, and the spots are almost gone, but nothing is right with this picture because Perry is walking toward me, his pudgy little legs barely carrying him across the parking lot.

With a strangled cry, I scoop him up and pull him to my chest, holding him close to assuage my own fear more than his. I count to twelve. I always count to twelve. As slowly as I can. It doesn't matter that he's happy and cooing and completely unafraid. Or that he appeared so confident in his joyful desire to get to me.

What matters is how he got outside. I look up and see the screen sitting ajar and torn against the living room window that I forgot to close this morning. Lowering myself to the pavement, I press Perry against me and try not to faint from the fear at all the ways my baby could have been hurt.

Will

"We've still got that offer from Wilson Sporting Goods that you need to consider."

"Okay."

"And then there's the matter with the Children's Miracle League . . ."

"Yeah, yeah, I remember that."

"And then I need you to—"

"Okay, that's fine. Just let me know your thoughts."

"Will, are you even listening to me?"

"Of course I am." But I'm not. I'm busy fishing for loose change in my top dresser drawer because I knocked a big pile of it in here and I can't live with pennies and nickels floating around inside my socks. That would be uncomfortable in a game. There's also a lot of money in quarters, and I need them for the toll roads on the way to the stadium. Forever creating chores for myself, that's what I live for.

"You're not listening," Jerry says. "Call me back when you have time to—"

"Okay, I will." My voice sounds like it's inside a canyon, hollow and throaty and slightly whiny, but I can't muster the energy to care. I'm losing everything lately. First the game, now the money, pretty soon my mind. I latch onto a penny and toss it on the dresser. It spins three times before falling on its side. Pennies are worthless. Why were they created, anyway?

"Wait, while I have you on for one more second let me—"

I pretend not to hear Jerry's voice on the other end of the line, press the off button, then toss my phone on the bed. I love my agent, but I already agreed to call him back and he's long-winded and wound up tight. A call with him usually lasts upward of two hours, and I don't have time for that. The guy needs to get off the caffeine or the whiskey or the Prozac or whatever it is that has him going ninety to nothing and then—and *only* then—we'll talk. Unless he has good news. Like I've just been offered a five-year, fifteen-million-dollar contract to go back to the Yankees. Right now I would give anything to move back to New York. The atmosphere is more my style and—funnily enough—the people are friendlier.

Southern hospitality. What a joke.

If that happens, then Jerry can get hyped up on whatever vice he chooses, even lie there passed out with a contract curled up in his fist, for all I care. But never mind my agent's addictions. I have to be at the field in forty-five minutes. Before that I have a shower to take, bags of ice to buy for tonight's party, and an obscene amount of takeout to order. I should have done that last one yesterday, but my mind was on the game and sleeping—pretty much all I have room for lately. Not to complain. I don't believe in complaining.

For the love of God, my wallet just fell behind the dresser. If the day could end now, everyone around me might be better off. I get down on my knees, fish the thing out, and toss it on the bed. Reaching into my top dresser drawer, I pull out my deodorant and a clean pair of underwear. Everything about this day sucks, including this underwear. My favorite pair is still lying unwashed on the laundry room floor, which means we'll probably lose again.

I'm passing by my bedroom window when I see her. The very attractive but odd chick from the apartment next door.

She's in the parking lot, crouching next to her car with what looks like a Handi Wipe in one hand and her purse in the other. She's facing away from me as she scrubs back and forth, examines a spot, repeats the process all over again, and then duckwalks on her heels a couple of feet in the direction of the bumper. The car shines as though it's been through a wash more than once today, but she keeps going until she's circled the entire Camry. Then, just when I think she's finished acting nuts, a ball of white fur waddles up next to the back right tire.

For one second she freezes—I can see her eyes widen from here, that's how frightened she is. She looks at the animal, then toward the apartment building, lips moving at a frantic pace. At first I think she has a phobia of cats—maybe she was attacked by one as a child?—but then she lunges for the cat and just stands there with the poor thing squeezed to her chest. I swear her lips are moving; is she counting? She sits down on the pavement for a long moment, then stands and darts for her car in one swift motion. Settling the animal under an arm, she reaches inside her glove box and pulls out something that looks . . . that looks like . . . *oh you've got to be kidding me.*

It's a leash. She pulls out a leash and wrangles the cat. *Her* cat, clearly. She works a collar and leash around the poor animal's neck while it wiggles and fights in her arms. I can hear it wail from here, and I swear a three-inch scratch just materialized on the lady's wrist, blood scattering in tiny, veinlike streaks across her skin. But if it's there she doesn't notice. She just continues to play tug-of-war with the cat and collar, until finally, finally she sets the thing down. The Persian shakes, a full-body shiver that starts at the head and reverberates down its back end with a flick of its tail. The thing is mad, but when I see her point an index finger and shake it at the animal, it practically sighs. Backbone falls, head droops, tail comes down.

Mad, sure. Mad and apparently resigned to this type of insane treatment.

They take off walking, the woman pulling and the white mass of fur dragging behind her like a reluctant snowball that just doesn't feel like coming apart all over the pavement. I would think about rescuing the poor thing if the sight wasn't so freaking funny. Plus—I have to admit—the view isn't bad. The woman has a nice butt, despite her weird ways, and I'm not too blind to notice. I stand and watch them a few more minutes, shaking my head and laughing to myself. The world is full of nutjobs, and—lucky me—a first-rate one lives right next door.

It hits me when they turn a corner and her blonde ponytail disappears from view. I'm wasting too much time. I now have thirty minutes to make practice. Everything else—the food, the ice—will have to wait.

I head straight for the shower.

Chapter 3

Olivia

I was glued to the television earlier, watching news coverage of some horrendous, out-of-control forest fires in Idaho—they are currently destroying so much of that beautiful state, at least it looks beautiful, though I've never actually been there—so I'm already exhausted from being awake an hour past my bedtime. And now this.

Horrible music—at least I think it's music, it's hard to tell with all that screeching and pounding—woke me up fifteen minutes ago, and I'm mad. Don't we have some sort of apartment complex rules about loud noises after midnight? I mean really, my wall mirror is vibrating because of the noise. With the throb of a drumbeat filtering through the baseboards, I shuffle into the kitchen and open the top drawer—the one by the refrigerator where I store all the junk like paper clips and thumbtacks and loose twist ties and random paperwork—and cringe. Without giving myself time to think about straightening the awfulness that is this particular drawer, I locate our apartment complex guidelines and flip through the section on disruptions. I trace line after line with an index finger, searching . . . searching . . . until there it is. *The noise volume should not exceed fifty-five decibels after midnight, at which time the offending resident will be fined a maximum of one hundred dollars for every hour the violation continues.*

I sigh. Great. Just great. It's one a.m. and I've heard a rumor that he's a professional athlete.

Who throws a party at one a.m.? Don't they know how late it is? Normal people are trying to sleep. I realize I'm tapping my foot to the beat and make myself stop. When did I become such a traitor to my own body?

With a glare at my foot and a hand to my head to ward off an oncoming headache, I look around and spot the vacuum cleaner. It sits dead in the middle of the living room floor. The smell of smoke has gone, along with the machine's ability to suck anything bigger than a piece of lint.

"Perry, Momma is going to fix this vacuum cleaner if it takes me the rest of the night. Do you want to help me? No? You'd rather sleep? That's fine, I think I can manage by myself anyway." My cat is half human, so I treat him that way. Other people might think it's weird, but other people aren't here. Of course he doesn't respond, just moves a paw a little to the left and continues breathing softly. I try not to feel slighted at his lack of interest and pick up a screwdriver.

I'm not sure what to do with it, but something tells me that with one turn of a screw it might—

The vacuum falls into pieces between my legs. I look at the screwdriver in my hand and look at the screw on the floor, wondering which just committed the greater offense and baffled as to how one turn could create such a mess. A giant mound of carpet dust sits in a pile in front of me, and a little blows in front of my face. I sneeze. Then sneeze again. In a rush of panic, I remember the children's Benadryl on my grocery list earlier this morning—the children's kind works better, it just does—but I do *not* remember buying any. I stumble into the bathroom and yank open the cabinet door, then breathe a sigh of relief. A shiny new box, thank goodness. I threw away the remnants of my last bottle because of contamination—you can't keep medicine after an illness, you know. The risk of reinfecting oneself is just too great. Same with thermometers. After a persistent cold or a rough bout of the flu, it's vital to toss them in the trash. I open the lid and measure out two teaspoons of the pink liquid, then bring the plastic cup to my lips.

Right as I open my mouth, a wall hanging crashes to the floor. The cup drops from my hands. When I try to grab it, I knock the bottle off the countertop. Benadryl gushes everywhere, all over the newly mopped floor that still smells like Pine-Sol. I love the smell of Pine-Sol, and now all I can smell is cherries.

That stupid man.

That stupid, stupid man.

My picture, shattered. My medicine, gone. My cat, awake.

He glares at me and yawns before flopping backward onto the sofa and closing his eyes again.

"I'm sorry, Perry. Go back to sleep. I'll be back in a minute."

I sneeze and pat him on the head, then head for the front door. I'm going to give what's-his-name ballplayer a piece of my mind. But before I do that . . .

I reach for the screwdriver. I'm going next door to threaten a stranger. Something tells me I might need a weapon.

Will

For someone who loves a good party and all the perks that come with it, even I think this gathering is out of control. I put out a fire a few minutes ago—a literal fire that started when someone knocked over a candle in the kitchen and a nearby hand towel soaked up the flames.

I heard a scream behind me, then turned to find some idiot girl just staring at the blaze with a hand over her mouth, watching in horror as the fire began to travel toward a stack of napkins sitting just to the left of a bottle of gin.

What kind of person just stares at a fire and makes no move to extinguish it?

More than a little annoyed, I barked some insult at her that I don't even remember and swept the mess into the sink with my bare hands—burning my throwing hand in the process, so that's just great—then turned on the faucet. Within seconds, the smell of ash replaced the scent of burn, thank goodness. I'd no sooner ended that debacle when a loud crash sounded from the living room. Pushing past the helpless chick, I headed into the other room in time to see someone throwing a punch at Ricky Taylor, the backup pitcher that we need in one piece since I keep getting pulled from games. The punch sent him sailing into the living room wall. It only took a second to break up that fight—which apparently started over a flippant comment some guy made about Ricky's date. I never quite got the story of who was truly at fault, and I don't care. Nothing important was damaged—neither Ricky's face nor my drywall—but I've just about had enough. One more disturbance and I'm sending everyone home. Ridiculous because it's only one a.m. Who ends a party this early? Old, boring people, that's who.

Maybe I'm getting old.

Scratch that. No matter how old I get, I will never actually age. Or become boring. For that reason, the party rages on, no matter how tired of it I might get.

"Will, someone's at the door for you," Blake, our catcher and my best friend on the team up to this point, yells over at me.

I glance at him over my shoulder, holding one Solo cup between my teeth, a stack of five in one hand, and three empty soda cans in the other.

"Who is it?" My words are muffled, and I don't know how he understands them with all the crap I'm currently biting and holding, but he does.

"I don't know, man. Some girl."

I toss everything into a nearby trash bag that's overflowing with discarded bottles, cans, and empty chip bags, then rub my hands on my jeans and turn to face him. The bag needs to go out, but I'll do it later.

"Is she cute?" It's a ridiculous question but not without merit. If a lady shows up at my door during a party, her looks make a difference. Especially if she wants an invitation to stay. I don't give them out to just anyone.

Blake wanders over to me with his forehead scrunched up, eyebrows pushed together. Nothing rattles the man, ever; something about his expression makes my pulse kick up a notch.

"She looks ticked off, dude. And she's carrying a screwdriver." He drops his voice to a whisper I can barely hear. "I don't know, man . . . a crazy fan girl?"

"As long as it isn't the crazy chick from next door."

It occurs to me a second too late that I say this louder than I intended. What if it is her and she heard me?

I look toward the front door, but all I can see is a flash of what look like blue flannel pants at the edge of the doorway and the pointed end of said sharp object. It's aimed straight out as if she's prepared to stab me upon arrival. I latch onto Blake's forearm and take a step forward.

"You're coming with me."

He shrugs out of my grip. "Dude, we can't both get stabbed, not this late in the season. Not with the All-Star Game coming up. Besides, she's here to see you, not me."

I just look at him a long moment and then roll my eyes. After the fire, after the fight . . . I'm not in the mood to deal with crazy. Not by myself. Not on top of everything else. We lost again tonight, and despite the fact that I didn't even play, my name keeps coming up on the ESPN sound bites, and not because the announcers are flattering me. Tonight's favorite line was *everything's taken a turn for the worse since Vandergriff showed up.*

Since Vandergriff showed up. As if I just walked on the field with a glove and ball and forced the higher-ups to put me in the game. As if I wouldn't give anything to go back to New York. As if I'm not spending every waking moment just waiting for a call to send me back down to the minors instead. This trade is quite possibly the worst thing that ever happened to me.

Resigned and more than a little ticked off, I head to the door, hoping maybe the chick on the other side of it just wants an autograph. Maybe just an invite. Maybe she's normal, good looking, and here to turn my night around. I fight a smile just thinking about the possibilities.

Until I see her.

And the idiot grin drops from my face.

Good looking? Absolutely.

Fan girl? Not so much.

Just my luck, I'm definitely dealing with crazy.

Chapter 4

Olivia

A man I've never seen before stands at the open doorway and checks me out from head to toe with an amused grin and zero shame. It isn't that I underestimated the size of this party or that I arrived with a screwdriver in hand, holding it as though prepared to strike. The man clearly thinks I look ridiculous. And I do.

I'm wielding a hot-pink screwdriver and wearing flannel pajama pants and a cartoon-covered T-shirt to what looks like an intimidating gathering of the more sophisticated crowd. With a frown, I peer over the man's shoulders to scan the living room. How does this apartment look so much bigger than mine? I know for a fact we share the same floor plan, even if this one is reversed. It isn't fair. Discount furnishings should not make that much of a difference in how a place presents itself. I peel my eyes away from the expensive decor and take in the people.

Dear God, why didn't I stay in bed and suffer through the music?

The people look well put together, and I'm wearing SpongeBob.

Women wearing barely-there dresses dance way too close with men who are clearly interested in much more than music. Nearly everyone holds a wine glass or soda can—liquid sloshing all over a cream-colored woven wool rug that had to cost more than my last week's salary. I notice a particularly large red circle. That stain is going to be tough to remove. I should know. I spilled apple juice all over the side of my left breast before I went to bed, and not even a Tide stain stick took it away, and those things are supposed to take away everything.

Suddenly aware of how bad the spot must look, I shift positions to cover it, but no amount of arm crossing will help. So I do the only thing I can do in this unfortunate situation. When I see that noise-ordinance-offending neighbor of mine walking toward me in his designer jeans and formfitting white button-up, I stand tall and force my chin upward a bit. If I can't look fashionable—or even clean—at least I can look tough.

My resolve falters for a second. My neighbor is incredibly good looking, and he sure does have nice arms.

"What do you want?" he asks, surprising me with his directness. All thoughts of his physique vanish—for the most part—and I glare up at him. The least he could do is smile. I'm not *that* tough, and something tells me he might have a nice smile . . .

Why on earth am I thinking about his smile *or* his arms? I. Am. Pathetic. I deepen my glare and harden my lips a bit. Toughness back. I'm finished being derailed.

"I want you to turn off the music," I say. "Normal, rule-abiding people are trying to sleep. Do you have any idea what time it is?"

I squirm when his gaze rakes me up and down, catches on my chest—darn stain!—and rises to my hair. It hangs loose around my shoulders, my blonde waves completely wild and out of control. I feel naked and exposed and horribly unkempt. Why didn't I think to pull my hair back before stomping over here?

"It's one o'clock in the morning, and this party is just getting started," he says, pulling me out of my internal scolding. My eyes lock on a lazy grin barely this side of legal, and much to my chagrin, I feel myself blush. My face grows hotter when he keeps talking. "If you wanted an invitation, all you had to do was ask. No need to act offended. Now, want something to drink? A beer? A Coke?"

This man. He sounds like a southerner, but he is so clearly not from around here. I heard the way he softened his *r*. Northerners are rude people. Plus, no one from this area wears his hair long like that, all hanging in his eyes and shaggy like John Mayer in his *Continuum* days.

I love John Mayer and that album.

Focus, Olivia.

And then there's the fact that I don't even know his name, which makes insulting him a very hard thing to do. But I try, because I'm not a quitter. First, there's the matter of his question.

"No, I don't want a beer or a Coke. Both are bad for you, especially soda. Did you know one can of Coke can clean a rusty car engine?" He just stares at me. *Why is he just staring at me?* I keep talking. It's the only thing I know to do. "And for your information, I'm not acting. And furthermore, I have a date and we're trying to watch a movie. We can't even hear it over all the racket you're making."

Judging from the way his expression changes from amused to unbelieving, it's the wrong thing to say.

"First of all, it's a carburetor. And yes, I've heard." He pauses. "More importantly, you're on a date. Right now. Wearing that." Three statements that might normally be delivered as questions, except he doesn't say them that way. He just insulted me three different times with ten well-placed words.

"Yes, I'm on a date. And I don't appreciate your unbelieving tone." I am suddenly jittery, and my hands become bendy and poppy—specifically my knuckles. It's the general way I react to telling outright lies.

His gaze pauses entirely too long on my midsection before swinging back up to my eyes. "Well, by all means, invite the lucky guy over here too. This party might actually benefit from a little scruff. But just so you know, you have a bit of dirt on your nose, some weird spot on your chest, your hair's a bit tangled, and you might want to consider changing clothes. I personally don't mind the pajamas, but a few people here might be bothered by the idea that you haven't showered today."

"I did too shower today." It's a ridiculously defensive thing to say. Do I look that bad? My hand finds my nose and furiously begins to rub back and forth. I'd go for the breast, but he might get the wrong idea. When I catch sight of his grin, I drop my hand to my side and decide not to care about either. Dirt or no dirt, stain or no stain, I can't let him get the best of me.

"For your information, neither myself nor my date is one for parties. We're more of the . . ." I search for the right words to polish off this lie.

"Netflix and chill type?" Another insult, this time delivered in four words. What kind of person does he think I am? He picks up a bag of trash and hoists it to his waist, then makes a move to walk around me and out the door.

I take a single step to the side to let him pass, hating the way my Hello Kitty slippers sink against the pavement. Further proof of my awkwardness. *Hello Kitty? Seriously, Olivia?*

"Yes, we're the Netflix type," I rush to say. "But not the chill."

He smirks at me; it slides way under my skin. "That's a shock."

That man. "Where are you going?" I hate to sound like I care, because I don't. But he can't just leave me standing here like a fool.

"I'm carrying this to the dumpster in the parking lot. Feel free to walk with me, unless you'd like to head inside and help yourself to some food. Might want to get your date first though."

I don't like the way he says "date," stringing it into more than one syllable, light on the long *a* and heavy on the sarcasm. I also don't like the way he walks away, leaving me standing there with a screwdriver in one hand and what is left of my very fragile dignity in the other. An internal tug-of-war lasts until he rounds the corner and disappears from view. That's when I do the only thing a lying girl wearing pajamas and childish slippers at a high-class party can do.

I follow him.

Will

She's uptight, and I'm a jerk. I know I'm a jerk, but come on. I'd rather be a jerk than be that uptight. This chick is about as likely to have a date waiting for her at home as I am to have a bride waiting for me at the altar tomorrow morning. I shudder just thinking about that horrific possibility and smile to myself when I hear her padded footsteps coming up behind me. Hello Kitty. I about choked on my laughter when I saw those. As if SpongeBob wasn't enough, even though I remember really liking that show. It's funny. A little more on the adult humor side than the kid side. This chick must think so too.

I switch the bag to my left hand and keep walking. The invitation to follow me was sincere, even though it was delivered as casually as I could manage. What can I say? The lady's hot, despite her obvious lack of taste in bedtime attire. Flannel pants? Has she ever heard of Victoria's Secret? The least she could do is buy those same pants in leopard-print satin. Anything would be an improvement on the way she's currently dressed.

But attire aside . . . her hair. It almost did me in. I've only ever seen her with it pulled back into a tight ponytail. The waves threw me. The desire to run my fingers through the strands nearly flattened me. Of course I've had that same reaction to plenty of women before, but never to one wearing an outfit that might belong on the cover of the Sears Christmas catalog I remember thumbing through when I was a kid.

I smell lavender or something behind me. Holy crap, this woman. *Remember, Will, she's nuts. She walks her cat on a leash.*

I keep walking, trying to remind myself of her craziness and arming myself with the same *who cares* attitude that has worked well for me in life so far.

"You're welcome to walk beside me, unless you're enjoying the view too much from back there."

I smile to myself when a flash of blue flannel comes into my line of vision.

"Oh please, enough with the ego. You're walking too fast, and I'm wearing slippers."

"Could have waited for me at the apartment."

"Looking the way I do? That wasn't much of an option."

"You look great." The words are out before I can stop them. *Wow . . . wow . . . wow. Settle down, Will.* I gather up what's left of my resolve to remain cool and stuff it in my pocket. There. Now I just need to remember to use it. "For a girl wearing those ridiculous slippers."

"For your information, my grandmother gave me these slippers and I wear them in her memory. And also . . . there was a dumpster much closer to your apartment that you could have used. Would have saved you some time."

Two things about this. One, now I feel like an even bigger jerk. A dead grandmother, and I just made fun of her gift. It occurs to me that she could be lying in the same way she was lying about having a date waiting at home, but I doubt it. There's a special place in hell for people who lie about dead grandparents, and I can't see this girl living comfortably in it. Too uptight for warm conditions, and she'd probably be concerned about frizz. And two, I know about the other dumpster just like I knew she would follow me, and I wanted it to take a while.

"I haven't lived here long, so I didn't know about the closer one. I'll make sure to use it next time." I lift the lid, toss the garbage inside, rub my hands together, and face her. "A woman like you shouldn't be out this late at night. I have half a mind to grab your date by the throat and remind him of that fact."

"A woman like me?"

I swallow and try to come up with something to say. Anything besides the fact that she's attractive. "Alone. It isn't safe, and those shoes aren't made for running."

Even in the moonlight, I can see her frown. "He didn't know I would be gone this long," she says with a tiny shake in her voice.

I wonder if she hears it. I wonder if she knows how bad she is at lying. I don't point it out, because frankly, it's cute.

"Then I'll walk you back. That alright?"

She looks to the left and then to the right as if trying to decide if I'm safe or an ax murderer poised to kill her somewhere between the dumpster and the parking lot.

"You walked with me this far all by yourself, remember? I promise not to harm you on the way back."

She relents with a soft smile.

"Okay, thank you. I don't really like being out this late at night."

I don't tell her I could have guessed as much. I also don't tell her she has a nice voice when it isn't raised to yell at me. Soft like butter, warm like honey. Both things lickable, and I should not be thinking about licking anything where this girl is involved. I shove my hands in my pockets and take a deep breath of the night air. Maybe if I suck hard enough, I'll be able to get a big mouthful of my sanity and swallow it back down where it belongs.

"I've seen you outside. You have a dog, right?"

No idea why I feel the need to lie, but I do. Sue me and call me a sinner.

"A cat. A Persian named Perry. I've had him since I was sixteen."

I glance over at her. "Which makes him . . . ?"

"Thirteen. Which is old for a cat, but the vet thinks he'll live for several more years."

"Nine lives and all." I hate small talk; such a waste of time, especially with women. On a normal night, I usually give it five minutes to figure out if we're on the same page. What she wants, what I want. But tonight is anything but normal.

"Exactly. Plus, I'm very careful where he's concerned. I never let him out by himself, and he rides in a car seat next to me."

I trip over a crack in the blacktop and look at her out of the corner of my eye. Thank God I stop the laugh that nearly breaks free. She's not kidding. But it's a cat, not a baby.

"Sounds very responsible," I say, making a point of keeping my eyes off her. If I look at her, I'll lose it. Thankfully we reach her door, and I keep my composure.

"Thank you. I'm sorry, but I don't think I caught your name?" she says. She's very timid when she isn't angry. I have a thing for strong women, so I'm not sure which I prefer. But then one more glance at her hair makes neither one matter, because the hair trumps everything.

For a second I forget what we're talking about.

"Oh. It's Will. Will Vandergriff." I wait for the flash of recognition. It never comes. I think about doing a fake windup and pitch to see if that jogs a memory for her but decide that would look stupid. When she just looks at me, a crease deepening between her eyebrows, I'm certain of it.

"Well, neighbor Will, thanks for walking me safely to my door. I'm sure my date will be happy to hear you're such a gentleman."

"Glad to know. Maybe I could step in and meet him? Tell him I found some flannel-pj-wearing chick wielding a screwdriver on my doorstep."

"Yeah, I wouldn't do that. He's probably sound asleep on the sofa by now. Plus, he was pretty mad about your music. If he is awake, I wouldn't want him to beat you up or anything." Her chin comes up, but she bites her bottom lip. I stare at the way she rolls it around in her teeth for a second longer than I should. Women should not bite their lips unless they want a man to join in the fun. To every guy I know, this is a turn-on. I'm no exception.

I force my eyes away. "Since we're neighbors, you should tell me your name too. It's only fair, so I don't have to call you the cat chick."

"It's Olivia," she says.

I was expecting something else. Jane, maybe. Definitely not Olivia. It's perfect. A beautiful name for a beautiful—

"Goodnight, Will."

She takes a step back, and the door closes behind her. I stand outside it for a second. Maybe thirty. Maybe a hundred. Long enough to mostly convince myself once again that the lady next door is crazy. *Remember the leash, Will? She's nuts.*

It isn't hard for the mantra to stick. I've thought she was weird for a while, after all.

The harder part will be trying to forget that smile.

And good lord.

That hair.

Chapter 5

Olivia

The day after I met Will what's-his-name-that-I'm-trying-to-forget, the birds sang a little louder over the roof of my apartment. I love waking up to their sound—especially during that pleasant time of year when the school calendar is turning its last page, when I'm down to just a few remaining check marks in my day planner until I can pack up my classroom and close the door for the summer. I have so many plans for June and July: research and embark on my newfound passion of organic herb gardening, finally paint my kitchen a lovely shade of blue I've already selected from a color wheel at Lowe's Home Improvement, go for walks, play with Perry, enroll us both in a Mommy and Me cat day camp that we used to enjoy but have found ourselves missing the last two summers due to a particularly violent bout with the flu on my part and an insufferably bad mood on his.

Cat depression is a serious thing and can last quite a long time. It was news to me . . . and to our veterinarian. But we're past it now. Perry's back to his delightful, lazy self, thank goodness.

As I was saying, the day after I met Will, I woke up to a world colored a brighter red. A warmer orange. A sunnier yellow. A regular rainbow lighting up the sky.

Until I had the bright idea to google him. It's something I'm not proud of, something I regret. He plays baseball for the Rangers—a perfectly fine profession, a job that many women would be overjoyed to align themselves with. Women concerned about status, women who love to rub shoulders with wealth and high society. Fortunately or unfortunately, I'm not one of them. For me his job comes with all kinds of drawbacks, the main one being that I don't like baseball players. I have my reasons, every single one of them valid. But his profession isn't even the real problem.

The problem is his number.

It's thirteen.

Of course it's thirteen.

All my life, I've had nothing but bad luck with the number thirteen. I know it's a cliché, and I hate being part of a cliché. But the problems. So many have piled up around me that I now avoid the number at all possible costs.

At a hotel, I will not stay on the thirteenth floor.

At a grocery store, I will not shop on aisle thirteen.

At a movie theater, I steer clear of that row.

On a staircase, I count up to twelve and hurdle the thirteenth step.

I won't even read books with the number thirteen in the title. I've probably missed out on a few good ones, but I figure that's the author's fault.

The only thing I haven't managed to avoid is the thirteenth day of the month. So I get my revenge the only way I know how: dress in black, keep my head down, and pretend I'm in mourning all day.

Not hard to do, since the thirteenth day of the month is also the day that—

"Ms. Pratt?"

I look up from the stack of papers I'm grading and meet the cautious gaze of little Avery Hardy. The black cloud surrounding my Monday morning mood lifts a little at the sight of his sweet face. For some reason, my repulsion for all things unclean stops with him. Avery wears ill-fitting, mostly unwashed clothes to school every day, and he wears a baseball cap backward because I never have the heart to tell him to remove it. As for showers . . . there's no way he takes one more than once or twice a week. His family is poor, but I've seen his brothers. They seem generally well-kempt and energetic, which tells me Avery bears the brunt of their family's lack of resources.

He is late to school again, a somewhat common occurrence; right now I'm in the middle of my planning period, and recess isn't over for another twenty minutes. He looks troubled. I've seen him this way before, but today is different.

I set my pen down. "What is it, Avery?"

The backpack slung over his shoulder looks almost as big as the top half of his body. His small stature, along with his too-short jeans and the sneakers that have a tiny hole at the toe, means he is often made fun of. For a moment I think this is what he wants to talk about. I'm wrong.

"Thank you for bringing the bag by my house last Friday."

I smile, relieved that he isn't here to discuss more. "You're welcome. I'm glad you found it."

"Well, see," he swallows and looks around the room. At my computer, at my desk, at the floor. At everything but me. It's the common sign of insecurity, isn't it? Being unable to look people in the eye. If more people could make eye contact and couple it with the truth, there might be less hurt and more understanding in this world.

It isn't until he shifts from one foot to the other that I finally notice it; he's holding a hand to his middle. Pressing. Cradling. My heart sinks into my stomach; this isn't the first time I've seen him this way. I can't believe I didn't hear the noises coming from his stomach before now. "My brother found it before I did, and . . ."

He looks out the window, his mind locked inside a recent memory. One he has likely revisited a hundred times in the past forty-eight hours.

"You need something to eat?"

At my words, his gaze flicks back to me. "Do you have anything?"

It's nine thirty in the morning. Lunch is hours away, and breakfast was over a long time ago. I stand from my desk and make my way to the cabinet across the room.

"Yes, I do. Do you want to eat in here or take it next door?" There's a parent room next to mine, one that mothers and the occasional father use to plan parties, help with bulletin board cutouts, organize take-home folders for children. In the morning, it's always empty.

"Here, if that's okay," he says. "I promise not to get in your way."

His tiny voice breaks my heart a little. Something tells me Avery is often made to feel inferior. It's an emotion I recognize. Taking a deep breath, I produce a blue and pink floral bag that holds the hummus wrap, bag of pretzels, and apple that would have served as my own lunch later in the day and hand it to him. I've already checked the calendar. Cafeteria taco day isn't my favorite, but it will work.

"Of course I don't mind. You can sit right here next to me."

When his eyes go wide, I smile.

Avery reaches for the bag and smiles back, then unloads the contents onto the desk in front of him. While he digs in, I sit down at my desk, feeling much heavier inside than I did just a few short minutes ago, the black cloud firmly hovering over my head once again. Avery has done nothing to deserve the life he's been given, nor the situation he's been saddled with.

Brothers.

Why is it that so many unfair things in life point back to them?

Will

Sweat slides into my eye for the second time in as many minutes, but there's not much I can do to stop the burning sensation it creates. I remove my cap and swipe at my forehead with my forearm, only to have a fresh stream slide over my eyebrow and drip off my eyelashes. I squeeze my eyes shut, fighting a brief wave of blackness. The heat is nearly unbearable. Despite the early evening hour, the sun still manages to beat down on me with a fervor that has me feeling like I'm roasting in hell's oven. A couple more inches on the horizon, and the sun will finally disappear under the stands behind me. Thank God. It's the end of May in Dallas, and I have no idea how I'll survive living here and playing on this field for an entire summer. For miles around, there are no hills, no trees, no nothing but wide open spaces. Just an amusement park next door that somehow only adds to the sweltering conditions. Probably all that pavement. Or the mass of smelly, sweat-covered bodies walking around, holding roasted corn and funnel cakes. The only saving grace: this time next week we're in Seattle. It's at least twenty degrees cooler there. I've already checked the forecast.

I slip my cap on and glance up for a second, and that's when I spot a flash of long blonde hair that has my heart both dropping with dread and skipping from interest. Funny how the sight of a woman can give me those simultaneous reactions—especially a hot one, even if she's a bit weird. I squeeze one eye shut to see a little better.

It isn't her, just some other girl with pretty hair who doesn't interest me in the least. With a shrug of irritation, I swallow a wave of disappointment and face home plate again. Why doesn't that girl in the stands interest me? More importantly, why *does* Olivia, my crazy cat-lady neighbor?

Olivia.

The name bounces around my insides like a swarm of newly freed butterflies. I shake my head. What am I doing? Mentally writing poetry over a whacked-out chick who probably doesn't understand anything about baseball or the importance of the game? Disgusted with myself, I roll my eyes and imagine flinging those butterflies into the dirt. There. Now they're immobile. Every last one of them.

I banish Olivia from my mind and focus on the game in front of me.

My throwing hand still hurts a little from the fire I put out a few nights ago, but pain has a way of lessening with a loss on the line. And right now we're down by two in the bottom of the fifth—both unfortunate runs caused directly by player error. Namely mine. At the bottom of the fourth, I overthrew a ball. An unusual mistake on my part, but completely defenseless. It sailed right over Blake's glove and ricocheted off the rail behind him, where it rolled and rolled until he scrambled to retrieve it and tossed it to first. That move stopped the bleeding, but not before major damage was done. Two runners in with men on at second and third. I can blame the heat, the injury, the errors that keep stacking up against us tonight, including a foul ball that could have been easily caught by our first baseman but wasn't—but if we go down tonight, the loss will be on me.

Everyone blames the pitcher. Almost always rightfully so.

I fully expect to be pulled at any moment.

I rub a sweaty hand on my pants leg and shift on the pitcher's mound, then glance at the scoreboard. Wishful thinking doesn't change the facts. Blake drops a hand between his knees, gives me the signal, then watches for my nod. I hear my name shouted from the stands—some supportive, a couple not so much—then force the cries of the crowd to fade into the background as I study the batter. I cock my arm back and throw with so much power that the ball flies past the swinging bat in front of me and straight into the catcher's mitt. I relish the sound the ball makes when it hits the palm of Blake's hand. I live for that sound. Often I even dream of it.

That's strike two. One more of those and we have the chance to redeem ourselves.

As long as I don't screw up again.

Blake points one finger, giving me the signal once more. He's asking for a fastball, but I want to throw a curveball. This guy hasn't hit one all night, and I'm confident a curve will close this inning out with no more damage done. I shake my head, and he flashes the signal again. I'm not happy about it, but it's his call. Sweat trickles into my eyes again as I look left, look right, grip the ball in my fist, and throw. It sails toward home plate. But this time I don't blink.

Not when the ball connects with the bat.

Not when it sails over my head.

And over the back wall.

Not when one runner and another make it home.

This keeps happening, over and over.

I'm pulled before the inning is over. That keeps happening too.

When the game ends and we lose by five, I'm blinking like a cursor sitting idle.

I keep telling myself to suck it up, that I'm a man's man, for God's sake. Blinking rapidly is the only way to hold the tears in, where they belong.

Chapter 6

Olivia

I've managed to make it all week without seeing him—Will, the player next door with a brain the size of a pea. I know a thing or two about sporty types, and trust me they don't have much else going for them. Certainly not smarts. And again—I haven't seen him all week. So of course I would run into him now when I'm on my way to my car and he's just climbing out of his brand-new black Lexus.

I try not to notice that I like his shoes.

Or how nice he looks in his designer jeans.

Or how his hair falls just in front of the expensive sunglasses that shield what I remember to be very nice blue eyes.

Or the way he reaches up to brush that wavy brown hair off his forehead.

Or the way my fingers suddenly itch with a desire to do it for him.

Or the way he flashes a brilliant smile in my direction when he notices me standing there.

Or the way he so casually tucks a worn copy of *Atlas Shrugged* under his arm.

So many things not to notice, but that one's the toughest.

Of course he would be reading one of my favorite books of all time, completely invalidating my thought from only seconds ago. I pull my purse straps a little higher on my shoulder and move to walk around him.

"Where are you off to in such a hurry?" he says. That voice. Is it too much to ask for it to be a little less husky and alluring?

"I'm going out with friends." I hate the way my own words wobble. The way I have to clear my throat to make sure my voice works the next time I'm forced to use it.

"Like that?"

My spine stiffens, and I look him straight in the eye. Suddenly I have no doubt my voice will work just fine. "Like what?"

He nods toward my head as if the gesture makes perfect sense. "With your hair pulled back so tight. You should wear it down. It looks nice that way."

The nerve. "As opposed to the way it looks now?"

He shrugs. "Nothing wrong with the way it looks now. It just doesn't scream *girl out for a good time.*"

My jaw drops and I respond before I think the better of it. "I'm not looking for a good time. I'm just going out to eat with friends."

I hate the way he smiles. I hate the way I like it.

"Then . . . perfect," he says, ruffling every hidden feather on me. "And I'm impressed. A date one weekend and out with friends the next? You're a busy girl." He reaches into the trunk for a suitcase, one I wish to grab and use to hit the top of his head. He doesn't have to say the word *date* so sarcastically or imply that tonight is equally unbelievable. Maybe he's right about the fake date, but I *am* going out. So what if it's completely against my will?

"Extremely busy, for your information. My schedule for June is entirely full already, and the summer hasn't even started."

He raises an eyebrow and closes the trunk of his car. "It must be a pretty good schedule, then. You and the furball headed to the beach?"

I straighten my shoulders. "No, we're not headed to the beach." I want to grab those defensive words and swallow them back down the minute they're out. Instead, I narrow my gaze and try to look unaffected. "And for your information, I have other friends besides just him."

"I didn't mean to imply that he's your only friend, just that you seem a bit busier than usual. That's not a bad thing."

Okay, that bothers me. "How would you know anything about my normal schedule? We just met last weekend."

His small laugh catches me off guard. "We might have just met in person, but I've seen you around. Nearly every day when I'm in town. You're the lady with the Handi Wipes you use on your car every afternoon. The lady who forces that poor fat cat to walk on a leash each afternoon. Right?"

"Perry is not fat, and I don't force him."

He switches his duffel bag to the other hand, and I see a flash of his number monogrammed on the side. My indignation deflates a bit and I take a step back. Why does *that* have to be his number?

"Forgive me," he says. "Chubby. And hairy."

For a moment I forget what we're talking about, but then it all comes rushing back and I'm angry again. "For your information—"

"Also, you like to use that phrase."

This stops me. "What phrase?"

"'For your information.' You use it a lot. I've counted at least three times in the few minutes we've talked. It's your fallback. Your go-to. Interesting."

"There's nothing interesting about it. I don't have a fallback or a go-to."

He slips off his sunglasses and hangs them from his shirt collar. "You have several. That phrase is just one of them."

"What are the others?" *Why did I ask that, and why did my voice shake?*

"You love the color blue, you hate imperfections, you grab the ends of your hair when you're nervous . . ."

I drop my hand from its grasp on my ponytail and hurl mental insults at my navy blouse. Whatever. It's time to go, anyway. Jocks not only have tiny brains, they also have next to zero manners. Plus there's the fact that he thinks I'm crazy, so why does his opinion matter?

"Listen, I'd love to stand around and let you analyze me for the rest of the night, but I have plans. And I'm late."

This time he winks at me, cocky and confident, like we're sharing a secret. "Well, don't let me keep you from getting started on that schedule of yours." He takes a step back and gestures toward my car door.

I walk around him, actually thankful Kelly talked me into going out and careful to hold my breath against the scent of his cologne. My mouth waters when I inhale a mix of mint and evergreen. It's like he's chewing gum in the middle of a Christmas tree farm. What kind of human smells like that?

"By the way, what restaurant are you going to?"

I keep my back to him, but my pulse is racing. "For your—" I pause, internally cursing the fact that he's right. I have a go-to phrase. "I'm meeting a friend at the Owner's Box in fifteen minutes."

"One of my favorite places to go, probably because of the name."

That makes me smile slightly, though I'm glad he can't see it. "I guess it would be, considering your profession." I open my door, then twist my head a bit to look at him in an effort to be polite. Plus, I just want to see him one more time. All in all, he isn't that bad, despite his arrogant attitude. "Have a nice night."

"You too." He tucks a hand inside his pocket and turns toward his apartment. "I'll see you around."

I shut my door, then catch a glimpse of myself in the rearview mirror. My hair is so tight. Almost severe. It's pulling my eyebrows up too far. How come I've never noticed before? I reach up and slide the elastic down the length of it before I realize what I've done. I can't believe that man talked me into changing my appearance. With a resigned sigh, I shake the curls free and let them fall past my shoulders, telling myself I wanted it that way anyway. Telling myself I would have restyled my hair even if he hadn't said he liked it this way. Telling myself I will never be seeing that maddening man again . . . that I'm glad about it.

But that's the thing about lying to yourself.

It hardly ever works.

—————

Will

"Why the heck are we here?" Blake asks the question for the second time, grabbing another roll and slathering it with butter. "Obviously it isn't to pick up women, since I'm married and you've done nothing but sit in that corner staring at nothing since we got here. I think you dragged me here under false pretenses. We haven't even ordered and I'm starving." He looks over his shoulder, then back at me. "What are you staring at, anyway?"

There's no way I'm answering that question. Instead, I gesture to the crowd around us. "What false pretenses? All I said was I wanted to eat. And as far as women go, you've got the best one so I don't know why you're complaining. You have something right there." I tap the indent below my lip and watch as he swipes a napkin across his chin. The place is crawling with women, both figuratively and literally. Across the room, there's a woman clutching the wall, doing some kind of dance against it that looks incredibly interesting even if it is weird. I stare for a second, then look away to scan the room again.

You came all this way, man. What now? I pick up the salt shaker and move it to the other side of the pepper shaker. Checkmate.

Maybe I was just curious. Maybe a part of me wanted to torment Olivia a bit. Maybe it was that my mind couldn't reconcile the idea of Olivia hanging out in a bar because the idea seemed so ridiculously out of character from the very little I know about her. Maybe it was just a simple desire to see what the odd chick from next door does for a good time. Whatever the reason, here I am at the Owner's Box with a handful of friends and teammates, trying to spy on the neighbor lady like a cat who doesn't know when to give it a rest. Curiosity kills those things, you know. I give myself a private eye roll, the irony not lost on me.

Blake holds up a finger for another drink. We're already on round two, though I haven't touched mine yet, preferring to sip water as I wage an internal debate with myself about what to do. She walked in a few minutes ago and is sitting at a table across the room—at least I think it's her, all I can see from here is a familiar flash of blonde and the blue silk blouse I remember from earlier—and she's alone. But she hasn't gone unnoticed. I glance at a blond guy in a tweed blazer a few feet away from me who keeps craning his neck to check her out. Who wears tweed in the summer anyway? Womanizers with no taste, that's who. The cat lady is clearly naïve—no telling what kind of trouble she could get herself into. Thank God I'm here to keep that from happening.

Decision made. I stand up.

Suddenly thirsty, I pick up my glass and down it by a third. Courage in a crystal goblet maybe, but I need some. For some reason I'm nervous, and I never get nervous. Not when I'm on the pitcher's mound, not ever.

Except now.

"I'll be right back." I plunk my glass on the table, wipe my mouth with the back of my hand, and start walking. No one ever got anywhere in life by standing around. Certainly not me.

"Where are you going?" Blake sets down his glass and looks up at me.

"I saw someone I need to talk to. I'll be right back."

"Finally, you're on the move. Maybe now we can start having some fun around here. What do you want to eat and I'll order?"

"A burger. A steak. I don't care," I call over my shoulder.

Blake opens a menu. "On it. I'm ordering you a salad, heavy on the olives. That's what you get for asking me to babysit you all night . . ."

I give the room an eye roll. I've never needed a babysitter, and I sure as heck don't need one now. I walk backward a few steps to call out to him over the loud music.

"If I don't come back, eat it for me." For one fleeting moment, I picture myself asking Olivia to have dinner with me. Then I'll ask her for a ride home. Then I picture one thing leading to another and now I'm smiling to myself like an idiot. Maybe I could offer to meet that stupid cat of hers. At least that could be my excuse to get inside her apartment. As for excuses to stay . . . I'll just have to make those up as I go.

"Hey, you."

I stand at the edge of her table, staring at the back of that severe ponytail, but she doesn't turn around. Unused to getting a nonreaction from women—even crazy ones who try to pretend they're not into me—I try again. "I saw you from across the room. Completely forgot you said you were coming here tonight."

I wait. Wait some more. What is it with her?

Finally, she turns.

My confidence wavers right along with my expression.

It isn't Olivia.

I blink. Look up. Scan the room for one second . . . five. Where is Olivia? And why isn't she here? And why isn't this her? And why does it matter?

The woman in front of me holds out a manicured hand: red nails, sharp points, good for scratching, fake. I study it for a second and finally reach out. Sharp edges aren't always bad. She offers a smile—the kind of practiced smile worn by pageant queens and sorority girls everywhere—all kinds of meaning hidden inside it.

"Hey, yourself. Aren't you Will Vandergriff?"

And that's all it takes. All it ever takes. Just like that, my mind empties of everything but blonde ponytails and suggestive expressions. I'm suddenly not particular about who either belong to.

I nod. Scan the room one more time for Olivia, because maybe I am just a little particular, then sit down in the seat she offers. Something about this girl seems a bit familiar, but I chalk it up to her predictable—though definitely bombshell—blonde look.

No matter. I spend the rest of the night getting to know the girl. Her name is Lexi. She's a dental assistant who works in downtown Dallas and . . . I never caught the rest. Because turns out it didn't matter. It wasn't that kind of night. It was the kind of night that goes down in memory, even if the memory is shrouded in a haze of too much drinking, too much dancing, and not enough talking.

But the best part about the evening? The part that I found out about just two hours later? A personal record for me, by the way.

Lexi doesn't have a cat.

Chapter 7

Olivia

The thing I like most about the end of the year is the smooth way it normally sails toward the finish line, gliding along the proverbial water with very few breaks or waves on the horizon. I realize this is abnormal; most of my teacher friends spend the last two weeks of school complaining about the immense amount of paperwork, the out-of-control children, the overwhelming calls from parents wanting last-minute meetings and verbal end-of-year assurances that their children will, in fact, graduate from eighth grade and move on to high school.

But that kind of chaos has never been an issue for me. I'm just fortunate, I guess.

"Ms. Pratt, we have a problem."

Mr. Ellis, our school's band director, walks into my classroom holding a sugared doughnut, white powder all over his lips like he just spent time inhaling cocaine the wrong way. Not that I've ever done cocaine or even know the *right* way, but I do have cable television and I do occasionally watch it. I learned a lot from *Breaking Bad*, primarily that you should never use acid to clean a bathtub. It spells disaster in so many ways, and all your efforts would be for nothing.

I briefly think about handing him a Handi Wipe, but decide against it when my stomach growls. Our principal personally delivers doughnuts to the teachers' lounge every Monday morning as an incentive for the staff to show up early, ready to face the week; sadly, it almost always works for me, though I haven't had one today. I make a mental note to grab one before lunch. It's the blueberry ones. The blueberry cake ones, specifically. They get me every time. Much more of a downfall than movie-theater popcorn.

Mr. Ellis plants a hand at the edge of my desk and glances at my chest—a move I'm used to, as is every other female teacher in this school. He knocks a small stack of papers to the floor but makes no move to pick them up. I try not to cringe as I close a tab on my computer and look up at him.

"What's the problem today?" I eye the papers. Unable to take the sight of them just lying there, I suppress an eye roll and crouch down to gather them up.

"Our guest speaker. He just cancelled."

My hand pauses mid-reach, and my skin tingles with a chill that travels like pointed fingers exactly down the middle of my spine. What did he say?

"What do you mean, our speaker cancelled?"

Tomorrow is the last day of school, and fourth-grade graduation is today. This afternoon. In three hours, to be exact. And I'm in charge of it. I was put in charge of it two months ago. In that time I ordered the decorations, chose the desserts, and booked the speaker—the vice president of our local community college. He's known to give inspiring speeches at these sorts of events. Sure, he has a tendency to go a bit long, and there is a rumor floating around that two kids and a father fell asleep in the front row during his last commencement speech, but that's probably just nonsense. There's no valid reason for the man to cancel at this short notice. No reason at all.

"Why in heaven's name would he cancel?"

"His wife was in a car accident earlier this morning and broke her leg. He's at the hospital with her now."

Maybe that's a valid reason. But of course it would happen today. If she was going to have an accident, why couldn't it be at a more convenient time, like tomorrow? Or next Tuesday, when summer vacation is in full swing?

I press a hand to my forehead and will my racing heart to slow.

"What are we going to do?" With a sick feeling weaving its way through my insides, I slowly stand and return the papers to my desk. "If I have to find a replacement, it has to be within"—I check the wall clock above the SMART Board and feel my eyes go wide—"two hours. And if I can't . . ." My words trail off. I'm too horrified to think of any other possibilities. I *have* to find someone, and fast.

I forgot to take my St. John's Wort this morning, and right now I'm severely aware of the deficiency in my nervous system. Heart palpitations, sweaty palms, labored breathing. All the classic symptoms of a nervous breakdown.

"If you can't, you'll have to give the speech yourself, I guess." Leave it to Mr. Ellis to verbalize what I refuse to acknowledge.

I feel my mouth drop. "I'm *not* making the speech myself. There are a lot of things I'm willing to do for this school, but public speaking isn't one of them." I walk a few steps toward the back of the room, then turn and retrace my steps. There's got to be a solution. Something that doesn't involve me, a case of hives, a quivering voice, and the very real possibility of passing out in front of three hundred people. I halt and face the band director. White powder dots his charcoal suit jacket. "Do you have any suggestions?"

He brushes sugar off his hands and onto his pants, then shrugs. "I have no ideas at all. Hopefully you'll think of something soon. Otherwise, happy speaking."

And with that, he walks out. I glare after him. There's white powder on the back of his pants too, but I say nothing. He can just walk around like that all day for all I care. Hopefully the kids will make fun of him. If I'm lucky, someone will kick him.

I spin to look at my desk. My students will be back from art class in five minutes. What am I going to do?

And then, like a bad nightmare that just keeps getting worse, I have an idea.

An awful idea.

The worst idea I've ever had as an adult—maybe even as a teenager, if I could remember back that far. With shoulders slumped in defeat, with feet dragging in protest, I make my way toward my classroom phone and pick up the receiver. I punch in four numbers and wait for the ring.

"Susan," I say, "can you find someone to cover my class for an hour? I need to run an errand."

The receptionist assures me she will find someone, and I hang up. Now I have only one thing to do. Maybe two. Both of which I dread more than I've ever dreaded anything in my life.

Swallow my pride.

And do a whole bunch of begging.

Will

It's freaking ten o'clock in the morning, the game went into extra innings last night and didn't end until almost eleven, I fell asleep some-time after three, and now some idiot won't stop banging on my door. It's pissing me off, to say the least, but the ignoring I've done for the last five minutes hasn't worked. The person keeps knocking. I fling back my comforter and jump out of bed. I'm about to pound whoever just woke me up, and I'm going to enjoy it.

I stalk into the living room wearing black boxer briefs and nothing else, and I don't give a crap. If someone wants to see me this badly, they're gonna see more than they bargained for. Without checking the peephole, I fling the door open and brace myself against the doorframe. Sunlight slams into my eyes. I blink at cream-colored floor tiles while my corneas burn—seriously, I probably won't even be able to see to pitch tonight. My career ruined by some lunatic with no manners. Never mind I'm already doing a decent job of ruining it myself.

I rub my eyes. "What do you want?"

It isn't until the words are out that I fully look up.

I wish to God I hadn't looked up. I wish I'd gotten dressed. I wish a lot of things.

Olivia. Olivia wearing a V-neck white tee and fitted black pants, looking more casually sexy than I've ever seen her look before. Her ponytail is looser, little strands falling around her face like even they don't want to obey her rigid rules today. The sight of her nearly flattens me, but then I remember I'm supposed to act cool. Ticked off. So I slam a glare into my expression and look at her.

There. That's better.

I start to ask her what she wants again, but then I see her look of horror. The way her cheeks redden at the same time the rest of her face drains to white. And then my evil side scratches its way to the surface. My cute neighbor is embarrassed and trying really hard not to look at me. Her eyes are locked on my forehead like the key to happiness and long life are tattooed somewhere along my hairline. She's mortified.

Now it's my job to keep her that way.

I inhale a deep breath, flex as much as my muscles will let me this early in the morning, and brace both hands at the top of the doorjamb.

I read somewhere that women like this sort of pose in a man. But a barely dressed one? She won't know what to do with herself.

"Did you want something, Olivia?"

I'm a terrible human. I should be shot. Someone should put me in my place. But right now, I'm having too much fun.

She fiddles with a gold hoop earring. "I need you."

When I wink, her eyes go wide from my nod to her unintended innuendo. It's all I can do not to laugh, especially when she looks on the verge of passing out.

"You need me, huh? Like, right now? Here in the entryway or . . . somewhere else?"

She sways for a second before catching herself on the doorframe. But when she does, her eyes narrow, chin goes up, hand falls to her side, and face gains back a little color. She clearly just reached her limit with me.

"I see what you're doing, and you can stop with the ego trip. I don't need you in *that* way, I need you to do me a favor. An important one. My job is on the line if you don't help me, so can you?"

Something about the way her gaze flicks to the side makes me think that last part might be an exaggeration, but I humor her anyway.

"Wow, something so important you might get fired from teaching. That sounds awful. What is it you need?"

She sighs, obviously annoyed. Women are cute when they're mad.

"I need—" She finally scans my frame and rolls her eyes. "Can you please put on some pants? It is ridiculous for someone your age to stand here unclothed in the middle of an open doorway. People can see you."

My age?

"What's that supposed to mean? I'm thirty-one, not sixty. And there's no one but you out here, so I don't see the problem."

She just looks at me. "Of course you don't. You're a man."

Did she seriously just pull a gender insult? "You know, if you need me to help you, you're going about it the wrong way. Insults don't usually work on me."

She bites the inside of her cheek, pulling her pink lips into a pout that is incredibly sexy, and she doesn't even know it.

"I'm sorry," she mumbles. "I need you to speak at a fourth-grade graduation ceremony. Say something motivational. Something encouraging. You can talk about the baseball thing you do." She waves her hand dismissively in front of her. "Can you help me? I would owe you forever."

Even the *baseball thing* comment doesn't offend me, because I'm still staring at her lips.

"Will, please?" she asks again.

This time the words register, and my gaze snaps to her eyes. One thing about men—a little lip biting . . . a little forehead scrunching . . . and definitely a little begging always work.

I run a hand through my hair. "Sure, I'll do it. What time do you need me there?"

Those lips morph into a smile so brilliant it sucks me right in. "In an hour? At Washington Elementary. Search for it on your phone, it's easy to find. You're a lifesaver. And don't forget I owe you." She pats my arm before backing out of the doorway. Pats my arm. Like I'm one of her students. Like she totally forgot about the sight of me—Will Vandergriff, famous baseball player, God's gift to a lot of American women—in Calvin Klein boxer briefs and a whole bunch of muscles. I'm a freaking *GQ* centerfold is what I am. Now I am offended.

And I won't forget. I definitely won't forget.

"You do owe me, but I'll be there," I say, moving to close the door. I leave it cracked for a moment, watching until she fades from view. When she rounds a corner, I shut the door completely.

Suddenly I'm tired. Worn out and sleepy and annoyed and more excited than I should be. It's that last thing that bothers me. No matter how pretty my neighbor appears to be, she isn't my type. She's too uptight to be even close to my type. The attraction I feel is ridiculous.

I head back to my bed. Obviously I need to sleep this thing off.

Sleep always helps.

Chapter 8

Olivia

"And so, once again, I would say to work hard. To be yourselves. To go out into the world and show them what you're made of. Because there's no one like you, no one with your ideas and your character and your outlook on life." There's movement behind me as someone snickers, causing the fourth graders on stage to shift in their seats and begin another round of whispering.

Sweat slides down the back of my neck, and my nose itches. It's the third time I've said these words line for line, but I didn't have time to write a speech. Even if I had, I have no idea what I might have said in place of this catastrophe. Public speaking isn't my thing; if we're being honest here, neither is private speaking. I'm an introvert to the highest degree. Some might think the trait doesn't pair well with grade-school teaching, but shy people will endure all sorts of things when they're passionate about a subject. I love children. I want this generation to love learning as much as I do.

I sweep my gaze across the audience, then immediately wish I hadn't. Yet another child yawns in the front row. That, in addition to the cell phone usage by nearly every person in attendance, the blank stares scattered everywhere, and the occasional eye roll from men and women alike, might make me pass out. This speech is terrible, the worst anyone has ever delivered at a commencement, more boring than an eight-member presidential debate; no one has to tell me that.

I catch Kelly's eye and send her a look. She shifts in her seat and bites back a smile, and it's at that precise moment that I know I'm going to kill Will Vandergriff for putting me through this. I'm going to tell him that right before I grip his neck with both hands and squeeze with all the strength I possess.

With a shaky hand, I tuck a strand of loose hair behind my ear and grip the paper in front of me—the one scratched with words like *encourage, motivate, talk about middle school*—the only notes I could come up with at the last minute, all completely useless. I begin what I hope is a very short wrap-up.

"So to the students onstage, go out there and conquer middle school. It's been a great year, but I know next year will be even better." I turn toward them and give a little fist pump to emphasize my lie, which I'm sure looks about as natural as my attempting to make a three-point shot in a basketball game. I remember fifth grade. It was the worst year of my middle school career, the year Sarah Davenport dubbed me "snot face" and blamed me for cheating off her test. Sarah was not the smartest girl in school, plus she spit through a very large gap in her front teeth every time she spoke, so I tried not to get too close to her. Definitely not close enough to cheat. I never did like Sarah, and I'm still not over it.

I rub sweaty palms on the back of my pants and utter my last words. "Thanks for coming, and have a great summer." People stand and stretch. The words *long, boring,* and *Why did Ms. Pratt have to be our speaker?* drift toward me, but I try my best to shrug them off.

Thank God it's over.

As I knew he would be, Mr. Ellis is at my side within seconds, a smug expression on his face and a faint smear of powdered sugar across his lapel. A little water could have cleaned it up, but I refrain from saying so even as smart-mouth comments work their way past his lips.

"Riveting speech, Ms. Pratt. What happened to the guest speaker you had supposedly lined up? Will Vandergriff, wasn't it? The Rangers player? It's always a pity when things don't quite work out the way we promise they will, isn't it?"

This man makes me insane. As soon as I finish choking the breath out of Will, I'm going to slap the cocky expression off Mr. Ellis's face. I swallow a sigh.

"I suppose it is a shame, though no one else came forward with any better ideas. Not even the person who broke the news to me and claims to personally know several local celebrities who might have been at least marginally entertaining. More so than me, don't you think?" It isn't like me to be so direct, even with him. But I'm flustered and sweaty, I've just given the worst performance of my life, and I'm not in the mood to deal with him. And as for Will . . .

I'll never forgive him for this.

I'm already thinking of ways to make living next door to me a source of constant misery for him. I could scatter kitty litter outside his front door, turn up my Chopin so the sound of classical music drifts through his walls in the afternoon, hang pictures late at night so the racket of a banging hammer keeps him awake. And there might be a few better ideas . . .

"Don't beat yourself up about your speech," Mr. Ellis continues, interrupting my plans for revenge. "I doubt anyone listened to much of what you had to say anyway." He squeezes my elbow and takes in my nonexistent cleavage again, staring a little longer than usual.

"Good lord, could you be more obvious?" Kelly appears and nails him with a scathing glare. "Take your eyes off her chest, Ellis. And I've heard you speak. You wouldn't have done any better."

His face reddens as his eyes meet my hard stare. He doesn't bother looking at Kelly. "You have a good day, now," he says, his jaw set. "Try not to be too discouraged. Only a few people fell asleep." He laughs to himself and walks off.

"I hate him, and I don't hate anyone."

"We all hate him, so you're in good company." Kelly looks around the room. "I didn't know about the speaker cancelling until right before we walked in. Sorry you had to do that by yourself."

I send her an imploring look. "Was it awful?"

And you know what they say: the truth is in the hesitation. "It wasn't terrible . . ."

"Oh shut up. It was awful."

"Pretty bad. But good news." She pats me on the shoulder. "A few people fell asleep, so not everyone will remember it."

"Thanks a lot."

"Anytime." She takes a few steps backward and motions for her class to join her. "I'll see you later."

"See you later." I'm left standing all by myself in a sea of jabbering people, wishing it wasn't my planning period. Forty-five minutes without children. Forty-five minutes in front of me to replay the disaster of the past hour. There are some things in life you just never get over. Embarrassment. The feeling of being unprepared for life's biggest moments. The dismissal of a coworker, even one you can't stand. And being abandoned by a man you were actually beginning to like.

I won't forget this.

And when I'm done, neither will my stupid, ball-playing neighbor.

Will

I turn my head sideways and lie here blinking into the very strong sunlight. As I study the dust particles floating in the air around me, I'm suddenly hit with a weird sense of urgency. A list flashes through my head as though I were turning the pages of a mental day planner. There's our pregame workout this afternoon. A team meeting an hour before the game. A couple of guys talked about going out for drinks after. I'm pretty sure my dry cleaning will be ready to be picked up in an hour.

Aw crap.

I was supposed to be somewhere in an hour. With Olivia. *For* Olivia. And it's been . . . I reach for my cell phone to check the time.

It's been almost three hours. The graduation ceremony is long over by now.

I flip onto my back and scrub a hand over my face, then leave an arm across my forehead.

The worry in her eyes when she told me about the cancelled speaker, the embarrassment I childishly made her endure at the sight of my mostly undressed self, the relief on her face when I said I would help her out. All those images and more assault me and heap layer upon layer of guilt into my subconscious. I have no idea how to apologize . . . no idea how to make it up to her . . . no idea how I will even face her.

The lady might be a little odd, but something deep in my bones tells me that she's sincere. She looked frightened earlier. Almost as if—

Oh dear God. What if she had to deliver the commencement speech herself?

The idea of Olivia up there saying words that I have no doubt would be completely off-the-cuff fills me with an unusual sense of remorse. No regrets, that's my motto. Maybe it's because she's my neighbor and I know I'll be faced with the consequences eventually, though I'm pretty sure her idea of punishment is on the same level of innocence as the rest of her seems to be. She would probably place a banana peel in my path or slam my car with hard-boiled eggs to prove whatever point she's trying to make. I laugh a little to myself just thinking about it.

Still.

I really need to be more careful with people's feelings. Really need to work at saying what I mean and keeping my word. Really need to think more about the careless decisions I make and the people they affect. The intent is always there, but the follow-through . . . let's just say I'm better at pitching than keeping my promises. Sometimes I even think—

The cell phone rings from its spot on my bedside table, and I groan from the desire to suppress the noise. I forgot to silence it again. Never smart, since some people have a sixth sense about when I'll be awake. If I could find whatever triggers that sixth sense, whatever invisible switch exists that tunes certain people into my every movement, I would disable it long enough to take a freaking shower. Instead, I reach for the phone and press the on button.

"Hello?" My voice is raspy and laced with annoyance.

"It's about time you answered," my agent barks. "I'm standing outside. You've got exactly five minutes to get your butt out of bed and answer your front door. You've made quite a mess of things, and somehow we've got to figure out a way to clean it up."

"What are you talking about? I mean, I know we've lost a few games and some of the fault lies with me, but—"

"I'm not talking about the losses."

At that, my blood stops flowing. I've never heard him so angry, so calmly enraged. I sit up and grip the phone, a dozen possible scenarios coming at me like water balloons thrown at a kids' birthday party, but

I'm too tired to duck, so I just sit here with drippy hair and busted latex on my face.

Maybe it's Olivia and her commencement speech, but that makes no sense. He doesn't even know Olivia.

Maybe it's the three games we've lost in a row, but then only one was directly my fault.

Maybe it's the other night when—

The possibilities fall in a heap around me as a nauseating sense of dread settles in my gut. The girl. The fingernails. The bar. The . . . after.

Surely that isn't the reason.

How did anyone even find out?

Chapter 9

Olivia

I saw him wave at me. He doesn't think I saw him, because I'm pretty good at pretending not to notice people—I hide behind my car under the pretense that it's dirty and needs a quick polish, I shove bags of groceries closer to my face to obstruct my vision, I slip on sunglasses and pretend to look off in the distance . . . the list is endless. When you like to keep to yourself, you'll do whatever it takes to make sure your alone status doesn't shift. But I saw him. I pushed my sunglasses a little higher on my nose, and I walked right by. When he called my name, I turned up the music on my phone and kept going down the road with Perry.

This cat and his stupid aversion to a leash. It makes no sense. We follow this routine every afternoon, though we're currently walking in the morning since today is the first official day of summer vacation and I'm able to do whatever I want. Now I want to enjoy a nice walk. Currently all I'm doing is dragging a twenty-pound feline behind me and cursing the eventual moment when I'll have to pick him up. It isn't that he's overly heavy; it's that the wind is blowing a little harder than normal and strands of his hair will be certain to fly up my nose, and I left the house without taking my allergy medication. I'm so forgetful lately. I don't understand what's causing this distracted state.

The music stops playing, replaced by the buzzing of my phone. My already precarious mood dips a little. The day is too nice for phone calls. I check the caller ID and frown. It's been a while since we talked, and I had hoped to keep it that way. It looks like she has other ideas. I give the world a great big eye roll and slide my phone on.

"Hello, Mother." There are other words I could add to that sentence, but I stop at the two most important ones and leave it at that.

"You can't ignore me forever, Olivia Jane."

Suddenly too exhausted to care about germs, I sit crossed-legged on the pavement and rest my chin on my palm. This road is mostly untraveled—a good thing since I'm currently curled up in the middle of it. "I realize that, hence my answering this call."

"Are you going to get in contact with him or not?" she continues. All at once I remember the mother of my early childhood, the woman who brushed my hair for hours and hours just because I loved the way it felt. The woman who read me the same bedtime story night after night after night because I was a bit OCD and she was too kind to draw attention to it. The mother who packed me a peanut butter sandwich with banana and raisins every day of preschool because it turns out you never quite rid yourself of compulsive issues even as you age.

That mother didn't last long.

By the time I hit kindergarten, she was replaced with someone obsessed with perfection and relentless in the pursuit of it for her children. Or, more accurately . . . for her older child. My brother. Star athlete poised for success, though success took a detour in the form of complete derailment. My mother, though . . . she's a still-beautiful woman turned bitter from intense anger at life and all the ways it wronged her. And wronged her it has: my father, my brother, some might say even me. But sometimes you have to let go. Even if it means moving far away from the family you love for the sole purpose of being able to breathe for the first time in your life.

As sad as it is to admit, I'm prepared for things to stay this way forever.

"I haven't decided whether to call him or not," I say. It's honest. I've lost sleep over my brother. I've cried over him. I've missed him and longed for one of his pep talks. But every single time my mind goes down that road, I've had to prevent myself from sliding into another state of depression over things I can't change. In the end, the responsibility lies with him. It's a concept my family has never been able to comprehend, not even when we were younger.

Except, only recently, me.

"He's your brother, Olivia Jane." I hate my middle name, especially when it's strung together with my first and used as a curse word.

"I'm aware of that, Mother. It's been a year. A few more months while I try to make up my mind won't hurt him." I squeeze my eyes shut to ward off an impending headache. "If I call him, I'll do it on his birthday."

She clears her throat, displeased with my answer.

"I sincerely hope you won't let another birthday go by without a word. Last year your silence nearly crushed him."

I open my eyes and stare at the loose bits of gravel resting beside my bare thigh.

I don't say that I've spent my life getting crushed.

I don't say that my life has always been about my older brother.

I don't say that no one ever thinks of me.

I don't say that it might be nice if someone—anyone—saw things from my perspective.

Instead, I say, "I won't. I love you," and hang up the phone with empty promises to call my mother back soon.

And then I curl into myself in the middle of the road, wondering what life would be like if someone cared that much about me.

A few minutes later I'm running. It's hard to run with a cat in your hands, which is why I make it only twenty yards—Perry's poor head jostling against my chest, his meows coming faster and louder in protest and duration—before I give up, lower him to the pavement, and proceed to drag him behind me again. A run would be a nice way to flee the demons that keep assaulting me when I replay the conversation with my mother, but Perry won't have it, and I can't figure out a way to make it work. I glance at the time on my phone. Perfect. In five minutes I'll officially be able to chalk up this last half hour as one I'd like to permanently forget.

My mother.

My brother.

That phone call.

The latest email from my principal this morning—another not-so-gentle reminder to set up next year's graduation speaker at least three months in advance to save myself repeated embarrassment, as though I hadn't done that this year. As though I needed yet another reminder that my speech sucked, and I rarely use words like suck because there are much more interesting words in the English language. More dignified. Less crass.

But it sucked. That's the best way to describe it.

I'm dwelling on this very sad fact when I look up and see him. And if there's actually a rock bottom in life—if it's possible to physically hit it—I just did.

Will Vandergriff.

Jogging right toward me.

And aside from scooping Perry up and holding him in front of my face, I have no way to hide. I glance at my cat, glance at Will's approaching form, panic, panic more, worry about the speed at which my heart is racing.

And then decide it's hopeless.

Twisting the loop of the leash in a tight ring around my wrist, I stand in the road and wait. I wish for the earth to open up and swallow me, for a tree to choose this exact moment to fall on me, for a car to flatten me perpendicular to the yellow lines, for a very out-of-place mountain lion to—

"What's that look on your face for?" Will comes to a halt in front of me. In his black fitted tee and gray gym shorts, he's all sweaty and wind-blown and perfect. Seriously, his brown hair looks like he just rolled out of bed—and *not* from sleeping. It makes me dislike him even more. I cross my arms over my chest, inadvertently choking Perry. He squeals. I look down and gasp when I see that I've accidently hung him by his own leash. I loosen the leash and plant what I hope is a menacing glare into my eyes.

"What look? The one that I hope communicates how much I'd like to kill you?" A friend once told me I had a way of sounding intensely threatening if I tried hard enough. That's the tone I'm going for now. Will doesn't flinch like I hoped, so it's hard to know if it worked.

"No, I mean the look of terror, the look that says you're afraid of me, the look that screams *someone find me a place to hide*. That look." He glances at Perry. "And speaking of killing, good job almost doing it to your furball."

I'm now fairly sure it didn't work. My eyes narrow because now he's just getting on my nerves. "Stop calling him that. I'm not afraid of you, and I certainly have no desire to hide." Lies, all lies. He doesn't need to know that.

"It sure looked like it." He takes a deep breath and rests his hands on very well-defined hips. And in those shorts, it's hard not to stare at—

"You mad at me?"

I force my eyes upward and focus on his question, telling myself his body is officially off-limits. Until he raises the hem of his tee and uses it to swipe at his forehead. It's so unfair, the way my eyes dart to his waistline and lock there, pulled in by some sort of athlete magnetic force that I've unfortunately been around my whole life. There's comfort in familiarity. But only for a second.

It takes work, but I make myself look away.

His body.

Is off-limits.

Starting right now.

Remember that, Olivia.

I blink at him.

"Why would I be mad at you?" My voice is shaky, slightly breathless. I swallow and command a little more venom in my tone. "For leaving me on my own? For breaking your word? For making me look like a fool in front of the entire student body and my coworkers? What about any of that could possibly make me mad?"

"Touché. I deserve that."

"You deserve it and more." I look toward the tree line behind Will's head, beginning to feel my anger ebb and morph into something that feels a bit too much like rejection. I'm best friends with the emotion and don't welcome it. Not when I've worked so hard for two years to keep it at bay. I gather up a little of my self-control and look at Will's face. "Why would you do that? If you didn't want to help, all you had to do was say so. There's nothing nice about standing up a woman, especially not when doing so causes her so much embarrassment."

The words are meant to sound like a lecture; instead they wind up sounding pathetic. Like a plea for an apology. Maybe that's what they are. A lock of hair escapes my ponytail and I push it off my forehead. When it falls again, I leave it alone and stare at the ground.

"Hey."

Will's voice is so soft that I can't help but look up. Our gazes lock—mine wrapped in rejection, his in apology.

"I'm sorry I stood you up. It wasn't intentional, but it was unfair. I hope you'll give me another chance." He reaches out and tucks that stray strand of hair behind my ear, and my breath catches in my throat. My lungs feel so small that there's no way I can grab enough air. His fingers brush the skin of my cheekbone and my face grows warm. I swallow, trying to remember how to speak.

"Fine. I'll give you another chance." I sound so weak, so absent of my former resolve. What happened to threatening? To intense? Instead I feel empty, drained, but there's not much to do. Life is what it is, and I apparently just decided to forgive Will. I wish there was a way to keep hating this guy, to keep thinking my neighbor is as shallow and brainless as the company he surrounds himself with, but he keeps proving me wrong. "But only one more. Two strikes and I'm done with you."

"The general rule is three."

"Well you only get two because I don't play by the rules." This is a bold statement. Slightly false. I'm a rule follower to the point that no one even likes to play Monopoly with me. Because if the bank says you're out of money, then you're out of money. There's no leniency, not even among friends.

"Not a rule follower?" Will grins as he processes my words. "That's great to hear, because I actually need you for something now. Something that a stricter woman might find a bit questionable."

My senses go on alert; my words come back to haunt me. I want to tell him that I'm strict, the strictest. That I believe in rules. That if people try to cheat even in the slightest, I no longer want to play the game.

Something tells me Will Vandergriff just played me.

Five minutes into his explanation of harassment, inappropriate behavior, and lawsuits, I'm certain of it.

Will

"You want me to what?"

Olivia's mouth is hanging open and she's laughing, but it's an insulting laughter. The kind an audience delivers when watching something unusually absurd, like a particularly bad *Saturday Night Live* skit or any rerun of the Kardashians. Don't ask me how I know about them; I just do. I even think I see a tear in the corner of her eye, and it's really starting to piss me off. I'm Will freaking Vandergriff. Nothing funny about that.

"I said I want you to pretend to be my girlfriend."

I bite out the words, and just like the first time, they make my stomach turn. But what else am I supposed to do? I can't think of any other option, and though it occurs to me that it's somewhat hypocritical of me to ask her for such a huge favor when I just stood her up at the precise moment she needed one from me . . . I'm desperate. I need her help now. Plus, if we're being entirely honest, I'm used to getting what I want from the opposite sex. Women like to be around me. Love it, actually. There's no reason to believe Olivia is an exception to this rule.

Except she's still laughing.

Wiping underneath her eyes.

And then there's the unfortunate fact that she says this:

"You're out of your mind."

She gives me a disgusted look, then turns to walk away. Now I'm mad. I stare after her for a moment, convinced she's only testing me— man, her butt looks good in those yoga pants—but she keeps walking. She's a good twenty yards away before I decide she isn't kidding. Olivia is leaving me helpless and all by myself in the middle of the road. Does she seriously not know who I am? I've got to stop her. I've also got to rescue my ego before it crash-lands on the pavement and she makes a point of stomping on it.

"Come on, Olivia," I call after her. I sound impatient. Probably not the best way to bring her over to my side. "I wouldn't ask you if it wasn't important. I need your help. And by the way, I never beg. That's how you know I'm sincere. I'm begging you to help me."

I think that last sentence might have sounded slightly sarcastic. Maybe a little degrading, especially since I put a little extra emphasis on the word *you*, as though by asking for her particular help I've stooped to an all-time low.

Pretty sure Olivia heard it.

She spins in a one-eighty and plants a hand on her hip, little bits of gravel shooting out from around her feet. I half-expect her to pick up a few of those rocks and hurl them in my direction, but she doesn't. I admire the self-control.

"Is that supposed to make me feel important—telling me you never beg? Is that supposed to make me feel honored that you would ask *me?*" Yep, she heard it. She presses a hand to her chest and bobs her head the way women do when they're mocking men. I swear it's either an innate skill or mothers everywhere teach their daughters how to do this before they can walk.

"No, you're not supposed to feel honored," I say. I mean, she is, but clearly Olivia isn't into that sort of thing. Maybe ballplayers don't impress her? "But will you help me anyway? I'll buy you dinner. And you know, a little travel might even be involved." I'm lying, but even from here, I can see the way her head tilts a bit, the way her shoulders straighten an inch. She's thinking . . . that last part might have actually worked.

"I hate travel. I hate dinner even more."

Maybe not.

"No one hates travel. And everyone eats dinner."

She crosses her arms over her chest. "True, but I like to do both alone."

Now we're caught in a stare down. "Why alone? That sounds awful."

"Not if you enjoy your own company."

She's got me there. I like to be surrounded by other people. A virtual football huddle in daily sixteen-hour stretches, minus time for sleeping. In the presence of only myself is not somewhere I normally like to be.

"Okay, scratch the travel. Would you consider just coming to one game?" That same strand of hair falls in her face and she blows it away.

"What night?"

"Tomorrow night, if that works. It's the start of our series against the Tigers."

"The Tigers . . ."

She looks so serious in thought that my lip twitches, but I fight against it. I can tell just by watching her that she's on the hook. Testing the idea. Nibbling at it. Thinking about taking a full bite. I take a second to study the pavement. Women. They're so predictable, no matter how different their personalities. I don't know what possessed me to think she wouldn't agree to my plan. Of course she would. I'm Will Vandergriff. The whole world is in love with me, even if I'm currently losing. Why do I keep forgetting that?

I'm full-on in the middle of my skyrocketing ego trip—no crash-landing involved, thank you very much—when she hits me with another comment.

"Okay, you have yourself a deal. But I have two requirements."

My spine chills as the control I thought I had over the situation inches its way downward. This is my game. No one tells me how to play it. Not her. Not anyone.

Still, I force myself to ask, "Which are?"

"You can't try to kiss me, not once." She blows that stubborn strand of hair off her forehead again and looks at me like she wishes it would be so easy to remove me. "You might think you're cute and all, but baseball players aren't my thing. Especially not you."

With those words, I'm looking at what used to be that skyrocketing ego lying in small chunks all around my feet. I consider stepping on them myself just to watch the way they flatten. It makes me think of pancakes, but suddenly I'm not at all hungry.

Why especially not me?

With this thought at the forefront of my mind, I brace myself for her second requirement. Surely it can't be as bad as the remark she just hit me with. Surely. Why don't I know any other available women in Dallas? My thoughts shoot to Lexi from the bar, but she's the reason I'm in this mess. So I'm left with Olivia. I lift a shoulder to indicate that I'm waiting for her to keep going. She mentioned two requirements after all. When she doesn't catch the hint, I roll my eyes.

"Fine, no kissing you. That shouldn't be too hard since you seem to have an aversion to my kind." *Do I sound hostile?* I force an ease into my tone, reminding myself that I need her help. "So are you going to tell me your second condition, or do you just want me to start guessing? No making out? No trying on your clothes, especially not your underwear? No weird celebrity name combining into something like Willovia or Olivilla . . . ?"

She looks at me like I've lost my mind, but then she does the oddest thing. She doesn't laugh. She just looks at the ground and smiles to herself. And maybe it should bother me when she bites her lower lip and uses her shoe to push a pebble out of the way. And maybe I should call the whole thing off when she looks up at me with a gleam in her eye that clearly has nothing to do with the joke I just made.

But that gleam is so bright. Mesmerizing. And I'm no longer a big-time baseball player with a self-image that could fill a bedroom and an oversize walk-in closet. I'm now just a guy powerless to do anything but stare at her blue eyes and wish I were closer to them.

"No, I'm not going to tell you yet. I'll tell you eventually," she says. "But for now let's just stick with the no kissing thing."

And with those words, I'm left realizing that I may have laid out the plans for a new game, but Olivia just made the rules.

Chapter 10

Olivia

"Olivia, are you coming?" Will's question hangs on the other end of the line, but I can't think of the right response. It's only been a few hours since we last talked, and I'm still not sure how I feel about this silly arrangement. I sigh and reach for Perry's back, stroking it back and forth, watching as my fingers make a jagged pathway through his white fur. After a moment he looks up at me and then scoots to the other end of my bed, plopping down next to my pillow with a sigh. Even he wants to be left alone tonight.

Still, Will is waiting. I sigh and look around the room. He wants me to go to dinner with him and work out a plan to convince the higher-ups at his work that we're a couple, but I don't want to. It isn't that the idea of dating him is bad or that I hate the thought of traveling—which I'm convinced was a lie on his part anyway; I have a fantastic ability to see through those sorts of things—it's that I don't think I can pull it off. There are just so many bad combinations looming in front of me: I hate baseball, being at a game might cause an all-too-familiar panic attack, I'm no good in social circles, and he wears a very unfortunate number.

That's the worst part. I can't get over that stupid number. Why does it have to be thirteen?

"Will, I think you need to find someone else. Someone prettier. Someone who's a better talker. Someone who knows a thing or two about your job."

That last part is laughable. I know more than most people about Will's job.

"I'm sitting here eating out of a bread basket by myself." He says it like he didn't even hear my suggestions. "Everything about this is pathetic."

"Order an entrée and you'll look more refined. Try the lobster bisque. I hear it's great there."

"I hate eating alone, and that's a soup. I hate soup."

"Is there anything you like?"

"I like cats. And schoolteachers."

"We both know you're lying."

I catch a glimpse of myself in the mirror. I'm wearing a rare dress and my hair is down. I guess it isn't a bad look for me. There are definitely prettier girls out there, but I might not be too bad to look at. It isn't entirely impossible that Will could eventually like me a little . . .

But I don't want him to like me. Nothing about it would work well. And he called me crazy. I keep forgetting that. Starting now, I vow to remember it. Eyeing a Sharpie, I consider writing *he thinks you're nuts* on my wrist so I'll have it to look at every time my thoughts begin to wander, but I decide against it. I've always wanted a tattoo. Maybe Will's right. Maybe I am crazy.

"Call up one of your teammates. See if they'll eat with you."

"Come on, Olivia. I'll order a bottle of wine and we'll just talk." The clink of silverware sounds over the line. "Please help me with this. As for all those things you're afraid of—I'll teach you everything you need to know about my job, you won't have to talk all that much at the game, and as for being pretty . . ." He clears his throat. "You'll put all the other players' wives and girlfriends to shame."

I smile like an idiot. He's being kind because he needs my help, but I can't wipe the traitorous grin from my face no matter how hard I scold myself for it.

"Fine. But I only like Moscato, and I don't drink much. A glass is fine, no need for a bottle."

He laughs. "I'll get a glass for you, but the bottle is for me."

I hang up with a promise to be there in ten minutes, my nerves tripling in threat and volume as they bounce around inside my chest. I don't think I can do this. It's more than I bargained for. Why did he have to go out with that girl anyway? Why do men make such dumb decisions like picking up women in bars? Especially when the rest of us are perfectly content to just go there and eat.

It does make me the tiniest bit happy to know he first thought the woman was me.

I sit at the edge of my bed and force myself not to go there. Then I count to ten. When I hit nine, I put my head in my hands and decide to keep going. This case of stage fright is going to require more numbers than usual.

At thirty-two I stand up and smooth out my dress, feeling only marginally better than before.

At forty I grab the Sharpie and scrawl out the words on my wrist. Somehow this needs to stick.

At forty-nine I reach for my purse.

At fifty-two I open the front door.

At fifty-seven I'm starting up my engine.

At seventy-six I'm pulling onto the freeway.

I lose count somewhere in the mid-hundreds, but by then I'm maneuvering into the restaurant's parking lot and climbing out of my vehicle. With shaking limbs, I walk toward the restaurant's main entrance. I don't know what I'm so nervous about. I came here to tell Will Vandergriff to find another girl, not to offer myself as a living sacrifice that would certainly get trampled underfoot somewhere around third base. It won't be hard to turn him down. There's absolutely no reason to worry.

I almost have myself convinced that nonchalance is a new way of life when I walk inside, give the hostess Will's name, and scan the room in search of him. I spot him sitting in a corner by himself. He sips a glass of wine, one arm resting across the back of the chair next to him. He's the epitome of casual confidence as he smiles at the couple sitting at a neighboring table, nodding in answer to a question they've just asked. The couple has clearly spotted a star, and he's giving them what they want. Conversation. Camaraderie. A few minutes of exclusivity.

As I watch him, my resolve falters.

Because that's when I realize I have everything in common with that couple seated next to him. Just like them, I am starstruck and pulled in by his magnetism. And even though I am me and Will is famous and the idea is so laughable it's absurd, for a moment I entertain the idea that Will Vandergriff could be mine. Suddenly it's what I want more than anything.

Even if every second of it will be pretend.

Will

One look at her walking in my direction, and I'm hit with so many things at once.

She's going to turn me down.

She hates my job.

She may also hate me.

That one stumps me, because it's something I've never encountered before. People like me. Everyone likes me. Fans like me. Maybe not the

Rangers fans as of late, but they'll come around eventually. I think. But never mind them; they're not important. Announcers like me. Players like me. Women for sure. *You can't kiss me.* Those four words have played through my mind on repeat since she said them. Women might like me, but Olivia isn't a normal woman. And she still hasn't told me her second requirement, says she won't until our arrangement is over. On the one hand, I dread finding out; on the other, it means I get to spend a little more time with her even when everything is finished.

And I definitely want to spend more time with her. That much is clear just by the sight of her walking toward me. Watching her, I'm speechless . . . breathless . . . lacking in confidence and intelligence and the basic ability to think in more than single syllables that aren't even real words.

She's so freaking hot.

I've never seen anyone hotter in my life.

She's wearing a short blue dress and heels—she looks so good that now I see her fascination with the color—the hem skirting her tanned and toned thighs in a way that has my imagination running in all kinds of directions, none of them anything I could ever say out loud. Her hair is down again and styled in perfect little waves that fall well past her shoulders. Summer has been great to her so far. The number of men in the room who turn to look her way doesn't surprise me; the fact that Olivia doesn't seem to notice does. I'm around sexy women all the time. The difference is that every single one of them knows it.

Suddenly it feels warm in here. Overly warm. For all the complaining I've done about playing baseball on a Texas field, being in this room with Olivia this close to me is worse. Much worse.

"It's about time you showed up. Another five minutes, and I was out of here," I say, forcing indifference into my tone. I look up, tracing the outline of her lips with my gaze. I've never seen lips like hers before. How have I never seen lips like hers before? I pick up my half-empty wineglass and take a long sip to soothe my painfully dry throat. Then

I do it again in hopes of getting a buzz going. I will need it to endure sitting across from her.

"Found someone else to take my place already, have you?" She pulls out her chair and lowers herself into the seat across from me. I probably should have done the gentlemanly thing and pulled it out for her myself, but this isn't a date. This is a business arrangement, and I want it over and done with as fast as possible. Finished. She goes her way and I go mine. At least that's what I tell myself a few times, hoping to make it stick.

She smiles at me. Her eyes look bluer than I remember.

It didn't stick.

And there's not even a little buzz.

Annoyed with myself, I clear my throat. "Yes, as a matter of fact I have. Our waitress said she would help me for a thirty percent tip, so I agreed. As soon as she's off work, we're going out for drinks to talk terms." The topic of conversation chooses that moment to refill our water glasses and hand Olivia a menu. After a quiet "thank you" from Olivia, our waitress walks away.

Olivia leans toward me and drops her voice. "She's at least fifty, but maybe you're into the whole cougar thing."

"The older the better. Seventy is more my style, gray hair and all," I say, and for a long moment we just stare at each other. Olivia opens her mouth like she wants to say something but seems to think the better of it. She bites her lip—that perfect lower lip—and fidgets in place. For one fleeting moment I wonder if she has ever dated anyone seriously before, but then dismiss the idea. Of course she has. Every twenty-nine-year-old woman has had at least a few relationships. Haven't they?

"Will, I really think someone else would do a better job than me. And really, I don't even know why you would want me in the first place." She reaches for her silverware and rearranges it next to the plate, tallest to shortest, spoon on the outside.

It's a good question. Why do I want her? I scramble for an explanation that sounds halfway believable and take a deep breath.

"I've lived here two months, and the only women I know are the girlfriends and wives of my fellow teammates. Asking any of them would make me look like even more of a jerk than I already do. No offense." Her face falls; there seems to be no end to my douche-baggery. Unable to take back the words, I keep going. "Also, you're innocent. No one would ever suspect you of acting." Two plates are delivered and placed in front of us. I pick up my fork and watch while Olivia butters a roll and breaks it into small pieces. "And I promise it will only be for a few days. Once the controversy dies down . . ."

She stops, takes a moment to swallow, and looks at me. "You were caught drinking and driving with the team owner's stepdaughter in your car. I hate to break it to you, but there's a tiny chance the controversy won't die down."

Olivia is smarter than I thought. She's right. I'm in more trouble than anyone knows, even myself. But right now it's all speculation— Lexi's word against mine, and she's the one who decided to talk.

"I wasn't exactly caught; she's just telling everyone about it. Right now the only strike against me is her claim."

"Except for the fact that she has pictures of the two of you kissing in the car and at her apartment, none of which are attractive, by the way. I've seen them online. She looks sick and slobbery and you look like a stupid, overeager teenager."

I shift positions. "First of all, those pictures don't tell the whole story. Second of all, she was sick. She threw up about ten minutes after we got to her apartment. And as for me . . . the fact that we're having this conversation at all kind of validates that opinion."

She tries to hold back a smile but isn't quite successful. I reach for my wineglass again. Olivia has a way of pointing out my flaws, and I don't like it. But she has a point, and I have a problem. One I haven't quite figured out how to remedy. That's where she comes in. I'm hoping that Olivia will have a solution I haven't yet thought of. She's a teacher, after all. Somewhere inside of all the neuroses that make up her quirky personality, she has a fully functioning brain. And considering the fact that she doesn't drink, her brain cells are probably much more active than mine.

I take a deep breath and look around the restaurant, then settle my gaze on Olivia once again. I decide to turn on the charm and force a little innuendo into my tone. It's worked well for me in the past. "Maybe we could come up with an explanation for that. Maybe if people think it wasn't just me and Lexi there that night . . ."

I should have known it wouldn't work with Olivia. She practically rolls her eyes and looks at me with disgust.

"The little pathway that your thoughts are traveling down right now? I don't walk that way." She leans forward to make sure I'm really getting it. "Here's the deal. I'll help you, but the minute you start implying I've done something sleazy just to clean up your own reputation, I'm out. And if it comes to that, you'll have two girls ready to tell stories about you." Her lip trembles from anger, and I wish I could take that idea back. She isn't used to being so direct, but I've forced her hand with my arrogant attitude. "Do right by me, Will. All the time. Okay?"

Right then I would agree to anything just to keep her from being upset.

"You have my word."

With a sigh, she picks up her fork and stabs at her salad. When she shoves a bite in her mouth and begins to chew, I grow a little calmer. Until I see—

"What's on your wrist?"

Olivia drops her arm into her lap.

"None of your business. Now, when do we start?"

Chapter 11

Olivia

My palms start sweating before I climb out of my car. Despite the preferred parking pass that Will forced me to hang from my rearview mirror, which would have given me front row access, I park in the back of the lot, farthest from the gate. That way I don't have to worry about someone knocking into my car and putting an obnoxious ding in the side. I used a wipe on the white finish this morning to erase all the smudge marks caused by last night's rain; now it shines. The last thing I need is a dent I'm unable to remove. I hate being powerless to fix things. This way, that possibility can be avoided.

Plus, the long walk to the stadium will do me good. I want the extra time to make sure my mind is in control and my breathing in order, and to keep the rising panic attack currently stuck in my chest from completely overtaking me and making me look like a fool in front of a box full of people I'm supposed to impress. I press a hand to my stomach and stop between a red sports car and a blue Town & Country.

What am I doing?

I have no idea what I'm doing.

I mean, I know what I'm doing because I've been here before, but what am I doing here now?

I have no idea how to impress people. No idea how to engage in meaningful conversation. The graduation ceremony is a painful reminder of that cold reality. I'm a bore. Entertainment at its worst. A marginally decent alternative to counting sheep for the sleep deprived.

I brace myself on the hood of the red car and count to ten, aware that I'm causing an entire handprint's worth of smudge marks on this poor person's vehicle, but it can't be helped. This is going to be awful. If I don't trip over my own two feet on my way to the suite, I'll most certainly blurt out some random boring fact I remember from my childhood and get Will into more trouble than he's already in. No one cares that there are ninety feet between the bases on a major-league field. Or that to hit a home run, the average player needs to both hit the ball a minimum of four hundred feet *and* clear the center field wall, which itself is an average of seven feet tall. Or that Tropicana Field, home of the Tampa Bay Rays, is the smallest major-league field in America and that Dodger Stadium in Los Angeles is the largest—seating forty thousand and fifty-six thousand respectively. Or that this particular ballpark—Globe Life Field in Arlington—seats forty-eight thousand if you don't count the grassy area.

These are the facts I entertained myself with while I watched from the stands as my brother played the game—reading them in brochures that my father carried around in his briefcase, listening as my grandfather recounted all the fields he had been to as a boy, asking to be told again and again and again because that's what girls with attention deficits do, even when it drives everyone around them crazy. These are the things I remember most. These are the things I could talk about at endless length to anyone who might want to listen.

But I can't.

Because these are the things that no one cares about.

It's the story of my life, magnified and getting ready to unfold in front of very important people, and I'm the idiot who agreed to participate. And for what?

For what?

That's when I remember. It's funny how sometimes it only takes a fleeting mental image of hair color or a remembered piece of worn fabric to bring everything into alignment . . . to make panic subside and purpose slide into the empty space. And just like that, mine does. I'm doing this for a reason. A very valid and important one. One that I'll likely remember for the rest of my life if all goes according to plan.

Clutching the VIP lanyard that dangles from my neck, I walk toward Will Call to retrieve my ticket, then check the name of the suite that I'm expected to be at in the next five minutes, not that the name Coca-Cola means anything to me. Who names a suite after a soda, anyway? That's not very classy. Spotting an usher to my right, I smooth out the lines on my royal-blue cotton top and head toward him. Even though I love the color blue, I feel a little odd wearing it in a shade this bright, but today called for it.

Hearing a low hum that has nothing to do with the field, I stop walking and glance to my left. There it is, Six Flags, only one short mile away. If I were smarter I would walk over there and hop on a water ride, then let it soak me to the point that I'm too unpresentable to show up tonight. And then with dripping hair and a new outlook on life, I could get myself a funnel cake. I love funnel cake. Love it. But I hate being wet. And I'm not that smart. It's a trait often falsely attributed to schoolteachers.

With a sigh, I tear my eyes away and head for the gate.

A few seconds later I'm inside an elevator, riding upward with two women and a man who look like they belong here. All are dressed a little too high-class for a ball game—the man in jeans and dress shoes, both women in red heels and hair extensions, all three wearing custom-made Rangers shirts—I know fashion when I see it. When the doors open and they walk purposefully down a hallway of gray steel doors with titles over the top—titles like the Hank Aaron Suite and the Walter Johnson Suite—my hunch is confirmed. They know what they're doing.

That makes everyone but me.

It isn't until I open the door to The Coca-Cola Suite and step over the threshold that I realize just how much in the dark I actually am. A woman with the brightest red hair I've ever seen walks toward me with a Julia Roberts smile on her face and what looks like a glass of brandy in her hand.

"You must be Olivia. We've all been expecting you."

When half the heads in the room swivel toward me, I swallow the desire to bolt and force down a new wave of panic.

Will has talked about me.

A million awful scenarios flash through my mind. Cats. Screwdrivers. Graduation speeches. Sitting alone on an abandoned road. More images hit me full force and then dissolve into a plume of overwhelming confusion. Although the lady smiles at me, I'm not sure whether it's genuine or polite.

Because I have no idea what he told them.

———

Will

Everything about this game feels different, and not only because we're finally winning. It's the bottom of the sixth, and I haven't made a single mistake. No walks, no stolen bases despite four real attempts so far, and the Detroit Tigers haven't scored a single run—unusual for them. Blake has played impeccably the entire game, and anyone who has managed to make it to third has been tagged out by him before their feet hit home. This isn't normal. Still, the feeling has me riding an elusive wave of euphoria, and the change feels good. Something I could easily become addicted to if given the opportunity.

I just wish I could pinpoint the cause.

For a brief second, I wonder how Olivia is handling things up in the suite. Hopefully she's doing a decent job of acting like she adores me. Shouldn't be too hard, considering it's only one game and I'm . . . you know . . . me.

Shaking my head, I put my overthinking ways aside for now, pull my cap low over my forehead, get into position, and acknowledge the signal for a fastball—something we haven't used much tonight. I'm glad for it; we're ahead by five and I want to see the margin increase. Nothing gives a team more confidence than getting so far in the lead there's almost no chance to lose. The opportunity doesn't arise often and certainly hasn't for us lately, but when it does, the best thing to do is grab onto it and let it carry you through to the end. Our season is nearly halfway over; despite our recent losing streak we still have a decent chance of coming out ahead. If we play things right, we could see ourselves in first place soon. Not a bad way to wind up, considering how the season started.

The batter gets set, but then Blake shakes his head and points two fingers, changing signals. My eyebrows go up. It isn't like him to change mid-play, and I don't want a curveball. I want a fastball and shake my head in a silent argument, convinced the fastball is the way to go. He points two fingers again—he's stubborn like that—then points away from the batter. I've been straying a bit to the outside; I get the message. I think about arguing more but relent, then wind up and sail the ball right into the center of his glove. I resist an eye roll. Blake was right. He'll drop a few *I told you so*'s after the game because that's what he does, and I'll suck it up and deal with it.

"Strike!" The umpire's shout is music to my ears.

When that same word consistently flies out of his mouth, when I'm replaced in the seventh and our backup pitcher continues the same flawless streak, when runners continue to make it home for the remainder of the game, it's all like a platinum-selling album playing from the overhead sound system. I've never heard a more beautiful word said so many times in one night.

Before I know it, the ninth inning is over and I'm yanking off my hat and running toward my teammates. We're celebrating on the field, shouting in the dugout, and all I can think is *I'm back.* I'm on my game. I'm not going anywhere. Not even with this stupid accusation following me around.

And that's when the euphoria fades. And that's when it dawns on me in the same way an oil spill might slowly ruin a picturesque fishing hole. A few hours ago I jumped in the water, swam around for a while, and now I'm covered in sludge and surrounded by dead fish.

Way to go, idiot.

I'm screwed.

Screwed.

So incredibly screwed.

Because Olivia.

Olivia is the one thing that was different about tonight. The only change I've made in a long string of sketchy playing.

And just like my teammates and almost everyone else I know who makes a career out of this game, I'm a bit of a superstitious sort. Before every game, my socks go on first the left foot, then the right—Nike symbol facing out and slightly toward the back of my calf. I eat a turkey sandwich on rye with Swiss in the mornings, then chase it with two cups of black coffee. Normally I like the drink loaded with sugar and cream, but not on game days. And I take three showers—one the second I wake up, another right before practice, and another right after the game. I love the feel of dirt on my hands and dust in my mouth during a game, but all of it has to come off immediately after. It's just the way I've always been. But all of this poses a problem.

For Olivia.

Because something tells me that crazy chick just turned into my good-luck charm.

And because of that unfortunate fact, starting tonight . . .

She's not going anywhere.

Chapter 12

Olivia

"No."

"Why not?"

"Because I said so."

Seriously, I feel like we're in preschool, engaging in a battle of four-year-old wills.

For nearly an hour I sat alone in the stands, waiting for him after the game like he asked me to. Had I known this conversation awaited, I would have run every stop sign and traffic light in an effort to get home quickly. Now I'm fast walking to my car with Will trailing behind me, asking me the same senseless question over and over. Men and their inability to listen.

He pushes against my car door before I reach the handle, preventing me from opening it. I shoot him a look.

"Move your hand, Will."

"Come on, Olivia. What could possibly be so bad about one more game? Were the women mean to you or something?"

I roll my eyes at his stupid question and yank on the handle. It won't budge. "Yes, they really hurt my feelings and wouldn't let me play with them at recess. Not sure I'll ever get over the trauma."

Will misses the sarcasm. "Who was it? I'll make them apologize."

I sigh. As though my biggest fear is not fitting in with the popular crowd. The women were perfectly nice, save for one brunette named Candy who kept pointing out that I'm a schoolteacher, and it wasn't a compliment. She repeatedly said the word in a long, drawn-out, pitying tone.

So you're a schoolteacher. Does that pay much?

So you're a schoolteacher. Do you find it hard to deal with kids?

So you're a schoolteacher. It must be nice not to have to work all summer.

That last one left my fingers itching with the desire to flick her on the nose, especially considering she'd just finished a long monologue about the painful aspects of Botox and not being able to find a good housekeeper, and then a list of complaints about a decorator who had the gall to take a twelve-week maternity leave in the middle of birthday season. To that I wondered, *There's such a thing as birthday season?* Not exactly the problems your average American woman faces. But I said nothing. I just kept talking to the woman who opened the door for me and whose name I forgot the moment she introduced herself.

Now I'm stuck in a parking lot with a belligerent Will, though I can't deny his willingness to defend me touches a pleasant little part of my mind. The part that also enjoys ice cream and a shoe sale at Dillard's, neither of which I entertain often and both of which I find completely unnecessary.

I shake my head to clear it, determined to stand my ground.

"Will, they weren't mean. But I'm not going back again."

"It's just for one game."

"That's what you said last time."

"But this time I mean it."

And that's when he gives himself away with a little eye flick to the side. It wouldn't be just one game. It would be another and another and another, except it makes no sense. Why in the world would he want me here at all? I'm not self-assured or beautiful or every guy's dream date, so what's the appeal? It takes all my self-control not to come out and ask him. I hardly want to seem unsure of myself.

We face each other in a standoff until I realize I've placed my hand on the door, fingers unwittingly overlapping his. With a start, I pull my hand back and lean against the door, then look at the pavement.

"Tell me why," I say.

Maybe I expect a lie or some dressed-up half-truth, I'm not sure. I don't, however, expect his simple honesty.

He raises a shoulder. "Because we won."

My eyebrows push together at the same time I feel a sinking inside me. I'm going to cave. I'm going to do it, what he wants. That doesn't mean I'm going to bend without at least appearing to resist.

"What does that have to do with me?"

Will takes a step back and leans against the car behind him. We both know I'm not going to climb in my car and drive away. He sighs and looks up into the night sky. Stars are everywhere, the Big Dipper shining brightly above his left shoulder. I get lost in the vision for a moment until he begins talking. And then my eyes lock on his. I'm suddenly not sure what's prettier.

"I have no idea, Olivia. All I know is that we've lost the last five games I've pitched, mostly due to my own errors." It pains him to admit it out loud, and he winces. "But tonight we won. Not only won, but I played one of the best games I've played all season. And maybe it's stupid, but . . ."

"You're superstitious."

It's a statement, not a question. I know baseball. I know players. Superstitions are as much a part of the job as a bat and ball. Some run deeper than others, but everyone has a ritual of some sort. For my brother, it was breakfast cereal. Frosted Flakes and almond milk eaten with the same spoon at the same time on every game-day morning. Everything in our home was store brand, but the Frosted Flakes were always the real kind. Nothing but the best for the star of our family.

An embarrassed grin curves Will's mouth. "Maybe I am, or maybe I just developed the trait tonight."

I tilt my head. "Do you put your socks on right foot first or left?"

He snickers and rolls his eyes. "Left, of course. You only do right if you want to lose."

I try not to laugh at the logic. But I can't make fun of him. I have superstitions of my own that I would rather not explain. Especially not to him. I study the ground for a long moment, at war with myself. Finally I relent. Anything else is just pretending.

"One more game. I'll go to one more game."

An eyebrow goes up in surprise. "You will?"

"One," I remind him.

"I mean, unless we win."

"Will . . ."

"Fine, one game. Probably."

"You're ridiculous."

Without thinking, I push against his chest and feel my face flush, but I'm not sure if it's from embarrassment or agitation. Either way, I like the way he's looking at me, a teasing glint in his eye that I'm sure a thousand women before me have fallen for.

"If you win," I say, more to distract myself than anything, "you can consider me your good-luck charm. But if I'm your good-luck charm, it's going to cost you a lot more than what I've already mentioned."

Will raises an eyebrow, something I'm beginning to notice he does quite often. "The only thing you've mentioned is that I can't kiss you. Is that costing me something?"

That teasing tone is still there. It's my raging blush that's new.

"N . . . no," I stammer. "I just meant that—"

"Tell you what," he interrupts. "If we win again and I can convince you to keep showing up, you can name your price."

He reaches forward and opens my car door, then gestures for me to climb inside. I should be relieved to be leaving. After all, overweight, half-blind cats are easier to handle than men who look like billboard posters and smell like wintergreen. But I can't ignore the part of me that deflates a bit.

"Sounds good to me," I say, forcing a lightness into my tone that I don't feel. "What night do you pitch again?"

"Monday."

"Fine. Then I'll be there Monday."

"Thank you. I'll see you around, Olivia. Maybe even later tonight at the dumpster."

I smile and slide behind the wheel, then look up at him.

"Dumpsters are your thing, not mine. I'll see you Monday," I remind him. "Same time, same place?"

He nods. "Same time, same place."

I back up and pull out of the lot. Just before I get to the main road, I glance in my rearview mirror.

Will is standing exactly where I left him, staring after me as I drive away.

———

Will

It's a long walk to my car on the other side of the stadium, but I haven't moved from my spot. There's no explaining why I'm staring after a car long gone, but here I am doing it.

I make my feet move just to feel less foolish.

I've been around a lot of women in my life—strangers and groupies and sisters of friends and friends of friends and nieces of colleagues.

Some I've dated, some I've spent time with out of obligation, out of pity or old-fashioned guilt. Nearly all of these relationships were to boost my own already inflated ego.

I've never had a problem with that until now.

There's something about Olivia. Something I can't put my finger on. She doesn't put up with my crap and has never once tried to impress me. Something tells me she would be just as interested in talking to the mailman as she is in talking to me. She isn't captivated by my job or by the perks that come with being famous. She makes me uneasy and self-conscious in ways I don't want to admit out loud. I haven't felt this way about anything since the first time I stepped up to the pitcher's mound in the major leagues. Arms shaky, chest tight, gut churning, all senses screaming at me not to throw up in the dirt. For a guy like me who's been lucky enough to see his biggest dream come true, it's a feeling you never forget.

For some reason, with her, I'm okay with all of it.

I fish my cell phone out of my back pocket and dial her number, trying to keep my voice even.

"Hello?" She's surprised I'm calling, probably looking at her phone to double-check the ID, probably agitated to be talking on the phone while driving. Olivia and her rules.

"Hey, it's me."

There's a long pause while I search for a way to fill the silence. I want to ask her over, I want to see her one more time . . . a few minutes longer . . . just a couple of seconds.

"I just wanted to say thanks again for coming."

I can't get up the nerve to ask her, and this is Olivia. Olivia, for God's sake. She's reduced me to a teenage boy nervous about asking a girl to dance.

"You're welcome, Will." There's confusion in her voice, like she knows I have more to say. A few beats pass before she must decide I don't. "I'll see you Monday?"

I pound the side of my head a couple of times with an open palm. "I'll see you then."

I hang up the phone and climb in my car. There was no point to that call except to make me look stupid. Starting now, I need to get it together. Because nothing rattles me. Nothing. Not fans or coaches or pressure or stress.

Certainly not a blonde neighbor with a weird affinity for cats.

I hold that thought for a second, really force it into my brain.

Because when it comes down to it, I prefer brunettes.

And I don't even like cats.

Chapter 13

Olivia

When I was five I had a fascination with perfume bottles. The shapes, the sizes, the gold-infused liquid floating around inside. And the scent. Nothing smelled better than my mother's hair after she spritzed the top layer with Chanel No. 5. She wore it every day, and I purposely chose the moments right after she sprayed it to ask to be picked up. I would bury myself in her neck and breathe deeply; nothing could soothe my mind, which spun with a million questions, more than the hint of spices coming from her soft skin.

Unable to handle my curiosity, one day I picked up a bottle and accidentally dropped it. Of course it broke, and Chanel No. 5 sloshed all over my hands and legs and clothing and hair, overwhelming my already overworked senses with the scent. I cried from the awful smell, and cried harder from the blood sluicing like raindrops off my right wrist. I didn't require stitches that day, but I did require a long bath. The smell still lingered afterward, and later that night at my brother's baseball game, my parents gave me stern instructions to sit on the hard ground in front of them while they moved three benches up.

My mother said the distance was to keep me away from the fans trying to enjoy the game. Even at five, I knew it was because I smelled bad. And you can't enjoy the sight of your favorite son making the most of his God-given talents if you have a throbbing headache caused by your disobedient daughter. So I sat in the dirt, alternately playing with blades of grass and watching the way my brother's jersey fluttered in the wind while he ran, the side-by-side numbers one and three doing what looked like a dance every time he rounded a base.

I'm back in the suite, and the scent of expensive cologne envelops me as I tug at my necklace and look down at the game. The Rangers are winning again, and I'm already trying to plan my exit strategy. Something tells me, where Will is concerned, it will be a hard battle to fight.

I keep my eyes on the game, feeling bad for pleading with the heavens for something to go horribly wrong, but I do it anyway. Clearly no one up there is listening to me because absolutely everything is going right. It's the way of my life, things working out for everyone but me.

It's the bottom of the ninth and, other than a breath-stealing moment when an outfielder dropped the ball and almost allowed a runner on third, the game has been nearly flawless. Even that mistake resulted in an out. As for Will—I didn't realize I would enjoy watching him this much. At the last game I was too nervous to take it in. This time I can barely tear my eyes away.

I'm impressed—by his passion, his skill, his nerve. But it is his strength that has me really enthralled. Every time someone has tried to steal a base, either he or what's-his-name the catcher has managed to get the runner out, no matter what direction he's coming from. Will has to be throwing the ball at lightning speed to make that happen. The guy is good. The guy is great.

It's all a bit bizarre. In all my years as a spectator, I don't recall ever seeing a game quite this perfect. I raise my phone and snap a picture to remember it.

As for the goings-on of this room, things haven't been as bad as I thought they might be, and that puzzles me even more. If I were to venture a guess, I might be tempted to say a few of these people actually like me. But I don't want to go overboard. It isn't often that a group of men and women—especially a group of cool people like the ones gathered here—take to me. I belong more to the bookworm crowd, and even then I prefer to skirt the outside edges. Fade into the background—that's my motto.

A thick strand of hair falls over my left shoulder, and I once again find myself longing for an elastic to pull it back.

"Who is your stylist?" Julia Roberts from the last game—*why can't I remember her name?*—asks me in a very southern drawl. We're sitting next to each other in the middle of a cluster of red chairs set apart from the blue ones making up the rest of the stadium. Like last time, she wears a designer tee with rhinestones along one sleeve. Also like then, I'm decidedly less put together. She takes a sip of a beer while I clutch a bag of uneaten popcorn. I suspect her name is actually Kimberly and I'm pretty sure she's married to the shortstop. Or the second baseman? But I forgot her name right after she introduced herself and I've been too self-conscious to ask for a reminder. As much as I love to remember random facts, I am terrible with first names. I almost always forget them the second they're said.

"Um, I usually just trim the ends myself. But once a year or so I stop by JCPenney for a professional cut." I take a sip of my Diet Coke, carefully this time because I already spilled a drop on my blouse earlier. It's finally dry and unnoticeable, especially since the sun has completely set, but I don't want a repeat of that mistake.

Julia what's-her-name eyes me up and down. "Honey, JCPenney is hardly professional. And the alternative is you trim it yourself? With hair that gorgeous, you need to take better care of it. The fact that you don't and still have this beautiful mane makes me hate you." I know she isn't being mean, just truthful. Like roses having thorns. They prick, you bleed, that's how it is. Her red fingernails flutter through the air like ladybugs looking for a spot to land as she takes another sip of her drink. A few bubbles remain on her lip before she licks them off.

I swallow and study the field. This is hard, blending in. I wish there was an easier way to do it, a way that doesn't involve conversation drifting to things I can't relate to. Hair . . . fashion . . . decorating . . . none of it interests me, but it's what most women want to talk about. I pick up a kernel of popcorn and focus on something I know, watching as a white jersey in a black helmet steps up to bat. He swings and misses. Strike one.

"Well, I mean there's not much to maintaining my hair other than regular brushing and making sure the split ends stay away." Even I think I sound like a teenage boy, but it can't be helped. I'm not much for layers and highlights, even though I naturally have plenty of both.

Black helmet swings again and tips the ball, a foul.

She surprises me by lifting a section of my hair and letting it fall through her fingers. She laughs. "There's more to it than that. No wonder Will likes you. You're one of the most gorgeous women I've ever seen, and you don't even know it. Isn't she gorgeous, Jerry?"

Jerry is Will's agent—I remember this much.

But I'm too busy thinking about her words to focus on his response. *Will likes me?* Like, really likes me or pretend likes me? All at once I remember it doesn't matter; we're both faking everything, and thank goodness it's only for one more night. I give myself an internal scolding and focus on the things happening around me.

"Yes, she's a pretty one. Almost as pretty as this game, and—"

I jump when Jerry screams. Then Julia Roberts screams. Then everyone around me screams and I decide I should scream too because I'm supposed to blend. Soon the entire stadium is on their feet, drinks and popcorn spilling everywhere as people hug and cheer and dance in the aisles. The Rangers just won their second game in a row, and they did it almost without error. This one will be talked about for days, headlining the ESPN news. I've watched enough of it to know.

I study the players as the team rallies at the mound and then heads for the dugout. Julia/Kimberly picks up her purse and slings it over her shoulder, then shakes Jerry's hand and a bunch of other hands before heading for the door. Just before she walks out, she looks over her shoulder at me.

"The game's over, sweetheart. Are you coming?"

I blink at her. I have no idea where I'm coming to because last night I waited in the stands and then left—albeit with Will following behind me—and I'd like to do the same tonight. Will never mentioned an alternate plan. I want to head home. I want to change into pajamas and climb into bed. I want a lot of things.

"Olivia, did you hear Kimberly?" Jerry says. "You're welcome to come with us if you want to meet up with Will."

I nod, more to myself than anyone.

Meet up with Will. I'm going to meet up with Will. And they are going to take me to him.

I pull my purse up to my shoulder and follow them.

Kimberly and Jerry. Her name is Kimberly after all.

I just wish I knew where we were going.

———

Will

The cheering and toasting and rallying with towels has been over for several minutes, I've showered and changed and hopefully gotten rid of the smell of dirt and leather, and all I can think is *Did Olivia already leave? What if she's not waiting for me?* She waited around in the stands last night, but tonight I wanted her to come into the tunnel. Tonight I wanted to show her off to my teammates. Tonight I've forgotten all about my preference for brunettes. Tonight I'm convinced she's actually a good-luck charm and the thought of sending her straight home is just—

Holy hell.

Holy freaking hell I hate brunettes.

Because platinum-blonde Olivia is better looking than ever.

I'm carrying car keys and a picture a little red-headed kid handed me just before the game—a drawing of himself wearing my number and a rough but cute-looking helmet. I fumble with the keys and nearly drop the picture. The taste of alcohol lingers on my lips, but instantly everything on me goes dry. Most of all my mouth. Kimberly and Jerry are walking this direction with Olivia trailing behind, but all I can see is her. She's wearing a royal-blue blouse that hugs all the good places, a snug-fitting pair of designer jeans, and black flats that tread lightly on the concrete floor. Her hair is down again. I don't know what it is about that hair, but every time I see it like this my senses just die. We played a great game tonight, but the only thing that matters right now is my fingers and their desire to touch that hair. I've received congratulations from everyone around me, but my prize just walked in the door, a picturesque supermodel who wants nothing more than to fade into the background. I can see that by the way she keeps her head down and her arms wrapped around her waist.

Enough of that. I want her to look at me. I want her to touch me. I want a lot of things all at once.

"Hey, Olivia," I say, sounding a little too eager. I immediately curse myself and make to appear aloof, but then she smiles. She smiles, and dear God how can that not light up a room? I look around—does no one else see the way this gray corridor is suddenly glowing? But my teammates are all too busy with their own families to notice. Not that Olivia is my family—the idea is crazy, even though I want to tell her right then that she's mine, but then she would leave, and so would her good luck. Time to turn on the charm. "What did you think of the game? Did you like watching me play?"

She shrugs. Not what I expected. "It was a good game—the parts that I saw, anyway." Her voice echoes a bit and she grabs the end of her hair. All I can do is stare. "I was worried you wouldn't be able to get that guy out in the fourth inning when he tried to steal second, but good job. Maybe next time just try throwing it a little faster so it won't be such a close call."

I blink. She just called me out on what was possibly the best game I've ever played, and no one calls me out except my coach and occasionally Jerry. Never a woman. That hair begins to twirl between her fingers, and any inclination I might have had to get mad evaporates. Maybe the hair-twirling thing is Olivia's way to flirt. Darn if I don't like it.

"So throw a little faster, huh?" Out of the corner of my eye, I see Jerry smirk.

"Yes, just a couple miles an hour more will probably do the trick. Flick your wrist a little more. It might work." She glances around the tunnel, looking as though she would rather be anywhere but here. Does she have any idea the things some women do to get back here? If she does, Olivia doesn't care to be one of them. She also isn't flirting. Or being mean. Or even arrogant. Olivia is serious. She's genuinely trying to help, and something tugs deep down inside me—something unfamiliar but not necessarily unwelcome.

No woman has called me out before, and there's a reason for that.

None have cared enough to.

Until now, they've all been too busy trying to impress me.

For a second I don't say anything. Maybe I'm in shock. Maybe it's confusion. Or it could just be the leftover desire to keep her good luck rubbing off on me. Whatever it is, I want Olivia to stick around for one more game.

I remember back to our last conversation and suppress an eye roll at my own predictability. She knew I would say that, and now I owe her all over again. But truthfully, I don't mind at all.

"Alright, I'll flick my wrist more next time." I shove one hand in my pocket and gesture toward the exit with the other. "Ready to go?"

This gets Olivia to look at me. "I'm not going home?"

Her eyebrows push together like she can't quite comprehend what I'm doing, and she's studying me.

As is Jerry.

And Kimberly.

I've never asked a woman to leave a game with me before, preferring instead to sneak out the back and pick up a stranger at a bar. Up until now, it's been my thing. Up until now, it's worked out pretty well. Odd how fast life throws you a curve. It's almost always when you're not wearing a helmet and your head winds up throbbing from the impact.

But judging from the looks on their faces, we both need to do a better job of faking this relationship.

"I mean, you can if you want to. But I thought maybe we could get some dinner first."

"But it's midnight. Aren't you tired?"

I'm exhausted, but I can't let her go yet. Not without knowing she'll stick with me a little bit longer.

"I'm a gamer, Olivia. And I'm wide awake." I twirl my keys and fist them in my palm. "Tell you what. You lead the way, and we'll go wherever you want. Deal?"

That's when I see it: a spark of interest. Something tells me Olivia likes being in charge. Something tells me it doesn't happen often.

"Deal," she says and gestures for me to follow her.

I can't help but smile to myself as we head down the hallway.

I saw the way she bit her lip to keep from smiling too.

Chapter 14

Olivia

At the look on his face, I'm suddenly second-guessing my decision. But he said I could pick. He said it was up to me. This place is my favorite, and I never get to come to it. For one thing, even though I once told Will differently, I hate eating alone unless it's inside my apartment. And for another . . . this is never anyone's first or second or third choice. Except mine.

Maybe this is more proof that I really am crazy.

"We can go somewhere else if you would rather." I snap the lid shut on a bottle of hand sanitizer and toss it into my seat, then shut the car door. Rubbing my hands together, I shiver. Is it possible to feel cold in July? The stars are bright and the temperature has to be pushing ninety. But Will is watching me, and his face is clouded with an expression I can't read, and I don't want him to think I'm strange. For some reason, his opinion matters to me. It's an annoying character trait I've only recently developed, and I'm not yet sure how I feel about it.

"Did you want some?" I nod toward my car, then realize what I just asked him and fight back a sigh. I'm offering to share my Germ-X. Our first night out together, and this is the conversation I lead with.

He shakes his head once. "No, I'm good." The grin he levels my way has probably shattered hearts all over the country. It's doing quite a number on mine right now. Closing the door to his car, he shoves a small ring of keys into his front pocket.

"Why are you smiling at me like that?"

He takes a step away from the car. "Because you picked this place. Although I have to say I'm a little surprised."

I rub my arms and fall in beside him, trying to work through my insecurities. "Why, do you hate it?"

He does a double take and glances at my arms. "You cold?" He puts his arm around me and leads us toward the door. The move surprises me, as does my reaction. It's funny how a body can go from cold to overheated in two sputtering heartbeats.

"No," he says. "I love this place. Have since I was five and my father brought me to one just like it after church on Sundays." He clears his throat. Something tells me there's more to that story. "I've just never met a woman who did. I've never even tried to bring a date here before, because I know exactly what they would say."

He opens the door and gestures for me to walk through first, a surprisingly gentlemanly thing to do. I like it. We're immediately greeted with the same scents I've spent my entire life hoping I'll encounter in heaven.

Butter.

Syrup.

Roasted pecans.

Grease.

I inhale without being too obvious, though I think Will hears me because of the quiet laughter coming from behind my head. Choosing to ignore it, I lead the way to my favorite booth and slide onto the left bench, the one facing the window in direct sight of the jukebox. Nothing excites me more than the reds and blues and purples lining the machine in rows of chasing lights. Feeling just like the little girl whose daddy used to have a quarter ready and waiting in his pocket, I reach for my purse and begin to search around. It's a mess. Although I am generally very organized, my bag is not. I brush aside a package of Tic Tacs, a ketchup packet from my last fast-food visit, and a comb before my fingers make contact with my wallet. I yank it out, proud of myself for stopping a little victory shout.

"What are you doing?" My pride fizzles when I look up into Will's amused face.

"Looking for a quarter."

An eyebrow goes up. "Quite the tipper."

I glare at him. "It's not for a tip, it's for the jukebox."

There it is, a look of interest. "They have one here? Can I pick?"

My insides deflate. I don't want him to be *that* interested. "I always pick." Okay, that sounded a little whiny, but still. I do. I always pick. And I always pick Madonna, followed by Prince, followed by David Bowie. I'm an eighties music kind of girl, have been since I was a kid. Despite what some may think, I've never quite grown up.

"When do you always pick?" Will says. "You just said you hardly ever come here."

"Well, not anymore. But I used to come here with my father all the time." There's something about the way his expression changes. I don't like it. "Why are you looking at me like that?"

"I didn't know you grew up here."

My top lip twitches upward. "I didn't. I grew up in Oklahoma. But we had a Waffle Shack just like this around the corner from my house—same layout and everything. Even the jukebox is identical. Like you, we used to spend Sunday mornings here. Sometimes after church, and on the days we would sleep in and skip, we would go after." Despite the late hour, a family steps out of a red minivan behind Will's head, a father and mother and boy and girl. The boy is older and wearing a baseball uniform. The girl is wearing a backward shirt and a forlorn expression. The family could have been mine. I used to dress myself like that on purpose, then chew on the tag all day long. I could never begin to count the times my mother scolded me for it, but it never seemed worth the trouble to make me turn the shirt around.

When the mother picks the girl up and settles her on a hip, the similarities vanish. I peel my eyes from them and focus on Will. "And always, my father would have a quarter ready. A quarter gets you three songs, you know."

Will smiles. I like the way he smiles, especially when I've caused it to happen. "Then I get to pick two, and you can pick one."

I slide out of my seat, watching out of the corner of my eye as he does the same. "Nice try, mister. It's my quarter. You get one song, and only because I'm feeling generous."

I lean against the machine and peer at the strips of black that highlight song titles. There are so many, but I already know which ones to choose. It's the same, every single time. Although relinquishing one to Will throws a kink into my playlist. But when he comes up behind me to look over my shoulder, all the lyrics in my head scramble and fade into a low hum that spreads into my fingers and toes. I swallow and remind myself to breathe.

"Find anything you like?" he says. When his warm breath feathers against my shoulder, I flinch as though jolted with electricity, then inwardly scold myself. We're having breakfast. At midnight. Everyone knows the hours between eleven and five don't even count as a date, barely even a get-together. Especially not when you're eating waffles.

It occurs to me that I might have just made that up, but I go with it in order to keep my thoughts in line.

"I already know my two. Have you found one you want?"

"I have." Will smiles at me and doesn't look away. It's the strangest thing, because the entire time he's stood here, he hasn't once looked at the selection. The only thing I've seen him study is me.

———

Will

I'm having trouble holding firm to my original opinion of Olivia, and I don't like it at all. I mean, I know the chick is hot—that's something I've come to accept. Kind of like the weather in spring is warm and windy, and the game of baseball is sweaty and incredibly fulfilling, and if I had a choice between digging my toes in the sand or digging my fingers through Olivia's hair, I'd choose the hair every single time. It's just the way things are. It is what it is—to use the world's most overused cliché. But then she throws me these curveballs and everything I've decided is true about her . . .

Might not be.

Take the hand sanitizer. One minute she's rubbing it all over her fingers and offering me some, like the germ freak she obviously is, but then the next she's practically caressing a dirty jukebox and licking sticky, syrup-covered fingers one by one. That was unfair and hard to watch, by the way. Practically had me self-combusting while sitting across from her. There's not much sexier than the sight of Olivia's lips as they move from finger to finger to finger. It took about half a second for my mind to crash into the gutter, and it still hasn't come out.

It is what it is, and all that crap.

Then she went and chose "Like a Virgin" and followed it up with "Let's Go Crazy." I've spent the last ten minutes trying to decide if there's some sort of intended innuendo in her song selection. Good thing I rounded both songs out with Sam Smith's "Safe with Me" or we might be in a whole lot of trouble.

But then there's the fact that she picked this place. The significance of it isn't lost on me, though I've spent the last half hour trying to shove the reality down. Way down. Deep down. Far down to a place I store my worst memories.

Except this place houses my very best one.

I signed my first contract to play minor-league ball inside a Waffle Shack just like this one. Most people pick fancy places; I wanted to do it here. I wore faded Levi's and a grin that didn't leave all day as I sat with my parents, my new agent, and an array of Yankees gear spread all over the table to make the most of the ongoing photo op. Newspaper reporters came; local television stations covered it. Afterward, I ordered this same stack of pancakes—bacon and a bowl of grits on the side— and drank this same kind of coffee and fiddled with this identical set of flatware. I was so nervous that day.

Much like how I'm feeling now.

When I told Olivia the story earlier, she responded with "I knew there was more," as she poured more syrup over her pecan waffle, but I didn't ask what she meant and it doesn't matter anyway. I haven't been to a Waffle Shack since and may not come ever again. After today, my experience with the place can only go downhill. For now, being here is as surreal as the company I'm keeping. After a minute, I snap myself out of my jog down memory lane and all the weird feelings it's conjured up and force myself to remember the reason I asked her to dinner.

"So Jerry texted me. Seems like you're getting along well with every-one in the suite. Sounds like they all liked you."

She shrugs and reaches for a piece of bacon, seemingly unaffected by the compliment that would make most other women I've met start giggling and hoping for another invitation. My theories about Olivia keep crumbling. Pretty soon I'm going to be left holding powdery ashes in my charcoal-stained hands.

She pulls her bacon in half. "I can't vouch for the last game; I was too nervous to talk. As for tonight, the only person I really talked to was Kimberly, and even then I couldn't remember her name. Do you think she looks like Julia Roberts? I kept calling her Julia in my mind until Jerry what's-his-name finally said her name out loud." In goes the bacon. Wide go my eyes.

Jerry what's-his-name. My agent. Only one of the five wealthiest agents in baseball, sought after by almost every young player trying to make a name for themselves. Jerry takes only the best now. These days, he can afford to be exclusive.

And Kimberly, a.k.a. Julia Roberts. Only the wife of Blake DeMarco, who is only the top-paid catcher in baseball. Most people can't believe he even plays for the Rangers, having come from the Mets on a fifteen-million-a-year trade two seasons ago. But hey, Olivia isn't fazed or intimidated, because Olivia doesn't know a thing about them.

Funny how it makes me like her even more.

"Kimberly's last name is DeMarco."

She pauses. From the way her lips part, maybe she does know at least a little. "Oh . . . then her husband isn't the shortstop, like I thought. Is he the catcher? Or the pitcher?"

I'm the pitcher. It's so hard not to get offended.

But Olivia is still talking. And I'm not sure, but I think maybe I saw a slight smile. "I probably shouldn't have spent so much time telling her about my split ends, then."

I nearly choke on my coffee. She says it almost as an afterthought as she takes a bite, and now my eyes are watering from the laughter I'm holding back. Maybe Olivia knows, maybe she doesn't. Either way, no wonder she was so well liked by everyone. A lot of wives and agents and higher-ups in professional sports like to be adored by the so-called lower class. They feed on it. They thrive because of it. But the DeMarcos and Jerry—kind-hearted people with deeply ingrained values—they're as humble as they come. A lot less ego-driven than even me. But they're great at what they do.

Olivia forks a bite of waffle into her mouth, and a drop of syrup remains behind on her upper lip. She licks it off, and I shift in my seat, forcing myself to look away. This woman and her odd, unassuming ways. Both are set to drive me out of my mind. And that tongue running across her lip . . .

Focus, Will.

I swallow and run a napkin over my mouth, then ball it up and sit back to look at her. Casual—it's the way I need to be. Unaffected—it's the way I need to act. I consider faking a yawn but decide against it. Olivia would probably tell me she's tired too and ready to go home, and that is not the best way to sell myself.

"So I was thinking—"

"I wondered how long it would take you to ask me."

I sigh. "You're not going to make this easy for me, are you?"

"Nope." She sets her fork across her plate and looks at me. "You realize this whole good-luck thing is silly, don't you?"

I clear my throat. "As a matter of fact, I do. I think superstitions in general are a joke. But for some reason when it comes to the game . . ."

"It's a habit you can't risk breaking." She finishes my thought for me. And she's right. Churchgoers, agnostics, atheists—we all have our routines. And once you find one that works, it's hard—if not impossible—not to start relying on it. The second we start losing again is the second Olivia can have her life back. If she's willing to help me, that is.

"So would you mind coming back for my next game? We'll be home again, and I would love to have you there. For the right price, that is."

"What day?"

"Saturday."

She smiles. "I'll come, and don't worry about owing me. You don't. For now, at least. Start asking me to travel and my demands will go up."

I pick up my water and smile through a sip. The thought has crossed my mind. The next four games are on the road, but it's too soon to ask her about attending those. Nice to know it's a possibility. Something tells me she'll agree the moment I bring it up. This thing with Olivia is getting easier and easier.

I turn my gaze out the window as if something far more interesting is taking place in the parking lot and give myself a mental high five. There's nothing to see but our two cars and the red glow of a teenager smoking a cigarette. Normally the sight would bother me. Right now I could almost strut out there and take a celebratory drag myself.

"There is one thing, though," Olivia says, running a finger around the rim of her water glass.

I shoot her a cautious glance. "I thought you said no demands until later."

She shrugs. "It's not really a demand. It's more of a concern."

I scratch my chin and blink at her in frustration. Women and their ability to parse words. Something tells me to dread her next ones.

"What's your concern?"

"Perry. I hate leaving him home alone so much in the summer. The school year is bad enough."

I knew I was right to be worried.

I want to tell her he's a cat. I want to say that as long as she leaves out some Meow Mix and an easy-access litter box, there is nothing else he will need. But she's looking at me like we have a problem to solve, one that I'm clueless about.

"Maybe you should pet him a little more before you leave?" It's a stupid thing to say, and I can tell by the way her chin goes up that she doesn't like it.

"What's that going to solve?" She looks at me through narrowed eyes.

"It might make him less lonely?"

It's a cat. We're talking about a cat. I can't believe my life has come to this, but here we are and all I want to do is walk away from this meaningless conversation. Olivia has other ideas.

"I don't know, Will. I left Perry home alone tonight and I hate to do that to him so much . . ."

Her eyebrows push together and I can't believe this is happening.

Is she already thinking of backing out?

Is she really choosing a cat over me?

Who is this woman and where did she come from?

I play with the fork in front of me as dejection threatens to take over my mood. I'm better than a stupid cat. Way better. Everyone in America thinks so.

Except Olivia. The one person who freaking matters.

And then I have an idea. This might take a little creative manipulating on my part. Plus I might have to ignore a few protests. Come to think of it, things might be best if I don't say a word to anyone. But I think this just might work.

Chapter 15

Olivia

I'm not sure I should be doing this. I'm not even sure it's legal, and for that reason I keep looking over my shoulder, waiting for the door to open . . . waiting for a security guard to burst through and tell me to get out, to put my hands in the air, to drop the evidence and follow him to God knows where.

Except the evidence is a cat.

And I have permission to be here.

And both seem ridiculous.

And not a soul would believe me.

Because I'm the only one back here.

Everyone else is happily eating popcorn in the stands like normal spectators do, not confined to a locker room with a cat as though it's a newborn and I need a place to nurse. I can't believe I agreed to this. I mean, sure I didn't want to leave him for too many days in a row, and sure, the thought of coming here without him made me more nervous than I care to admit.

But.

He's a cat.

And I want popcorn.

And although Will was so sweet for offering to do this, I can't help but think he is a little strange for suggesting it in the first place. Who brings a cat to a ball game and hides him in a locker room?

Me. That would be me.

For the dozenth time since walking in here, I silently curse myself for agreeing to Will's stupid plan. For even bringing the subject up in the first place.

I jump at a noise outside the dressing room, my shoulders slumping in relief when the only thing I hear is a collective roar coming from the television screen hanging above my head. I glance up to see Will throw a perfect strike, then toss his hat when the umpire calls it a ball and the guy walks to first base. The bases are now loaded. My mouth falls open, and I yell out a *Come on!* at the screen. That wasn't a ball. There's no way he should walk. The bulging veins that appear in Will's forehead when he jogs toward the umpire tell me he agrees with my assessment. I watch as several players and coaches alternately walk and run toward home plate, mouths moving and arms flying as often as the swear words I can clearly make out. Television censors need to do a better job of enforcing seven-second delays, because no kid is going to believe that those men were all saying "fun" when their parents try to claim it at home. Nothing about this is fun. Even I'm mad, and I don't get mad. They might lose, and what does that mean for me being a good-luck charm? They can't lose. Losing isn't an option and—

I stiffen. Close my mouth. Realize what I'm doing. Reach for the remote and shut off the television.

I will not become my mother.

I will not become my father.

I will not watch someone like my brother, even if I did promise to be here.

I don't *do* baseball. I may have agreed to show up to the games this week because of some stupid superstitious belief of Will's that I'm somehow good luck for his game, but that doesn't mean I have to watch it all unfold. Starting now, he'll have to be satisfied with my presence alone, even if it is in a back room with a cat who doesn't respect boundaries. I look around for Perry and gasp.

"Perry, get out of there!"

When I wasn't looking, he managed to wedge himself between a gym bag and a practice jersey stuffed inside Will's locker. I know this is Will's locker because the number thirteen is plastered everywhere. On the bag. On the jersey. On the locker itself—a gold-plated one-three that mocks me from where I'm standing. I walk quickly and snatch up Perry, clutching him to me, swiping at his fur as though I can magically erase the aftereffects of lying across that number with my bare hands. It's stupid. I know it's stupid, but I can't help myself. This is my cat and it's my job to protect him, so I grab a towel and keep working, ignoring his meows of protest as I keep envisioning that awful number stuck to his fur like a permanent tattoo.

Thirteen.

Even as I think it, I remember the reason I'm here in the first place. Maybe I shouldn't judge Will's belief in my good luck so harshly.

I grab the remote just as a deafening bang comes from the doorway.

"Why aren't you watching the game? You're supposed to be watching the game." An angry Will bursts in and walks past me, ripping off his glove and jersey in the process. I'm no genius, but it's the top of the eighth inning, and they don't normally give players breaks to freshen up their wardrobes.

"Why are you in here? You're supposed to be playing a game."

He shoots me a look for turning his words around on him, but I look down at Perry and pretend not to notice.

"I got kicked out."

That gets me to look up. "Kicked out? Then what am I here for?" I stand to retrieve Perry's cat carrier, then set it on a desk and attempt to stuff him inside. He shrieks—of course he shrieks, because my cat refuses to learn the meaning of cooperation—and I pray no one else walks in here. "So much for me turning your game around. I'm going home."

"They reversed the call after watching the playback. The guy was out, we're now ahead by one, and they only have one more chance at bat. You're staying here."

Joy. Utter and complete joy. Life has a way of never working out for me. With one hand keeping Perry inside the carrier despite his loud protests, I latch the door closed and lean a hip on the desk, then scoot over a fraction when I see some sort of stain on the edge. Coffee? Grease? I can't tell, but I don't want to touch it. "That isn't fair. I saw the umpire call a walk. It isn't my fault he changed his mind. Why am I being punished?"

"You're not being punished. We made a deal, remember? I still don't even know half of what I agreed to."

"Nor do you need to. It was a stupid deal anyway," I mutter, even though the words aren't true. It was a great deal, benefiting my cause much more than Will's. Still, I don't expect the silence as my words hang between us. When I can't stand it anymore, I fix my sights on Will. He simply stares at me, though I'm quite certain he's fighting a smile.

"What's so funny? You just got kicked out of a game. If you ask me, I brought you bad luck today, not good."

He pulls off a sweaty undershirt, and I'm left staring at his very slick, bare chest. "I get kicked out all the time; today isn't special."

He's in such good shape. I think he said something, but it's really hard to concentrate. It takes effort, but I force my eyes to his face and blush when I catch him watching me.

"Bad temper?" My stupid face is on fire.

He grins but says nothing as he runs a towel across his forehead. He doesn't take his eyes off me. And that smile . . .

"Terrible on the field. Off the field I'm a teddy bear."

Finally I snap out of it. "A teddy bear with terrible judgment. Why did you let me come in here with Perry? And what are you smiling at? Stop smiling at me." Really, it's unnerving, like he can see inside my mind and he's discovered a secret that he still hasn't shared with me. I don't like people knowing things about me when I don't know them first.

"You really hate this game, don't you?" he asks, surprising me. He's still using that towel and what I really want to do is grab it and use it to cover his eyes. I don't like people seeing me this clearly.

I don't hate baseball. I don't. It's just that . . . my memories of it are . . . it's not something . . .

Okay, I kind of hate it.

Perry won't shut up. He's swiping a paw at me and whining and scratching so much that what I really want to do is deposit him outside. Let him run a few bases and maybe get hit by a ball . . .

I can't believe I just had that thought about my cat. I love my cat. Would die for my cat. This whole situation is messing with my head.

"I don't exactly hate the game. I just have bad memories of it." I shrug and scan the room, mostly to avoid making eye contact with him. Will knows things; he's way more perceptive than what his job requires, and that makes me nervous. I've spent my life protecting myself, building an invisible barrier between me and anyone who might try to get too close. Without knowing it, Will began removing the barrier brick by brick on the first day we met. Somehow I need to keep him from making his way inside the barrier. It only takes a few bricks to create a hole big enough to crawl through.

I have an idea. I once heard the best way to disarm people is to deliver the truth . . . at least parts of it. So I start with that.

"My brother played. Let's just say it consumed my life for a lot of years."

His smile fades into concern, but not the pleasant kind. "I didn't know you had a brother. He played in high school?"

It suddenly feels very warm in here, and I'm sweating. "He played in the minor leagues . . . made it to the majors for one season." I've said enough and have no desire to keep going. Will has other ideas.

"Who did he play for?" I can see the wheels turning in his mind and I need a stick. Some sort of stick to shove in there to stop the movement, stop the rotating, stop the pieces from falling into place. My plan for disarmament isn't working quite right.

"He played for the Cardinals. Now don't you have something you need to do? Like shower or watch your team or—"

"What position?"

He's getting too close. "Pitcher. Why?" I take a step back.

"Why did he quit? I assume he quit, because I don't recognize the name."

I cross my arms in front of me and try to press out a lie. Something to stop this conversation from continuing, because various people could try to discover Olivia, analyze Olivia, pity Olivia . . . but Will Vandergriff won't be one of them.

"I don't see what—"

And because apparently God decided to choose today to finally smile on me, the door opens and two men walk in the room. Both look mad until one of them spots me and points; then his expression grows livid. He shoots a glare at Will, stops midstride, and plants his feet in the middle of the floor.

"Why is she in here?" he bellows. "And why in God's name is there a cat peeing on my desk?"

———

Will

I've had better evenings, but I can't say many have been as eventful.

We're sitting in my car because I wasn't ready to call it a night, and because Olivia looks like she will be wound up for a while anyway. No way she's headed to bed anytime soon, not after the night we just had.

"Would you please stop worrying? He didn't ruin anything except a schedule, and schedules are easy to print again. Heck, I'll print out a hundred of them and hand them straight to the manager if it'll make you feel better."

She takes a sip from a water bottle and spills a little on her shirt. "He used the restroom on your coach's desk. One, how did he get out of his kennel when I wasn't looking? I'm sure I latched it fully. And two, this might be the most embarrassing thing that's ever happened in my life."

Used the restroom. I nearly laugh at the use of such a proper term to describe a cat but decide it wouldn't go over well. Instead, I look over at her. She's sitting straight up with her knees pulled to her chest, her elbow resting on the door as she glares out the passenger window. She's cute when she's mortified, and I want to tell her so. I want to reach over and do more than just say things, but I figure now might not be the time.

Never. Never might actually be the time.

"I don't know, Olivia. You came to a party full of players and their girlfriends in blue flannel pants and a *Family Guy* T-shirt. That might have been a tad more embarrassing, don't you think?"

The glare she sends my way is the kind of teacher death stare I remember receiving in middle school. Nice to know educators across America are still fond of using it.

"It was *SpongeBob*, not *Family Guy*, and this beats even that. At least when I knocked on your door, I had a way to defend myself. This time all I had was a box of Kleenex and the equivalent of an entire stadium full of wounded pride because you didn't tell them I would be in the room. How did you forget to tell them I would be in the room?"

Oh. That.

Well see, I didn't tell them because I didn't expect it to be a big deal. Reporters are always walking in and out of the locker room, along with team doctors and trainers and the occasional random passerby. What harm would Olivia cause? All I wanted her to do was watch the game in the vicinity of the field and then be there when the game was over, so what did it matter? Besides, it worked. That's the important thing.

"We won. Remember that." It's weak, and I swear her hand jerks with the impulse to reach over and smack me. I admire her self-control, while at the same time wanting her to at least congratulate me on a game well played. Because up until the moment I was thrown out—a fairly common occurrence, I wasn't lying about that—I was playing what might be considered the best game of my life.

Funny how that keeps happening lately.

"Congratulations on your win." Her words are flat, missing the enthusiasm I was looking for. "I suppose this means you want me to keep coming?"

I grip the wheel to assuage my irritation.

"Yes, if you can find the time."

She sighs, long and laboriously. "I assume I don't have a choice."

I chew on my bottom lip to keep from saying more, but come on. I don't get her. I've never met anyone like her in my life. What kind of single woman resents the idea of hanging with a man like me? And just for argument's sake, take me out of the equation. What kind of a woman sounds so completely put out by the chance to hang with an entire team of single men like me? Most women would kill to be in her spot. Pay money to be in her spot. Pay . . . other things to be in her spot. It leaves me with only one conclusion.

"You're not into men, are you?"

I'm a ballplayer, but I've never seen an arm shoot out so fast. I don't even have time to duck before a fist slams me on the shoulder, and heck if it didn't hurt a little.

"Ow!"

"Don't say that again. What, just because I'm not falling at your feet, that means I don't like men?"

Yes, of course it does.

"No, of course it doesn't."

"Of course I like men. Get over yourself, Will. I'm not a big fan of the game, and I like being home. How do those two things add up to a question about my sexuality?"

Perry meows from the kennel, but I don't care. The cat is fine, and we both know he doesn't need a litter box. I drum a few fingers on my knee, taking a moment to rub my shoulder with my left hand.

"For your information, I wasn't trying to offend. Just wanting to understand you."

When she isn't quick to respond, I steal a glance at her. The way she's pinching the corners of her mouth, it's clear she's trying to swallow a smile.

"What's so funny?" I say.

"Now you sound like me. *For your information . . .*"

I run a hand over my face. "Good lord, not that. Anything but that."

This time when her arm shoots out, I catch it in my hand. "Nice try. Not going to happen a second time." She looks at me and giggles before stopping herself. I've never heard the sound escape her lips. It's unlike her, unnatural. I want to hear it again.

"I really hurt you, didn't I?" she says.

My shoulder. It's probably going to bruise. But I'm a man, so I can't admit it.

"Maybe a little," I say, wimping out. "You definitely don't hit like a girl."

She nods. It's a faraway nod—like she's lost in a memory—and her smile fades just a bit. "I have an older brother. What can I say?"

There really is nothing to say. A million questions float through my mind, but I can't pinpoint which one to ask.

It isn't until she steps out of my car and into her own, we follow each other to the apartment building, and I walk her back to her door that I remember. There was one. And now it's too late to ask.

She never did tell me why her brother no longer plays.

Chapter 16

Olivia

It's my worst habit, but I can't help it. I'm getting closer to my destination, and the closer I get, the longer and higher I go, eventually getting too anxious to keep climbing. Then I start over. Like decades-old vinyl that hasn't been played in forever, the words come out slow at times . . . faster at others. And I always skip. Always skip.

Thirteen.

I never ever say thirteen.

The words are a whisper and said like a plea.

"One, two, three, f-four, five . . ."

I hate the way I count. I've tried to stop so many times, but my counselor says that's like asking an alcoholic to stop drinking, and most alcoholics take their very first drinks as teenagers, sometimes even adults. I started this stupid counting thing when I was four. I still remember the exact moment it happened. I still remember the weird way it helped, and the way it forever locked numbers in my brain as the fastest way to clear a troubled mind.

"Olivia, get up there."

"But it's too high, Momma. What if I fall? What if I get scared and I can't get down?" I held onto the denim fabric of my mother's shorts and tried not to cry, thinking as long as my fingers touched them, leaving wouldn't be a reality.

"Olivia, you're embarrassing your brother. Everyone else is taking a little brother or sister. Do you want him to be the only one who doesn't have someone?"

I looked around at all the other kids not wearing baseball uniforms. All of them were at least a head taller than me, and the youngest one was in third grade. She was the only girl who played with me at ball games. I wasn't in third grade because I still wore Rugrats sneakers and no one wore Rugrats sneakers after they turned six. My brother told me so right after he threatened to swipe mine and throw them in a dumpster when I wasn't looking.

"Can't he take someone else?" Even the tears already dripping down my cheeks didn't move my mother. When she had something in her mind, it stayed there. Except right now I was in her mind, and she was making me leave.

She pulled my arms off her thigh like I was a suction cup stuck to a refrigerator. Even now, I hear the sound every time I remember that day. While my mother pushed, my brother grabbed my arm and began to pull.

"There isn't anyone else. You're it. Now stop crying, go with your brother, and sit down. There's a seat belt. Nothing bad will happen."

My nose ran and dripped down my saliva-sticky chin. "But Momma—"

My cries didn't affect her. My wailing didn't work either. The McClain County State Champions banner strung over my head fluttered in the light breeze. The Take Your Sibling to the Fair sign fell over and skidded to the right. The way my mother looked at it and then snapped her gaze to me made me think she believed it was my fault.

"Stop it, Olivia." The whispered words came out on a bite. "The news-paper is here, and you are not to embarrass your brother." She gave a single nod. "Just count to thirty and it will all be over."

My brother dragged me to the seat while I kicked and screamed and cried and watched my mother. She pressed a hand to her red cheek and blew out some air like I was the biggest battle she'd ever faced, then shook her head and began to commiserate with a friend. Both of them shot me dirty looks, and the woman standing next to her wore red lipstick so she looked especially mean.

The seat belt clicked around my midsection, and I buried my face in the bar.

My brother yanked me backward, pressed his arm into my stomach, and yelled at me to keep my eyes open.

The roller coaster began to move at the same time I began to count.

One two three four . . .

At thirteen, the car jolted to a stop.

Upside down.

Everyone around us screamed—my brother, his friends, the other kids in the car, our parents on the ground—but no one screamed louder than me.

I was just the only one screaming numbers.

At seventy-five the car began to move.

At ninety-six I was finally upright again.

It wasn't until one hundred eighty-seven that both of my feet were on the ground.

At two hundred ten my mother said, "That wasn't so bad, was it?"

Counting hadn't helped at all that day.

But just like on that roller coaster, counting somehow became a habit that stuck.

———

"Who are you?"

The gruff male voice comes from nowhere, and I abruptly jump on the bottom step. I've been caught stealing, except I haven't. I'm actually dropping off a bag of food in secret for the third time this week, and I do not think the discovery will go over well. Or be believed. I've had a fear of getting caught since I started coming here. But who gets caught dropping off food, not to mention hiding it under an old wooden plank? Most people ring doorbells.

I take a step back, intimidated by the man's size. One look at his unbuttoned shirt and bulging belly, and I'm certain nothing good will come from this encounter. I swallow and force myself to speak.

"You must be Mr. Hardy," I say, holding out a shaking hand. "My name is Olivia Pratt. I was Avery's fourth-grade teacher last year. It's nice to meet you." I don't add that in the nine months I had Avery in class, I never once met the man, and that it would have been nice to have done so before now. I don't add that parental involvement is the most critical aspect of children's education—coming before test scores or AP classes or number of books read in order of importance.

Parents—they are the key.

Avery's parents—they never helped at all.

He studies my hand like it's a threat before slowly taking it in his own.

"Name's Wayne." He nods. "I'm Avery's dad." He lets go and rubs his hand on his pant leg. "I must say, it's a little embarrassing that I'm just now meeting you. But it's kind of hard to make school functions when you're working four jobs. Wish that weren't the case, though."

I blink. That was unexpected. Plus, the man is better spoken than I had imagined he would be. "Four jobs? How on earth do you manage that? Don't you have other children?"

He smiles. It's a kind smile, and it makes me even more uncomfortable. Mr. Hardy is cracking the perception I've had of him for nearly a year.

"Three if you count the ones living here. Six when you add the little ones who live with their mother. They live in Oklahoma City, but they'll be here tomorrow night. It's my weekend to have them."

"I see. Are they school-age?" I'm making small talk and I'm not a fan of small talk, but sometimes the mouth keeps going when the brain can't think of what to say.

"All but one. She's only four." He glances at the floorboard, still askew from my poor attempt at covering up the food. "What are you doing here? Looks like you were sneaking something."

I swallow the temptation to be indignant. After all, the man is right. "I was just putting a bag under your porch. For Avery." Saying the words feels like a betrayal, because what will happen now? I bring food for him three times a week and have for the entire school year. If I have to stop now because of the greediness of his father when I know his brothers already rough him up for it . . .

"Are you the one that keeps dropping off food for him? I see him eating pretzels and applesauce when he thinks I'm not looking, and I'm certainly not the one buying them."

My chin betrays my bravado by trembling. Because now that he knows, I'll have to stop. And how will I be able to live with myself, knowing a child is suffering because of my carelessness? If only I had been more discreet. If only I hadn't been so busy counting my nerves away to notice the man approach.

"I am. I'm sorry if that offends you. That isn't my intent. I just want to help."

His head tilts to the side as he studies me. Slowly, his upper lip slides left. "That doesn't offend me at all. Thought maybe the kid was stealing, so I'm glad to learn that isn't the case. Embarrasses me a little, but it helps to know that someone is keeping at least one of my kids from going hungry. I just wish I could be the one to do it myself, but I guess that doesn't matter, does it?"

I can't move. I'm frozen for a second. Even though I'm an introvert, people sometimes accuse me of talking too much when I'm nervous, and usually they're right. But now I'm faced with the rare instance of having absolutely nothing to say. Mr. Hardy leans down to pick up the bag, then rifles through the contents. Apples, three bananas, a package of animal crackers, and a box of saltines. Since I've never been entirely sure of Avery's situation, the easiest thing has been to pack things he can shove underneath his bed for safekeeping.

"I'll see to it that Avery gets this. That all right with you?"

I nod, and then test out my voice. It shakes, but miraculously works. "That would be wonderful, thank you." I back off the porch and turn to leave.

"That's very nice of you, ma'am. Thanks for stopping by."

I look over my shoulder and smile. I try to make it genuine, despite my flustered state. "It was nice to meet you, as well."

And all the way to my car, the only thing I can think is that it was. Nice to meet him. Confusing, but nice.

Sometimes people throw you. Sometimes they do the unexpected. Sometimes your preconceived notions are not only way off base but completely unfounded and laced with judgment. For someone like me, that's an especially painful thing to admit.

Starting today, I'm finished judging Avery's home life.

Starting tomorrow, I'm buying food for the whole lot of them.

———

Will

"Are you sure she's not the same chick that came to your party? The one wearing the *Family Guy* T-shirt?"

See? I'm not the only one who thought it was *Family Guy*.

"Nope, different girl." Lies are shooting off my tongue like sparks from a match. But sometimes lies are necessary, even if telling the wrong one might send you to hell.

"Then where did you meet her?"

"I told you, at a bar a few weeks back." This particular lie is bitter and one I should probably go over with Olivia, but I have a reputation to uphold despite also having one to clean up. It's bad enough that everyone saw me willingly leave with her after the game a few nights ago; if I told them we met over loud music and a cat, I'd never hear the end of it.

I wind up and throw a ball into Blake's glove. He tosses it back to me. "Yeah, but . . . Guys and Dolls? That seems like kind of a strange place for someone like Olivia."

Someone like Olivia. A few hours and a couple bags of peanuts, and the whole world knows her. I slip off my glove and scratch the back of my neck.

"She was working part-time as a waitress. Needed the money, I guess. Don't judge her for it."

Blake holds up his hands. "I'm not judging her. Kimberly loved the woman. But I don't know, man. She said the only job Olivia talked about was teaching at an elementary school. Said she doesn't sound like the bar type. Said she seemed too nice for that."

Kimberly said. Kimberly said.

As though nice people don't go to bars. What does that make me?

"It was a bar." The words have fangs, and I swallow and throw again. "She was working and it was early, but that's where we met. She's a great girl. It's been fun ever since." I emphasize fun in a way that would have Olivia slapping me if she were nearby, but she's not here, and again . . . my reputation. It's real and it needs mending.

As for slapping me, I have no doubt she will do it eventually, and this time not just on the arm.

"Don't have too much fun, man. Or have you already forgotten what happened when you had fun with the owner's stepdaughter?"

He makes quote marks around the word *fun* with his fingers, and the reminder pisses me off. Aren't catchers supposed to have bad memories from getting hit in the head so much? Didn't I read that somewhere?

"I haven't forgotten. I doubt I'll be allowed to forget anytime soon." And I won't be. Just this morning I got my fourth call from Jerry. Turns out Lexi hadn't yet turned twenty-one when we had our little date. The news made me want to hang myself with my own size-eleven shoelaces, because why was she at a bar? Why wasn't anyone taking better care of her? Why was I too stupid to walk away when I realized she wasn't Olivia? It doesn't matter that her birthday was two days later. What matters is that her stepfather is furious to the point that he's talking trade. Me, that is. Myself for some pitcher in the minors what doesn't have half my talent and is so young that he hasn't yet started down the pathway toward recklessness that all of us wind up on. Heck, I'm coming out on the other side, despite this latest revelation.

The only good news is that Lexi has yet to press charges. Now that she's an adult, the choice is no longer her parents', not that I think they'd sue. I'm too good a player, and her stepfather has threatened this sort of thing before. I'm hoping her conscience settles heavily on her, because—when it comes down to it—I wasn't that drunk. Four beers does not add up to alcohol poisoning, even if the memories are fuzzy. It doesn't even add up to a good night's sleep. I should know; I haven't had one of those in years.

"Good. I'd hate to see you traded, even though I believe that will happen about as much as I believe the Cubs will win the World Series next year. This'll die down, it's just a matter of how long it will take."

At that, I laugh. Poor Cubs. They don't stand a chance, and I say this as a loyal Cubs fan. It sucks to face so much disappointment year after year. I wonder what happened to that fan that reached down and caught that ball in the play-offs all those years ago. He was in protective custody right after, but I haven't heard anything about him in years. The Cubs haven't had that good of a chance since then.

I send a ball behind me and brace myself as another comes toward me. "Hopefully not too long. I'm already sick of it."

"Especially now that you're dating Olivia. She'll do good things for your reputation, I'm sure of it."

I don't say that this is my plan; that it has been all along. I don't say that Olivia is exactly what I need to rescue myself from—

"Speaking of," Blake says, and I feel my spine stiffen. I hate it when people say *speaking of* to me. It usually means my own words are on their way back to bite me. "Kimberly asked me to invite you guys over Thursday night for dinner. It will just be the four of us, so don't say no. Think you could talk Olivia into it?"

Suddenly the pain in the palm of my hand is a good thing. It distracts nicely from the iron fist of dread now curling in my stomach. First the games and now this. It's one thing to convince the woman to be my fake date for a few weeks. It's another to actually take her on one. I can't afford for the lines to get blurred here, no matter how attractive I sometimes find her.

She's a job. A means to an end. Something to use and dispose of, as crass as that may sound. She knew the stakes when she agreed to my plan. As far as the newest date, though, what choice do I have?

"I'm sure she would love to," I say.

Maybe she will, maybe she won't. Either way, why do I feel like I just slipped a noose around my own neck . . . like all that's left for me to do is jump, flail a bit, and die?

Chapter 17

Olivia

"No, I haven't kissed him."

I'm immediately assaulted by shrieking, so I pull the phone away from my ear. But not far enough away to avoid hearing the next question.

"If I haven't kissed him, what would possess you to think I've spent the night at his place?"

"I don't know, Olivia. Wishful thinking? You're dating Will Vandergriff. Surely it hasn't been entirely chaste up to this point." I should have known my silence would prompt her next statement. "Please tell me it hasn't been entirely chaste up to this point."

I squeeze my eyes shut and put the phone on speaker, then lay it on the counter in front of me. This is not how I pictured getting ready for my first date with Will. "Define chaste."

Kelly sighs. "With or without a dictionary? Here's my version: no hand-holding, no kissing, no making out, no nothing. Apparently you actually meant it when you said you don't like ballplayers."

I roll my eyes even as Will's words come back to haunt me. *You obviously have an aversion to my kind.* "Then I guess it's been entirely chaste. Except just because I once said that doesn't mean I still feel that way."

"Then what are you waiting for, Olivia? I read an article online about you two dating. People know. It isn't like you can hide it. But more importantly, you can't keep worrying so much about letting a guy in. Especially not when it's Will Vandergriff."

"He has a reputation, you know."

There's a pause on the other end of the line. "I know. But . . . he's Will Vandergriff."

I let my mascara wand fall. So much for looking out for me. "You keep saying his name like it's a big deal."

"Because he is a big deal."

Of course I know this, but why does he have to be? A better question: why am I starting to like him? To like someone means letting them get to know you. To let them get to know you means taking a risk that your heart will get broken. I'm not sure my heart can take it. What if I'm left trying to piece together something that will never function right again?

With that image in my mind and a promise to call her later and fill her in on the details, I hang up the phone and get to work on my other eye.

———

I tried to talk him into letting me meet him at the DeMarcos' home, seeing that it's only a five-minute drive from our apartment complex— yes, Will and I live in the same nice part of town, but no, it's nothing like the neighborhood we're headed to—but he wouldn't have anything to do with the idea. I shift in the seat next to him and look down at my hands. They're sweaty and sticky and bendy and my knuckles just popped.

"It's so hot in here. Can you turn up the air?"

Will reaches for the control and turns the knob. "It isn't hot, you're just nervous. Calm down. You'll be fine."

Calm down and *You'll be fine*, the dumbest five words in the human language. And this. This is proof that he still barely knows me. I can't calm down. I won't be fine. Introductions to people and places always have me feeling anxious, and not in the way most people are anxious. We're talking heart palpitations and irrational fears of getting sick. Right now I think I feel the flu coming on, but no, it isn't flu season. Leprosy. That might be it.

"Olivia, if you crack your knuckles one more time they're going to be the size of mine."

"That's a myth, you know. Knuckles don't enlarge from being popped."

"Still, I hate the sound. It's freezing in here." He turns the air down, and immediately my sweat glands rise up in protest. Why didn't I drive myself?

He claimed a desire to spend time with me, saying the drive would be a good time to brush up on some facts and go over our stories, making sure they match. I believe him for the most part, except that we've been driving a couple of minutes without going over anything, and I'm not the only one staring at a meltdown. Will is nervous. Really nervous. Almost as if he's headed to an interview and the DeMarcos are the ones who might hire him. He keeps gripping and ungripping the steering wheel, knuckles going from white to pink to white again in seconds. He's glanced over at me more times than he's looked at the road, which make *me* nervous. What if he thinks I look bad? In a short black racer back dress and ballerina flats, I don't *think* I dressed wrong. The dress came from the Nordstrom sale rack last season. Could it look too cheap?

Will glances at me again, his gaze darting from my face to my chest to my lap and back to the windshield before starting all over again. Now I'm not so sure.

"I'm nervous enough without your scrutiny, and you're really starting to put me on edge. Why do you keep looking at me like that?" I uncross and cross my legs. He's staring at them like he's waiting for one of them to unleash itself and rise up to kick him. I'm a lady. Ladies don't kick, at least not too often.

"Like what?" He bites a fingernail, something I've never seen him do.

"Like I'm the hands-down loser on 'who wore it best?' Like you want nothing more than to drop me off at the closest Goodwill to find a better outfit?" Now I'm biting a nail, something *I* never do.

He gives me the once-over; the way he stares has me reaching for the ends of my hair.

"You look great. Hardly in need of a new outfit."

"Then what is the problem?" I try to hold his gaze, but I feel myself blushing, so I turn to face the window. For all my bravado, I have no idea how to behave around men.

Will grips the wheel again and takes a deep breath. Whatever is on his mind, it's really bothering him. To pass the time while I wait for him to speak up, I take inventory of his car. I never knew a Lexus would be this nice—but it's exactly the kind of car you might expect someone with his stature and career to drive. It's black and it's big and it's leather and it's loaded. The seats feel air-conditioned, but that can't be right. I've never heard of cooled seats, only hot ones in the summer. But it's late July and these seats feel great. I wasn't scalded even once when I slid in beside him.

I sneak a glance out of the corner of my eye.

He's dressed in designer jeans and a white T-shirt that did not come from a package of three at a discount store. No, his shirt cost more than a few dollars, probably more than I made teaching all of last Wednesday and part of Thursday. I never knew a casual shirt could look so sexy on a man, or so elegant. Between that and the thick, dark hair that curls around his neckline and the cologne that has me wanting to scoot a little closer, he has me rethinking the way I look all over again.

It's hard to sit next to a guy like him and not feel very much like a girl who falls short. I pick at a piece of invisible lint and study my shoes, wishing they would carry me somewhere far from here.

"I told them we met in a bar."

I frown at my lap. "You told who we met in a bar?"

"Blake and Kimberly."

"But we didn't meet at a bar. We met outside your apartment." I'm confused. Why the need to lie?

"That's true," he says. But there's something about his tone. The insecurity I was plagued with moments ago falls away and is replaced by something else. Not exactly anger. More like a warning buzz that travels down—no, up; no, down—my spine. It might be a pleasant feeling in a different situation.

"What do you mean, a bar?"

He shrugs, but it's anything but casual. "I mean, a bar." He scratches his chin, fidgets. There's more. Something he isn't saying.

"What bar?"

Silence. Will says nothing, and that says everything.

This time I enunciate very carefully. "Will, what bar?"

My hand twitches with a desire to shove him even before he opens his mouth. There's the anger. I knew it would show up eventually. Holy anger. Justified anger. Anger that beats the heck out of a tingling spine, even though I can't explain the reason for it. I'm counting on Will to do that for me.

"Guys and Dolls."

"That's a strip club! You told them I was a stripper?"

His mouth falls open. "No. A waitress!"

"Is that supposed to make me feel better?" I'm sweating and shivering all at once, which is just great because now I'm convinced I'm coming down with leprosy. I lunge for my purse. Where is my phone? I need to look up the symptoms.

"No, but at least I didn't make them think you took off your clothes for—"

"We met at your doorway." I can't deal with him talking about me being naked. Where the heck is my phone? "I was holding a screwdriver and thinking about stabbing you with it. Thinking about it again right now, in fact. *A strip club?*" Is he insane? I pull my purse to my lap and shift in my seat to face him better. A face-off through my very narrowed eyes. "Isn't that what you're trying to get away from? Isn't that exactly how you got in trouble with the owner's stepdaughter? Do you want me to call her up and join forces? Is that what you're saying?"

Something people don't know about me: I can be forceful if pushed hard enough. From the way Will swallows, he just found out.

"Will you stop with the twenty questions?" he blurts. "I promise I'll clear it up. Just let me figure out a way and—what are you looking for?"

"I can't find my phone." Keys and gum wrappers are flying. "Fix it, Will." Stupid man and his stupid ego. There is nothing wrong with dating a schoolteacher, so why the need to fancy it up? Or dirty it down, depending on your view. "Fix it, or I walk. I mean it."

"Your phone is in the cup holder. Don't walk. I promise I'll—"

"No, never mind. I'll clear it up myself." I roll my eyes and grab my phone. Athletes. Especially the professional ones who haven't spent much time in the real world. Clearly he's been hit on the head one too many times with a few too many baseballs. "I'm a schoolteacher, Will. I work with kids. You're not the only one with a reputation that needs to be kept intact. Let me think of something. Just follow my lead and agree to everything I say. Got it?"

Good news. I don't have leprosy. But I may have a bad case of pneumonia. I toss my phone in my purse and give up on both diseases because now I have a headache. It's probably an aneurysm.

"Got it." Will pulls into a driveway that stretches toward the biggest house I've ever seen up close, and visions of the next hour flash across my brain. That man. That man and his penchant for making up stories. I mean, it isn't like the truth is such a bad thing and . . .

My thoughts fade away into nothingness at the sight in front of me. Waves of insecurity rise up and over me again.

This isn't a home. It's three homes. Five. Maybe even twelve, shoved under one roof. I take a picture even though I know it won't do the home justice when I show it to Kelly later.

I'm getting ready to walk into the biggest house I have ever seen, and I'm wearing a dress off the Nordstrom sale rack, and our hosts think I'm a stripper. This is proof that everything hates me.

Even the gods of good judgment.

Will

Out from under the microscope of my two judgmental eyes, Olivia is different. Almost as if I have shoved her into a cocoon of my own making, where wings are held tight and breath is taken within the confines of minimal space. And now that we're out . . . Olivia has become a butterfly with a wingspan so wide and beautiful it fills this entire room.

And once again, I've become a freaking poet.

She has no idea how beautiful she is, or how effortlessly she puts others at ease. Maybe it's an act or a perfectly honed skill developed on the back of many panic attacks, but Olivia has a way with others. A grace that's hard to find. A kindness that exposes itself despite her desire to blend into the background. From my spot on the massive white leather sofa, I look away from the goddess in front of me and down into my glass. The mixture of rum and Coke is a lot heavier on the carbonation than it should be. The loneliness in my gut is a lot deeper than it should be.

"You've lost your knack for mixing drinks," I say, swirling the ice and watching it spin. I'm not in the mood for conversation or company. Olivia still hasn't explained away our meeting, and I have no idea what she's going to say.

"Everyone's a critic." Blake slips the glass from my hand and walks over to the bar. Adding a scoop of ice, he pours in more liquid and stirs it with a straw before handing it back to me. He sits a few feet away and props up his feet on the round table in front of us. "There you go, princess. If you want more, go get it yourself."

I don't comment, just take a sip—stronger, harder, burns on the way down; more my style—and stare at the television and SportsCenter, trying to get lost in the highlights. For as long as I can remember, games have been my life. I don't appreciate Olivia's unwelcome distraction, even though I brought it on myself. But she wasn't supposed to be charming. She wasn't supposed to blend with my friends and teammates. She wasn't supposed to be so damn beautiful. I never should have told her to pull her hair free of that tight ponytail. She should have kept it severe and unflattering and then maybe my nerves wouldn't be so on edge, my fingers itching to touch the stupid strands every time she walks by.

Except it's not just the hair. It's the eyes. It's the jawline.

It's the body.

The very hot body in that very appealing black dress.

I steal another glance her way just in time to see her laughing at some dumb joke Kimberly just told. My back teeth grind together as my jaw works back and forth. The way she sits there so at ease, sinking into the navy chair as though it was made for her. It makes me wonder about the real Olivia. Who is she besides the neurotic neighbor with an odd affinity for cats and a strange obsession with numbers?

"You know, instead of sitting here pouting, you could go over there and join their conversation." Blake takes a sip of his gin and tonic and rests the glass on the arm of the sofa, never taking his eyes off the television. "I've never seen a man so miserable around a woman, especially one he's supposed to be dating."

I shoot him a look. "I'm not miserable. Just thinking. What do you think they're talking about? Girl stuff?" The question sounds stupid as soon as I say it. I'm a twelve-year-old boy in middle school dealing with acne and wondering if the girl he likes will go with another boy to the dance. Thank God only Blake heard me. Thank God he's a good man.

"Hey, you two," he calls over the noise of a commercial. "Will wants to know if you're talking about girl stuff over there. And then I want to know what 'girl stuff' actually means."

He's a demon. A freaking demon that hell spit out and dumped on me.

"Thanks, dude," I mutter. "Thanks for that."

"Well, if you must know," Kimberly says with a look at me. "Olivia just told me about the real way you met. Not fair making us believe you met in a strip club, Will. Especially when the true story is so much better."

Blake does a double take at me. "What's the true story?"

He doesn't look away.

So I do the only thing I can do, considering the pressure I'm under. I stand up, walk over to Olivia's side, pull her up, sit down in the spot I just pulled her from, and drag her onto my lap. Immediately she goes rigid. She's uncomfortable. She scoots to the farthest edge of my knee. She's sitting like I'm a wooden plank and splinters are wedging into her backside.

Funny, I suddenly just got really comfortable.

"I think I'll let Olivia tell it since I'm sure she remembers the story better than me." I run a hand across her lower back, then move my hand a littler lower and do it again because I like to feel her squirm. When her hand comes around to grab mine, I move to her butt. A nice butt it is, though from the way her fingernails try to dig into my palm, I'm fairly certain she doesn't like me touching it.

She gives up and turns to Blake. Alarm bells go off in my head when I see the beginning of a wicked smile curve her lips. To mute the ringing a bit, I cup my hand around one butt cheek and begin a slow circle. If Olivia is going to give it, she can also learn to take it.

"I'll tell you, Blake. And who knows, by the time I'm done you'll probably have learned about a whole new side of Will . . . one you never knew existed."

I shift positions and drop my hand, resisting the urge to dump her to the floor. Something tells me even the chance to feel her butt won't make up for whatever it is she's about to say. My discomfort descends like a freaking lightning strike at the same time hers melts away.

For good reason.

Did you know you can physically feel your self-image detach itself, suspend in front of you, and fall away?

Well you can. You really can.

Chapter 18

Olivia

I'm sitting in a silent car, fiddling with the hem of my dress, but the silence is not necessarily a bad thing. A lot can be discovered when no one is talking. Companionship. Camaraderie. Peacefulness. The way another person breathes . . . the rhythm of their unique in and out, back and forth. A quiet that settles deep inside the bones. A quiet that's hard to come by in today's busy world, especially with the way social media has taken over every aspect of our lives and completely consumed the minds of—

"I can't believe you told them I rescued your cat outside a strip club."

I should have known a thunderous storm cloud was brewing in the driver's seat. So much for the quiet.

"You're the one who insisted on adding a strip club. Not my fault I felt the need to alter your story." I swing my leg back and forth. He glares at it, which only makes me swing it harder.

"A cat. I don't rescue cats."

"You do when they're stuck in rain gutters."

"I hate cats."

"Not Persians. They're your favorite."

"And why in God's name was he supposedly in a rain gutter in the first place?"

"Because he slipped off his leash and ran away from me and he knew I wouldn't be able to climb that high. Were you not paying attention, sweetie?"

"You realize the leash part makes you sound crazy."

"Yeah, the thing about that is . . . I don't care. I don't have a reputation to uphold with the DeMarcos. And funny enough, they seemed to like me anyway. Who would have thought it?"

"Not me. Definitely not me."

"Oh, but you did. That's why you asked me to come here with you in the first place."

At that, I know I have him. He goes quiet. Too quiet. Suddenly I don't like it. Talking with Will is a lot more fun than wondering what he's thinking. And although my made-up story was fun to tell—especially the additional parts about me not working at Guys and Dolls but at the PetSmart across the street that Will frequently visits to check the latest in our hamster collection; I work there because, you know, I need the extra money that teaching just doesn't offer—I do feel bad. Will is a man. A famous man. A very famous man with very wealthy friends, and the last thing I want to do is embarrass him.

Maybe not the last thing. Maybe more like the second-to-last thing. Or maybe the third-to-last.

I sigh. "Are you mad?"

Suddenly, he looks tired. Too tired. It makes me wonder just how much traveling the country and punishing his body have cost him.

He runs a hand down his forehead and rests it at his jawline.

"I'm not mad."

At first I don't believe him, especially when he says nothing else. But then I see it. The jerk of his neck muscle. The way his tongue slides across his bottom lip. The way he pinches his lips together to fight what might be the threat of a smile. And then I can't resist.

"It was kind of funny, wasn't it? And the look on your face while I was talking . . ."

Finally, his grin breaks free. "Remind me never to cross you again. You're brutal in your storytelling. Must be that education degree."

I shrug and send him a knowing smile. "I've always been able to lay down a fantasy world if the occasion calls for it. And your stripper story definitely called for it. And speaking of strippers, the next time you try to grab my butt I will personally break your hand. Then you won't have much of a career at all anymore."

He pretends to think. "Might be worth it. You have a nice butt."

Dang it if I don't blush. "Of course I do. Just keep your hands off."

"I don't pay much attention to hollow threats."

That man and his stupid comebacks. I have nothing to offer in return because I'm too busy trying not to remember what his hand felt like. Not as unpleasant as I wish it had been.

He turns right at the light and pulls into our apartment complex. Turning into a space, he parks and shuts off the engine. I've been on dates before. A few, all very proper and routine. But it's weird to know that we're coming home to the same place, at least technically speaking. I'm not sure how a woman handles the drop-off when the guy doing the dropping lives one door over. Suddenly I'm nervous and feeling very foolish for it. Especially because his hand was on me an hour ago and a goodnight kiss seems like something I shouldn't be worried about.

"Hollow threat or not, I'm glad you're not mad."

"I'm not mad. Except—"

He opens my door, and I step out to face him. He's close. Closer than normal—one arm resting on the door and the other planted on the top of the car—and my pulse begins to hammer in that tender spot right beside the throat.

"Except what?"

His eyes flicker between me and the door. I've lost count of how many times his scent has drifted toward me tonight. The evergreen and mint combination has become my new favorite, and right now it encases the air around me. It isn't easy being around something this pleasant. Or someone. I try to take a step back but wind up touching the car. I'm stuck and Will is filling the space around me.

"Except I need you to come to the games next week. Will you at least consider it?"

I don't have to ask him what he means. He wants me to pretend indefinitely. Keep pretending to be his girlfriend. Keep pretending we're together. Keep pretending I like him. What he doesn't know is that pretending all these things is getting easier and easier.

It's the truth that's getting harder to conceal.

Still, I make an effort to stand my ground out here in the parking lot. "I don't know if it's a good idea, Will. What if you start to depend on me too much and . . . and . . . I get sick or something and can't make a game? And what happens when you're on the road? We both know I can't go with you. Not with Perry and . . . and . . ." The ground is softening. Even this excuse sounds flimsy to me—is my cat the only thing I can come up with?

"If you get sick I'll hire a nurse. As for road games, we won't worry about those right now." He takes a step closer—I don't think he even realizes it. My heart takes a dip and then rises with a vengeance. "I need you, Olivia. Can you please come? I'll owe you forever."

Now it's my turn to pretend to think. I'm not quite finished when I feel myself begin to nod. Of course I nod. It's the only thing for me to do.

What Will doesn't know is—no matter what I've said in the past—he owes me nothing. If he asked me to travel, I would. If he asked me to kiss him, I would. There's almost nothing I wouldn't agree to at this point, and that scares me more than anything.

———

Will

Only a handful of weeks ago I was a happily unattached bachelor living a life most men only dream of. Now that dream has puncture holes in it the size of one beautiful blonde and a few nosy teammates and their wives, who all love Olivia. Ask about Olivia. Want Olivia around. Now I can barely manage to begin a thought without the name Olivia coming out on the tail end of it.

Take now. All I'm trying to do is make popcorn because even though we ate two hours ago I'm still so freaking hungry, but all I can think about is our conversation earlier in the car and the way she kept swinging her leg. I hate the way it affected me. I hate the way I kept looking at it. I hate myself for wanting to slap it as much as grab it, bring it to my mouth, and lick it. Sometimes I can't stand being a guy. No matter how often I glared at her, she wouldn't stop with the swinging.

With frustration at an all-time high, I give up on the popcorn and reach for a bag of chips just as the phone rings. Jerry's name lights up the screen, and my frustration climbs even higher at the same time my mood dips. I may have the best agent in the business, but I'm not in the right frame of mind to talk to him. I turn the phone on and press it to my ear. Saying hello isn't even necessary.

"Is it true?"

I pop a chip in my mouth, not bothering to disguise the noise it makes. "Is what true?"

"Is it true you went to the DeMarcos' tonight with Olivia? That's the rumor on the street."

I nearly choke, a sharp corner of the chip stabbing my esophagus on its way down. "Where did you hear that?" I cough and reach for water. The liquid burns on the way down. Not a good sign.

"It doesn't matter where I heard it. Two different people called me, and both are a little worried."

I rub the space between my eyebrows, wondering when I became a seventh-grade girl with gossiping classmates. Two people? What two people? And what are they worried about? And why the hell do I even care? I'm having a hard time convincing myself I don't, now that my palms are suddenly sweaty.

"Yeah, it's true. Why does it matter?" I toss in another chip and lick a salty finger, trying to convince myself I'm not interested in this conversation. But I am. Because it does matter. Even though it shouldn't, it matters. There's always something slightly disappointing in seeing a free guy tamed. I've spent my life taking pride in my bachelorhood, pretending not to be lonely, faking indifference about the idea of ever wanting more. Now I have two choices: use Olivia until she serves my purpose and discard her when the process is over, or admit that being around her is nice . . . that maybe this dating thing isn't as bad as I've deliberately talked myself into believing it is.

Tossing Olivia aside is getting harder and harder to imagine.

Which means I need to get a bit more creative in my thinking.

"It matters because you're already in trouble," Jerry says. "You already have one woman throwing out supposedly baseless accusations—"

"They are baseless."

"Fine," Jerry says. "But we don't need another woman causing problems, especially not with the team in first place. The last thing anyone needs is a distraction."

I roll the chip bag closed and shove it into the cabinet. "Olivia isn't causing problems. Nor is she a distraction."

And this is a serious fault of mine. One minute I'm telling myself to use Olivia and be done with it, and the next minute I'm defending her. I'm like one of those ball pendulum toys—swing left, swing right, knock into things, make a lot of noise, and ultimately go nowhere. My life used to have direction; now it's all over the place.

Still, I don't like being told what to do.

"Olivia isn't causing problems. And whatever happened to *any press is good press*? Isn't that still true?" I use a firmer tone than I need to, but I want to prove a point. To him. To me. Except I don't know exactly what the point is. "She's coming to ball games and hanging out with me at friends' houses. I don't see what is so wrong with that."

Jerry clears his throat.

"Any press is good press as long as it doesn't land you in jail. And you're missing the point. I wasn't talking about Olivia. She's not the problem."

At those words, my blood chills.

Hang up the phone. Don't listen to another word.

This is what I'm thinking. But here's the thing about me: on the field, I can talk myself into doing just about anything. But off the field, I'm not usually one for inward pep talks. If I were, I never would have gone to the door when Olivia was holding that screwdriver. I never would have agreed to Olivia's terms for our fake relationship—one term I've yet to even find out. And I certainly wouldn't have come up with a plan for the next four games, all of which I've decided need Olivia's heavy involvement.

Then again, maybe I'm not one for pep talks. But I am one for speaking up, even when it's against my better judgment.

"If she's not the problem, then what are you talking about?"

I hear a sniff. A shuffling of papers. A drop of a pen. A very labored sigh.

"I'm talking about Lexi. Now she's saying you got her drunk against her will and took advantage of her. And right now—*right now*—I need to know if she's telling the truth."

I never knew anger had a color, but all I can see is black when I slam my hand against the kitchen wall. The drywall cracks to the right of the refrigerator, and my wrist throbs from the pain. Not the smartest reaction, but I can't stand false claims against my character.

I can get women. Willing women. Plenty of them. Anytime I want them.

Never in my life have I even thought about taking advantage of one.

"Of course it isn't true." My voice is quiet, loud, a simmering pan of water, a violent explosion in a downtown skyscraper. I feel everything at once, and nothing at all.

But I have no idea what she wants.

The only thing I know is, starting now, not only do I need to use Olivia as a girlfriend.

I also need to use her as a weapon.

Chapter 19

Olivia

Courage comes and goes with me—comes when I take the initiative to care for a hungry and underdressed little boy, goes when I am thrust in the spotlight for others to gawk at. For the last minute it's been a tug of war between the two, and I'm tired of the uncertainty. Finally, and before I can do any more talking myself out of things, I grab the handle of my front door, open it, and step out into the dark night air.

It's cold out here. Go back inside. Get back in bed. This isn't you. You don't do things like this.

Shivering for reasons that have nothing to do with the imaginary cold, since this *is* still July, I make myself reach up and knock on the door next to mine before one more negative thought becomes my undoing. *He'll laugh, he'll think you're even crazier than he already does, he'll slam the door in your face, he'll think you're stupid.* Make that four negative thoughts. It isn't fun to be constantly self-critical, but it's my reality and one I've learned to live with fairly well.

I press my ear against the wooden panel and breathe a sigh of relief when nothing sounds on the other side. No voices. No footsteps. No signs that anyone is even awake. I press a little farther against it just to make sure, but still hear nothing. At least I was brave. At least I tried. Two high fives and a fist pump for my ability to step out of my comfort zone and—

The door flies open and I nearly fall forward, catching myself against the doorframe with an embarrassing slide. I knew I shouldn't have worn fuzzy socks. Fuzzy socks and smooth cement do not make for a safe combination.

"What are you doing?" Will's voice doesn't hold accusation, just curiosity. And if I really stop to analyze it, amusement.

I right myself, no thanks to him, and pull my white T-shirt down, aware that in my clumsiness the hem has risen halfway up my waist and exposed more than a fair share of bare skin.

"I came to check on you. I wasn't aware it was a crime."

His gaze moves to my midsection and stays there as he props a hand against the door.

"No crime at all," he says. "But maybe next time remember I have a peephole and you're never all that quiet when you walk out your front door." Peeling his eyes away from my waist—*take your time, mister*—he points up to the door and the tiny glass orb near the top of it. "If you're going to spy, you might want to be a little less conspicuous."

I cross my arms in front of me, my face heating from embarrassment. "I wasn't spying."

"You were spying, but I'm flattered."

My chin goes up, which only makes him smile. "I wasn't spying, I was—"

"Hey, Olivia?"

I try not to look at him because he's right and I'm caught and I don't feel like being the equivalent of an animal stuck in a trap. But I wind up looking at him anyway. This is his front door and I'm the foolish girl who knocked. I make a mental note to have my front door hinges oiled tomorrow.

"What?"

"Do you want to come in? Because if so, all you have to do is ask."

And this is what I was afraid of when I first heard the pounding on the other side of the wall. My first thought was *What if Will is hurt?* My second, *What if Will is mad?* My third, *Stop thinking about Will.* My fourth, *I can't.* My thoughts tend to come in fours. So I tossed back my blankets and climbed out of bed and walked over here before I could fully change my mind. Now I wish for nothing more than to be in that bed and dreaming of kittens and term papers. Instead . . .

"Sure."

What else could I possibly say?

I step over the threshold, wondering if there will ever be a time when I come to Will's apartment wearing something other than pajama pants and a tee that should have been tossed out with last decade's trash. I wore this thing in junior high and of course it's an image of *Family Guy*. I can't believe Will is right once again. I can't believe it still fits.

The room looks different when it's empty of partygoers and plastic cups. Although we share the same floor plan, that's where the similarities end. Unlike my apartment, with its floral fabrics and sturdy oak furnishings—most of which came from my grandparents, parents, and yard sales—Will's place is decidedly modern. It's elegantly classy—decked out in rich leathers, marble tabletops, stainless finishes, and faux animal fur. Thick panels in chocolate velvet line the windows and cascade to the floor, while substantial lamps and accent pieces give the room a decidedly upscale feel. Every inch of this space could be displayed on the cover of *Architectural Digest*, yet somehow it isn't stand-offish. Will has expensive taste, but none of it is flashy or assuming. I like it. I like it a lot.

The front door closes behind me.

"So why are you here?" he asks.

Thoughts of being a caged animal return to the forefront of my mind as panic threatens. *Why am I here?* Suddenly the truth seems so basic, so foolish, that I'm scrambling to find a more intelligent answer. This is Will Vandergriff. He's used to having people fawn all over him. He's used to being the center of attention. Who am I to think he needed my concern?

I'm nobody, that's who. A stupid girl who heard a noise, got worried, and decided to investigate. The answer sounds ridiculous even before I say it, but when life gets real and when all the dust settles, I am a girl who believes in the truth. Even if I'm helping him live a lie right now.

Feeling very self-conscious, I turn from my spot at the back of his sofa and look at him.

"I heard something hit your wall, and I was worried something bad had happened." I tug at the hem of my shirt and shrug. "I just wanted to make sure you were okay." *I'm dumb I'm dumb I'm dumb.* "So are you? Okay, I mean?"

When all he does is stare at me, I am certain I never should have come here.

———

Will

I have no idea what to say, because words and syllables seem to have fled my mind, along with any ability to process what she just said. I'm used to people caring about me, and I'm definitely used to concern. My list of well-wishers is as long as it is colorful, as flattering as it is fulfilling. I could list a few right now and barely scratch the surface.

There's my coach: *How's your hand?* And my agent: *How's the contract coming?*

There's the media: *Tell us about your love life.* And the fans: *You're my hero.*

There are my friends: *Can you get us tickets?* And my family: *Can you give us more money?*

But never, not once in the years since I signed for the major leagues, has anyone stopped by just because they cared about me. About my hand, my money, my health, my career . . . but not about me. That being the case, I feel a sudden need to test her.

"I got some bad news and punched the wall with my hand. Sorry it was loud."

Her eyes widen as her gaze flicks between my hand and my eyes. "Is it broken?"

"There's a small hole in it, but—"

She rolls her eyes. "Not the wall. Your hand. Did you break anything?"

I think maybe she's passing the test. "I'll be able to play Tuesday night, if that's what you're worried about." Crap. What about passing a test do I not understand? And do I sound as pissed off as I feel? And why am I pissed off in the first place? Olivia has never once seemed the type to want me for what I could do for her. In fact, with her, my career seems like more of a detriment than a benefit, which is the craziest thing of all.

"As if that matters to me," she says with a disgusted look. "Are you sure it isn't broken? Do you need me to drive you to the hospital?"

When she reaches for my hand and turns it over in hers—little worry lines appearing on her forehead as she presses one finger against each of my knuckles and looks for signs of injury—that's the moment. That's the moment when I would normally use the situation to my advantage: fake more pain than I actually feel, and see how far my acting could take me. Usually it takes me all the way, but tonight I'm not even going to try.

Olivia is different. And because of that, Olivia deserves different.

I make a fist, flexing and unflexing to prove that I'm all right. When her hand falls away, I can't deny my disappointment. Her touch felt nice. The nicest thing I've felt in a while.

"It's fine. No hospital necessary."

She nods. Hesitates. Says, "Good." Then turns to leave.

I can't believe how much I don't want her to leave.

"Do you want to stay for a while? Maybe watch a movie or something?" When she bites her lip in uncertainty—again, why is she uncertain? No woman is *ever* uncertain—I keep talking in an effort to keep her here. "Or not a movie. We could just talk. Hang out. Play cards."

Play cards?

It takes work not to strangle myself, but I somehow keep forging ahead.

"Or we could—"

"A movie is good," she finally answers. She glances over my shoulder and I swear I see the beginnings of a smile before she stops herself. "But just to warn you, I only like chick flicks. Mainly things that make me cry. Keep that in mind when you're picking something out, though it probably won't be a problem for you."

I blink when Olivia walks around me and into my living room. *What the heck?* That was unexpected and goes completely against what I know about her personality. The Olivia I know isn't playful or forward, she's timid and reserved. I turn to follow her, thinking the Olivia I know is cautious and slightly fearful and—

Crap.

I see her standing in front of my paused television and know that I've been discovered.

"Oh." A dozen other better, fouler words cross my mind, but I stop there.

There are a few things about myself that I would rather not admit, and Olivia just discovered one of them. The evidence is clear, and there's nothing I can do about it. I squeeze my eyes shut, feeling the beginning of a headache. Or public mortification. Right now it's hard to know the difference.

"About that . . . ," I begin, gesturing toward the television.

Olivia stops me. "What are you watching?" She laughs, turns to look at me over her shoulder, and then focuses on the television again.

I clear my throat. "Just a show."

She presses her lips together. "I see that. What show?"

I do not like her and I want her to leave right now. "*General Hospital.*"

Her shoulders shake. I'm not amused.

"That's what I thought. The question is, why?"

I look at the ceiling, suddenly thinking about Chicken Little. Why can't something fall on me right now? Is a big piece of drywall too much to ask?

"That's none of your business."

That doesn't faze her; she's full-on laughing. "Well, why don't we just finish this, since you're obviously so into it." She walks around the sofa, sits down, then reaches for a blanket. When I make no move to join her, she looks at me and jerks her head, indicating the spot next to her. I do the obedient thing and move. "But first, fill me in on the story line so I don't feel left out."

I try to be mad. I really try.

But there's this thing stopping me. This thing I can't deny, no matter how hard I want to.

I used to watch *General Hospital* with my grandmother when I was a kid—every afternoon after school, a bowl of popcorn between us and a Coke in each of our hands. She would explain the happenings of the Quartermaines and the Spencers to my young, naïve self. Maybe it's silly and maybe I should be embarrassed, but sitting in her living room on her old, worn-out sofa while we watched her "stories" is my favorite childhood memory. I would revisit those days right now if some genie in a bottle gave me the opportunity to make the wish.

But I can't, and it won't, and I know this. So out of determination and a good amount of nostalgia, I've held onto the habit for years, keeping it to myself because . . . well . . . I have a reputation to uphold and most men would frown on this sort of thing.

But Olivia . . . here . . . this is first time anyone has ever joined me in my little secret.

And as I tug on the end of Olivia's blanket, forcing her to share it with me, it hits me how much I like it.

———

From my spot on the sofa, I watch her. The show ended five minutes ago, but I lost interest long before that, when she fell asleep next to me. Her head rests on the arm of the sofa, a stone-colored faux-fur blanket tucked under her chin, both hands clutching it to keep it in place. In an earlier moment of restlessness, she stretched her legs out to get comfortable, and one foot now rests fully under my thigh. I haven't moved since, nor will I. That one simple touch has me feeling all sorts of inappropriate things, the main one being that I like this girl. Really like this girl.

And thoughts of attaching myself to someone—especially someone like Olivia—are as inappropriate as they come.

My thigh burns from the contact, and I know I should wake her. The right thing to do would be to gently shake her by the shoulders and whisper her name, and then see her to her apartment when she's coherent enough to walk. It's the right thing to do. The noble thing to do.

I don't believe much in being noble.

I lay my head on the back of the sofa and cover myself with the blanket as much as I can without pulling it hard enough to wake her.

Then I roll my head to the side and watch her a little longer until I eventually fall asleep.

Chapter 20

Olivia

"That boy is on fire."

At those words whispered behind me, I bristle. This is never going to end. I'm going to be asked and asked and asked to attend these baseball games and it's all starting to drive me a little crazy. What's worse, what's *really* worse, is that I don't necessarily hate it. Will is playing a good—scratch that—great game. He's managed to prevent three stolen bases, and now he just threw a guy out at third, pegging the third baseman's glove dead center like it was only a few feet away. Spectators like the middle-aged drunk guy behind me have been chattering about Will for the last few innings, something that should have me feeling proud for him. But I don't; instead, I'm bothered.

Will keeps looking up into the stands as if to see if I'm still watching. I am. Of course I am.

It's all ridiculous and I feel like a teenager. A foolish young girl playing a silly but dangerous game with her heart, mind, and soul.

I'll never forget the moment I woke up on his sofa this morning and caught him staring at me. He quickly turned away, but I saw it. The look in his eye that said this charade was turning into more than just me being a lucky charm. Everything is quickly changing from just a fun game to . . . something more.

But that doesn't mean I have to allow it.

Especially since I hate hate hate this game.

Maybe not as much as I used to, but I definitely still hate it.

"I don't know if you realize this, but you've done wonders for his ability lately." Kimberly waves at someone a few rows down. "I mean, he's always been good, but not this good. Who knew what he needed was a solid relationship to really settle him down?"

A solid relationship. One built on tales of stripper poles, fake cat rescues, and bribery. Solid is one word for it. Sordid and wrong are two others.

"Oh, I think it's just a coincidence," I say. "A pendulum swings both ways, you know. He couldn't lose forever; he had to start playing better eventually, right?" I study the field as though nothing enthralls me more than white jerseys and dirt stains, hoping that Kimberly will change the subject to something I'm more comfortable with. Like germs or junk food. I'd welcome makeup tips or more criticism of my choice of stylist in order to avoid the road we're headed down.

"To hear him talk, you've managed to single-handedly save his game."

My head snaps in her direction at this. Of course I know he thinks this, but I never expected him to admit it to anyone else.

"He said that? All I'm doing is sitting here, and I contribute absolutely nothing to help him . . ." I eye the back of Will's jersey, but all I can see is the number thirteen . . . on a blue jersey . . . years ago . . .

"Don't underestimate yourself, Olivia. Will hasn't had a lot of stability in his life. Sometimes all a person needs is someone who calms them down, gives them a little confidence where they didn't have it before. According to Blake, that's what happened to him when he met me. I think with Will, it might be the same thing. At least that's what he told Blake the night you were at our house."

She places two fingers in her mouth and delivers an ear-piercing whistle, but all I can hear is my heart pounding between my ears. This whole relationship is a sham, and good people like the DeMarcos are falling for it. And Will is encouraging it. It's one thing for him to lie to me, but how can he lie to his friends?

But the more prominent voice I hear is this: *What if he isn't lying?*

And then there's the matter of the tiny voice whispering, *You're lying too.*

A dull panic settles in my chest as I overanalyze what it could mean. He's a player. A gamer. Of baseball. I'm an elementary schoolteacher, and even I know the combination spells disaster. Everything I've ever wanted in my life—baseball represents the exact opposite. The only thing that would have me second-guessing the goodness of another person's heart. Baseball. Right up there with criminals on my list of No Way Will This Ever Happen Not If I Can Help It.

As if on cue and because karma has a way of dealing it to me, my phone buzzes from its spot on my lap. A text from my mother. It's all I can do not to let the phone slip between the seats and shatter all over the pavement twenty feet below.

```
Her: Have you called him?

No.

Her: Are you going to?

I haven't decided yet.

Her: You're being unfair, Olivia.
```

```
I don't see how not being ready to talk
to him is unfair, especially seeing how
we ended things.

Her: His court date has been moved up to
next week. I think your presence there
would mean the world to him and maybe
give him a little encouragement. Don't
ignore your brother, Olivia. He needs
you.
```

With shaking hands, I stare at the message on my phone while something that feels like a dagger pricks the outer edges of my heart. *He needs you, Olivia. Don't ignore your brother, Olivia.* I don't like the ribbons of jealousy that were threaded through my heart years ago, but they exist. I try never to play with them so as not to entangle them further, but sometimes a fingertip slips in, and I pull. Tighten. I can't help but acknowledge them. They knot and twist and cut in the form of a text. A spoken word. A feeling of inadequacy, even while sitting in a crowd at the request of someone who apparently thinks me not only adequate but necessary.

Don't ignore your brother, my mother said. I think long and hard about that request for a moment, and then decide to do her one better.

With a swipe of my hand, I delete the entire text thread and stand up. Picking up my bag, I start down the aisle and then walk up the steps, ignoring not only my brother . . .

But my mother and Will and even Kimberly, who calls after me, wondering where I'm going.

Will

I spin my key ring around my index finger so that the silver is nothing but a flashy blur. I've been to her apartment, I've driven up and down the neighborhood side streets, I've checked at the Waffle Shack—and that was all after I scoured the ballpark looking for her. According to Kimberly, she just left. She stood up with her bag, walked down the row of seats, didn't respond when Kimberly called her name, and never came back. It's the first time Olivia hasn't waited for me in the last four games, and to be honest I'm a little put out. At myself. How quickly things become a habit—before we even realize what's happening.

And Olivia has become a freaking habit.

If only I knew her well enough to know where she might try to hide. I stand in the middle of the Waffle Shack parking lot and turn a slow circle, trying and failing to weigh my options. The streetlight overhead isn't working; shards of busted white glass litter the grassy area in front of me. No matter, it's nice not to have a spotlight on my indecisiveness. Other than her quirks, her cat, and her obvious love for routine, I don't know much about Olivia. Where would she go?

Her love for routine.

The key ring stops spinning when I grip it in my fist. I climb into the car and start it up. Only five minutes pass before I am pulling into the lot and parking next to Olivia's car. For a guy who thrives on adventure and unpredictability, I'm learning to appreciate the opposite.

———

"If you're here to give a speech, you're about four weeks too late."

She doesn't even look up when she delivers the words. It's as though she expected me to come, expected me to find her.

"So this is your classroom?" I look around, take in the colorful banners taped to the ceiling, the names of well-known authors and inventors displayed for the children to learn. An intricate wooden club-house has been constructed in the far corner, the words "Reading Nook" painted over the top of it, pillows lined up from end to end to offer the kids comfortable places to sit. Buckets. Bins. Files. Organized. The place is very neatly arranged. Almost overly so.

"Yes," she says. Still no eye contact. "How did you get in?"

I shove my hands in my pockets. "I parked next to your car, and since it was parked next to the side door, I took a chance the door would be unlocked and followed the only light in this place. You probably shouldn't be here alone, you know."

She tucks her hair behind her ears. That hair . . .

"I'm alone all the time." I don't think she means it the way it sounds. My hunch is confirmed when I see her wince. "I mean, I'm *here* alone all the time. Darkness doesn't scare me."

"It scares me." I take in the room and try not to shudder. It's a partly true statement. I walk the rest of the way into the room, feeling all sorts of insecure and unsure, and none of it has to do with Olivia. I wasn't the best student—the worst, actually. This room might have me breaking into a cold sweat of unwelcome memories if I didn't have a job to do. Something tells me I'm going to need to sell myself to Olivia all over again. I've never had to do so much begging in my life.

"Why did you leave the game early?"

She gestures to the books in front of her. "I had things to do."

"At midnight on a Friday? Doesn't school start in a month?"

She sighs but still refuses to look at me, so I pull out a kid-sized chair and sit across from her. From this angle I can see that her shoes are off, revealing painted red toenails that surprise me a little. Olivia is conservative. Subdued. A fade-into-the-background kind of personality. Olivia is blue. I never figured Olivia for red.

Her bare legs are tucked underneath her, a tower of children's books perched in her lap, more piled on the floor in a perfect semicircle around her. I watch in silence as she checks the spine, opens to the first page, checks the spine again, then inserts each into the bookcase one by one. She's on the seventh one when I decide I can't take it anymore.

"Olivia, tell me why you left."

She finally gives me an obligatory glance before studying those stupid books again. "I told you, I needed to work."

I reach for a small paperclip lying on the floor and place it on the desk in front of me. "Don't lie to me, Olivia. The truth might hurt, but it's always better than making something up."

She hurls *Harry Potter and the Sorcerer's Stone* toward the bookcase. "Fine, you want the truth?" she practically shouts. "We're lying to everyone, and I don't like it. Especially to Kimberly, since she's never been anything but nice to me. Do you know that during the game she went on and on about what a great couple we make? How perfect I am for you, for your game? It didn't help that you kept looking up at me to make sure I was still there, as though you honestly think I'm the key to your winning streak."

I just look at her. "I do think you're the key to my winning streak. But I don't think all those things you mentioned are the real problem here."

I can feel her mentally lunging for me, gripping two hands around my neck, but she sits still, cool as a chilled glass of champagne. But everyone knows champagne is full of simmering bubbles that steal your breath on the way down.

"Now you're going to psychoanalyze me? What's the real problem then, Will? Enlighten me, please."

I'm not one to back down from a challenge. "I think you're starting to like me."

She rolls her eyes. "Get over yourself."

But I hear the way her voice catches on that last word. "Look at me, Olivia."

She doesn't, just jerks her head. "There's a mirror over there. Why don't you go look in it and admire your image? That should last awhile."

At that I laugh. I like the feisty side of her a little too much. "No, thanks. I've done that plenty today."

"Why does that not surprise me?" She rolls her eyes again, reaches up to rub the back of her neck. "Besides, I'm dating someone, remember? Or did you already forget that?"

So we're back to that. Olivia is terrible at lying.

I clear my throat. "I guess I did. And he's been okay with you attending all these games on my behalf? Going out to dinner with me? Hanging out in my apartment?"

She sniffs and looks down, her hair becoming a veil. "I haven't exactly mentioned your apartment, but he was fine with the rest. I just explained that I'm doing it as a favor for my neighbor."

For a moment, that comment stings. Here I am, developing somewhat of an obsession with the lady with the gorgeous blonde hair, and she sees me as only the guy who lives next door. What does this guy she's dating have that I don't have?

But then I remember there is no guy.

And then my devious side kicks in like the trusty sidekick it's always been.

"Think he would be interested in coming over for dinner this weekend? Just you and him, and then of course I could invite a date."

There's this thing I'm learning about Olivia. When she's caught, she pales to a nice shade similar to vanilla ice cream. And when she pales, she starts making up more crap.

"We can't. We're going away for the weekend." She plucks another book off the carpet and practically slams it into the bookcase. It falls on its side. She rights it with a jerk, but I see the way her hand shakes.

I sit back and watch her, enjoying the performance. "Sounds like fun. Where are you going?"

"Chicago." She says it a bit too quickly. "To see a play. And go to dinner."

It takes a lot of self-control not to make an obnoxious noise. I lock both hands behind my neck and lean back in my chair. "You're flying all the way to Chicago to see a play? Wow. Big spender."

Something on the carpet is suddenly very interesting to her. "Yes, his family is wealthy. It's a private plane. With a minibar."

With a minibar. Her emphasis on that is comical. "Who's keeping Perry?"

"What?" She says it too quickly, like a gasp.

"Who's keeping Perry? I wouldn't think he could stay home alone all weekend. Especially since you couldn't even bear to leave him while you went to a ball game." I'm a devil with little horned demons whispering into both ears. I don't give her time to answer. "I have an idea. Bring him to me and I'll take care of him. That way you can have a nice, long, worry-free weekend together. Stay an extra day if you want. What do you think?"

"What?" She looks sick.

"You keep saying that."

"It's just that I hate to ask you when—"

"But you didn't ask. I offered." I slowly stand and push the chair back underneath the desk. Discussion over. "Why don't you drop him off in the morning so you and the boyfriend can get an early start?"

The vanilla ice cream has softened and now looks like a bowl of melting snow.

"If . . . if you're sure," she says, her lip shaking. I almost feel sorry for her, but that's what a person gets for lying to me. Then, with a jolt, I remember something. She might be lying, but I think I'm the one who might suffer the consequences.

"Wait, so you won't be here for tomorrow's game?"

Her eyes widen. She forgot, same as me. And now we're both stuck in the middle of her outrageous story.

"I guess not. Is that okay?"

I pause, nod my head. But it isn't okay. Sure we've been winning, and sure the days of me claiming Olivia is the reason for it are probably already numbered, but I want her there. I haven't played a home game without her watching in a while. Whether I'm playing or not, there's a weird calmness that comes over me when I know she's in the stands. I'm already forced to play without her on the road; even though she said she would come, I haven't been brave enough to ask. Or maybe I just know how much my guard would drop in a hotel room, and how much hers would go up. Either way, we've won and lost without her there—something I've learned to live with.

Having her with me at home isn't something I'm ready to let go of. Not yet.

I sigh. "I guess it has to be. What time are you leaving?"

She stares straight ahead, dread and remorse pulling up matching chairs and getting comfortable on her shoulders. "I think seven." She nods slowly. "Yes, seven. That's what he said."

"When do you get back in town?"

She bites her bottom lip, thinks for a minute. "I think Sunday night?"

This is getting ridiculous. "So you won't be at Sunday's game either?"

"I guess not." Olivia shakes her head. She doesn't look happy. That makes two of us.

I pat the door frame and fake being supportive. "You should go home and get some sleep since you're leaving so early. See you in the morning." I make it through the doorway, then pop my head back inside to look at her. "Oh, and Olivia?"

"What?"

She looks cute sitting there . . . stuck . . . guilty . . . and lost. I nearly smile, even though I'm ticked off at both of us. At her for beginning this charade. At me for keeping it going.

"Don't forget the litter box."

She swallows. "I won't."

"Perfect. See you at seven."

I'm halfway to my car before the reality of the situation sets in. This isn't funny. Not at all. Of course there are the games and the lack of Olivia's presence. But even more . . .

How did I—Will Vandergriff, two-time cover guy on *Sports Illustrated*—get stuck babysitting a cat for the weekend?

I hate cats. Why do I keep forgetting that?

Chapter 21

Olivia

This is what my life has been reduced to for the past four hours. Sneaking. Crawling. Hiding. Peering. All forms of peeping Tom-ing. And for what reason? All because I'm spying on a cat. A couple years ago, a child in my old apartment building referred to me as a cat lady. I balked, glaring at him and holding Perry close to my chest, his leash slapping against my bare leg as we returned from our midafternoon walk. I've always looked back on that child with a bad taste in my mouth, because he was rude and inconsiderate and too bold for his own good.

Now I'm starting to wonder if maybe he was right.

I'm currently feeding my suspicion by crouching like a caged tiger in my own living room, my eyes level with the windowsill, watching intently as Will walks outside with Perry hooked under one arm—minus the leash; I'm going to kill him for that tomorrow because *he needs a leash*—and climbs into his car. The tires squeal a bit as he reverses, and he drives away with my baby as though it's perfectly normal to let a cat lie unsupervised while sunning himself against the back windshield. I don't care that it's a nice day or that it's probably a pleasant place for Perry to lie. What if Will crashes the car? What if Perry falls? Why has no one yet invented cat car seats? Why have I been reduced to this hermitlike existence for the entire weekend?

And on top of it all, now I'm missing the game.

I like going to Will's games.

I don't want to miss the game.

Me and my stupid mouth.

I stand up and stretch, my back screaming in protest from all the ways I've kept it hunched over all morning. Now that Will has finally departed, I no longer have to be so quiet. The dishwasher has remained off, as have the television set and the washing machine. Even my footsteps have been muted. I'm supposed to be living it up in Chicago at this very moment—attending a play, eating amazing food, having a great time with my made-up Prince Charming—not standing in my bathrobe still unshowered and looking half deranged. I'm aware of the noise the pipes make when water runs through them; I couldn't risk Will hearing that from the other side of the wall. Then I would be reduced to making up new stories to go along with my giant string of current lies, and all of it sounds so exhausting.

With a sigh, I fling off my robe and head for the bathroom. Thank goodness he's gone. I'm sick of being dirty.

As water streams down my back, all I can think is *why did I make up that story about going away for the weekend?* Why the need for a false boyfriend? I don't lie. I make a practice of being truthful at all times. It's a rule I put into place years ago out of necessity. Coming from a family of liars will do that to you. Then I meet Will Vandergriff, and in a matter of weeks all the tidy boxes I've spent years wrapping and stacking around myself have been torn open and left lying in shreds all around me. I want them back. I like my shiny red bows and my eight-by-eight cardboard. They're safe, and safe has my name stamped all over it.

I reach for a towel and am wrapping it around me when I hear a knock. A knock that frightens me more than anything, because I have no idea who it is. What if it's Will and I've been discovered? What if it's not Will and I'm about to be murdered? A dozen similar scenarios flit through my head as I slip into a bathrobe and tiptoe toward the door.

I can't help an eye roll. I'm tiptoeing toward my own door because of my own dumb lies. This feels like punishment, because it is.

I peer through the peephole and breathe a sigh of relief. I've barely managed to crack open the door when a hand pushes against it and Kelly barges inside. She's wearing a yellow spaghetti-strap swing dress and a don't-mess-with-me attitude.

"What are you doing here?" I ask her, aware that my wet hair is dripping down onto my white terry cloth robe. I'm even more aware that the door is wide open and I'm fully exposed to anyone who might've forgotten something and chosen this exact moment to walk by with an overweight Persian. Gripping my hairbrush in a tight fist, I lunge for the door and shut it. "What are you doing here?" I whisper again. "And keep your voice down."

"We're going out and you're coming with us, and this time we're not taking no for an answer," Kelly says, glancing over her shoulder at the empty apartment. "But why are we whispering?"

"Who's 'we'? And because he might come home and hear you." I nod toward Will's apartment as though the answer is obvious. "What if he comes home?"

She just looks at me as though I've lost it. Maybe I have. "'We' is a few teachers from school. We're going shopping and then having dinner at Joe's Bar later tonight. And who might hear you? Who might come home?"

"Will!"

She whips her head toward the doorway. "I hope so. Then maybe I could finally meet the guy." She looks way too excited for a woman who is on the verge of blowing my cover. "But why does it bother you?"

"Because he could see me!"

She frowns at me. "I thought you liked him."

"I do!"

She just stares at me. Kelly has been to my apartment before, but it's been a while. Several months, in fact. But it hasn't been so long that she's forgotten how to get around. She blows out an exasperated breath and starts dragging me toward the bedroom.

"Olivia, you sound a little crazy right now, but we'll deal with that later." She flings me into my room. "For now, get dressed. I'll be waiting for you in the living room." She's no longer whispering.

"But I don't want to go shopping. I don't need anything." I'm terrified of being caught, so I keep my voice low. I trip over a shoe on the floor, jabbing a pointed heel into the arch of my foot. I hop in place for a second and try not to cry.

Kelly looks me up and down from the open doorway. "You're a mess, and I said I'm not taking no for an answer. Get dressed, and wear something sexy."

"For the mall?"

"I told you, we're staying out all day. No more hiding inside this apartment for you, and no more cats." She moves to close the bedroom door, then opens it a fraction. "Oh, and wear your hair down. No more tight ponytails either. Not today."

I almost say that I've worn my hair down a lot lately, but something about that statement makes me nervous so I stay quiet. It's almost like she has a plan. I love plans. I live for plans. I might even die for a few. As long as they're my plans. I hate them when they're formulated by other people. The door closes and I'm faced with my own wild-eyed reflection. Somehow I have to roam around town all day hoping I don't eventually run into Will. He has an afternoon game, so that buys me a few hours. But then I have to get back home later without being seen. I don't know how this is going to happen, since things never work out that easily for me. So I do the only thing I can do in this situation.

I lie on my bed and shove a pillow over my face.

Five minutes later, I give up trying to figure it out and reach for a dress.

Will

"Now, why exactly are you doing this?" Blake asks me.

I find the muddiest puddle at the outer edge of the field and plop Perry next to it. After the game ended—we lost, by the way, no thanks to Olivia—I decided to extend the fun because who's here to stop me? Certainly not Olivia. She's back at home, trying to be quiet in that apartment of hers while convincing herself that I can't hear her moving around. But I heard her all morning. I heard when she pressed that glass against the kitchen wall and then promptly dropped and shattered it. I heard the curse word that was supposed to be under her breath but came out in front of an echo. Who knew Olivia cursed? I kinda liked it. I heard the broom as it swished across the floor, the pinging of broken glass as it rained into a trash can. I heard the television come on and then immediately shut off. Of course I heard all these things because I was doing a little ear pressing and wall hugging myself. We live in one of the nicest apartment buildings in Dallas. That doesn't mean it came equipped with the greatest insulation.

And now. Now I'm going to mess with her a bit. Just because I can.

"Because Olivia's cat needs to get out and live a little. See the world. Get a little dirty." Just as I hoped, Perry inches closer to the sticky puddle.

Blake just looks at me. "Does she know you have him? I thought you told me she's really protective of that thing."

He says *that thing* like Perry has a disease. A couple of days ago I would have agreed, but one day with him and I've come to realize he's not that bad. All he does is sleep, and when he's awake he seems so dang appreciative of his food bowl and being able to walk outside without a freaking leash. When I first tried to take him out this morning, he cowered in a corner, clearly afraid of what might be required. I scooped him up and walked outside, plopping him on the grass adjacent to the building. He studied me for a long moment before sprawling on the lawn. He spent a good twenty minutes just rolling around while I sat a few feet away and snapped pictures. Something tells me he's never been allowed to just be a cat before. As long as he's in my care, that's what he's going to do. I smile to myself when Perry places one front paw, then the other, into the mud.

"Yeah, she knows. I offered to keep him while she's out of town with her"—I stop myself before saying a sarcastic *boyfriend*—"mother."

"Doesn't sound like you're a big fan."

"I'm not," I lie. I've never even met the lady, and for the first time I wonder if Olivia might be right. The lies we're telling everyone are stacking up. "She's not real nice to Olivia, and that bothers me a little." That part is true at least. I've heard bits and pieces of their conversations. I've heard the frustration in Olivia's voice when the subject of her family comes up.

Blake picks up a discarded bat and tucks it under his arm. By now, Perry has completely submerged himself in the mud puddle; only the top part of his back remains cotton-ball white. I laugh. He's going to stay that way until Olivia "returns" tomorrow afternoon, and I can't wait to see the look on her face.

"How are you going to get that thing home without ruining your car?"

Crap. I hadn't thought that far ahead. He has a kennel, but he's never once gone into it willingly. Which means I'm going to have to pick him up and somehow shove him inside. He won't be the only one covered in mud before the night is over.

"I'll figure it out." The dread is real, but I guess it serves me right.

"You know he has a pine tar rag stuck to his side, don't you?"

"What?" Everything inside me sinks. My stomach. My brain. My bravado. I rush toward the cat to examine him, only to find that Blake isn't kidding. There's a small rag running from his stomach to his side. "Oh crap. How am I going to get it off?" I bend down and tug on the rag, tug a little more. Perry meows in protest, but that's the only thing that happens.

Pine tar is used by players to get a better grip on the bat, because it's sticky. Sticky like glue, sticky like, well . . . tar. And it's hard to get off your hands. There's no way it's coming off a cat's fur. Not without—

"Only one way I know of," Blake says. "You cut it off."

I can feel my mouth just hanging open, but it can't be helped. I can't cut it. Nothing gets past Olivia, and she will definitely notice this. This can't be fixed with a bath. There has to be another option besides cutting his hair. There has to be.

"Maybe I can—"

"You can cut it. That's about the only option I see."

I shoot Blake a look. "Thanks for your help."

He shrugs. "Wasn't my idea to bring him out onto the field."

A thousand curses on me and my stupid idea. "Who the heck left that rag out here?" It's a pointless question that doesn't deserve an answer, but I don't want to go down alone.

"Kind of a pointless question, considering the situation." I can always count on Blake to back up my thoughts. He begins to walk away.

"Where are you going?" The kennel is across the stadium, tucked inside the dugout. I need him to get it. I'm not picking up this muddy, tar-covered cat and carrying him across the field.

"I'm going home," he calls out. "Good luck. But if I were you, I'd stop showing up here with that furball in your possession. One more time bringing him into the locker room and your manhood will start to come into question, and I'm not kidding."

Right now, every trait I possess is being called into question. Especially my judgment.

"This is the last time, believe me."

"Have fun trying to get that thing in your car. And good luck with the cutting. I sure hope Olivia doesn't kill you. If you're still alive, I'll see you tomorrow."

———

Strange how quickly the fun and games can come to a screeching halt.

Despite a shower, I still have mud caked under my fingernails, Perry won't stop whining from the laundry room—the only place I will let him sleep because he's filthy and there's no way I'm letting him out to roam the house—and it's midnight. And Olivia just climbed out of a black Audi. Olivia is wearing a dress. Olivia is smiling. Olivia is smiling a little too wide.

She's never once looked like that after a date with me.

Never mind that all our dates are fake.

My stomach drops when I hear her begin to hum right outside my door.

My spirits don't rise when she slaps a hand over her mouth and looks wide-eyed toward my door, all at once remembering she's supposed to be quiet.

And just like that, the tables are turned. Now I'm the paranoid one.

I don't hear from her until late the next day.

By the time the sun sets and I give in and call her, I'm convinced she really does have a boyfriend and really did have a date, even if she didn't actually go to Chicago. There's no way she could have gone to Chicago and back in one evening, right?

I roll that question around in my mind for a while. When she finally knocks on my door, I've talked myself into believing that I'm the player who's been played all along.

Chapter 22

Olivia

Will came home from the game an hour ago—they lost again, both games while I was supposedly gone, which makes me feel even worse for all the lies I've told—and I've spent that hour trying to figure out how to handle this. If I head over to his apartment too early, he might suspect I was actually home all weekend. Or that my date was a disaster. Or that I'm just so desperate for companionship that I can't wait to have my cat back. Which is true, despite the good time I had last night.

Thinking back on it, I'm at a loss to explain why I haven't been out with those women before now. Especially considering I met someone.

David Nichols asked me to dance. He walked up to me at Joe's Bar, where I was standing in a corner clutching a ginger ale and wishing with everything in me that I could return home. I agreed despite myself, then followed him onto the wooden dance floor, my little black dress clinging to my thighs with each step. I had been self-conscious in it all night, but something about the way he looked at me made those thoughts slowly fade. We danced together through one and two and three songs. I was prepared to depart when the fourth song was a slow one, but he grabbed my hand and pulled me to him, and I didn't resist. He was attractive in all the right ways—dark blond hair that curled a bit at the collar, tanned skin that suggested he spent a lot of time outside, woodsy cologne that had me feeling all kinds of things that have lain dormant for far too long, and a sense of humor that kept me and the other women in stitches for nearly two hours.

When he asked me to go somewhere with him, I turned him down. But when he asked for my number, I gave it to him. What could it hurt? It isn't like I'm currently seeing anyone. It's not like I'm in a relationship that requires exclusivity or even partial disclosure. If he calls, I might agree to a date. Maybe even a second one. Maybe even a third. He was that charming, that memorable, that handsome.

I've spent all day hoping that his name won't appear on my phone screen.

Conversely, I've spent the same amount of time hoping to see Will's name light it up.

With a sigh, I turn my phone facedown on my kitchen table to eliminate the urge to constantly glance at the screen, then try to distract myself with dinner. One look into the refrigerator tells me that except for a loaf of bread, some milk, and a bundle of yellowing broccoli, there's nothing to eat in there. I close the door and lean against it, taking in the sparse kitchen and its meager contents. I'm hungry, but I refuse to go out. To go out means that Will might see me, and if Will sees me then my charade is up. I'm not ready to let go of it yet. The second I let go is the second I have to start lying again, and based on the last two weeks alone, I'm beginning to accept that my future standing in heaven is shaky at best.

Pushing off the refrigerator, I open a cabinet to find what's left of an old box of Cheerios. I pull one loop out and take a bite—not too stale—and then pour the contents into a bowl until the box empties.

Just as I reach for the milk, my phone begins to dance across the table. I set the carton on the counter, then lunge for the phone on the third ring. I look at it with a mixture of excitement and dread. It's Will. The relief at it not being David surprises me a little. I answer the call. He doesn't bother to wait for my hello.

"You've been home most of the afternoon. Are you planning on coming to get this cat anytime soon, or will I have to take him to the field again tomorrow too?"

Crap. He's mad.

I knock the milk off the counter. Thank goodness the lid was still on the carton.

"Did you win or lose?" I ask, pretending not to know the answer as I pick the carton off the floor and pour milk over the loops. When I take a bite, it's dry. Grainy. Gross. I carry the bowl to the sink and fill it with water.

"We lost both games, thanks to you. You better be at the next one. I won't take no for an answer."

I'm not stupid; this time I don't make fun of his superstition. I'm too busy trying to deny the little thrill that runs through me at his forcefulness.

"I will be," I say before I think better of it. *Did I just agree without a fight? To a ball game and spectators and hot dogs?* There's a long pause as I wait, as he waits, as both of us wait for the other to speak up. Finally, I hear him sigh.

"Darn right you will be. And Olivia?"

"What?"

"Come get your cat before I call animal control. He's driving me crazy, and pretty soon I won't be responsible for my actions."

I hang up the phone and head for the door.

———

Will

I watch her face as she walks through the living room. Even the scent of the three rib eye steaks I have warming in the oven fades away when she blanches. There it is, the look I was waiting for . . . the look that makes the whole weekend worth the trouble.

She stops at the edge of the room and stares. And that's when she whirls on me.

"What did you do to him?"

Her face is a mask of horror and anger, and both look prettier on her than I expected. Wrap those two emotions around the feistiness I saw from her a few days ago, and Olivia keeps getting more interesting.

"Just let him play around, that's all." I shrug like I don't know what she's talking about. I mean, sure Perry is covered in caked-on mud that starts at his ears and ends at all four paws—had to flick a little out of his eye earlier, poor thing—but come on, the woman needs to lighten up. Although something tells me that won't happen when she sees the bald spot on his—

"What is wrong with his fur?" Her cold eyes travel between me and the animal. I grab my coffee to ward off her chilliness and take a long sip.

"What do you mean?" The coffee burns going down. *Oh man oh man oh man.* Suddenly I'm hoping for third-degree burns, the kind that might rush me to a hospital and away from here.

Olivia kneels down in front of the animal and runs a hand across his left side. "Where is his hair?" It's a question, but it's delivered more like a threat. *Find his hair and return it to his back or I'm going to blow up this apartment with you inside. Find his hair and return it to his back or I'm going to join that chick and her lawsuit and tell the whole world about your mistreatment of animals.*

I rub the back of my neck and shift positions. "It's on his body."

"Half of it is. The other half seems to be missing."

"Hasn't he always been like that?" Dear God, I sound like a kid trying to dig his way out of a broken vase and ruined flowers. I have a feeling the only thing I'm digging is my own grave.

Olivia whips around to glare at me. "No, it hasn't always been like that! What did you do, Will? And don't tell me it just happened!"

I try. I try to come up with something, anything other than the truth of my own immaturity. But there's nothing. So I tell her the story, leaving out the part where I did it on purpose, because so what if I'm immature? I play ball for a living, not the stock market. It takes only a minute and when I'm finished she just stares at me. Is there anything worse than a woman's silent stare, especially when you know she's using it to figure out the best way to physically harm you?

"So you had to cut that thing off his back. Because it got stuck. After he rolled around outside in the mud. Even though he's never done that in his life."

She doesn't believe me. Time to deflect. Time to pass the blame. "We were on the field, actually. And it's not my fault that he wandered into a mud puddle. It's not my fault he had to come to the game today."

I leave out the part about all this happening yesterday. I leave out the part about how I practically tossed the furball into the mud and rolled him around in it myself, then dumped a little extra on his head just to make sure he was really good and dirty. When did I turn into such a child? And why is getting under Olivia's skin so much fun?

I force myself to stop overanalyzing my adolescent behavior and study her. She looks tired, like the weekend has taken its toll on her. Once again I find myself wondering about the boyfriend, about what I saw and heard last night when she came in from what looked like a very real date.

"How was Chicago? What play did you see?"

She hesitates, that fierceness wobbling for only a moment before she forces it back into place with a shake of her head.

"Don't change the subject. Do you have shampoo? You're going to help me give him a bath."

I blink at the way she ignores my question because it's an important one, one I've thought about all day. "I have shampoo in the shower, but I thought cats hated baths."

"They do, and now you get to see firsthand just how true that is. Congratulations." She scoops up Perry and holds him like a football in front of her—not bad form, but now probably isn't the best time to hit her with that compliment—and walks toward the kitchen sink. Dumping him inside, she keeps one hand on his back and turns to look at me. "Get the shampoo, please."

I'm so busy staring at her backside that it takes a few seconds to register that she issued an order. I have the shampoo in my hands before I remember that I don't take orders from anyone but my coach, but something tells me Olivia won't want to be compared to him.

"What will he do when the water hits his fur?" I stand back and eye the situation. What happens if his claws come out and he scratches my pitching hand? Too big an injury and it won't matter that Olivia is at the game. It won't make a difference if she's sitting in my freaking lap reciting the Rosary if my hand is too marred and bloody to play.

"I'm more concerned about what he'll do when it hits his bare skin, but I guess you should have thought of that before you decided to let him get so dirty." She turns on the spray nozzle and aims it at his back. And that's when all hell breaks loose. You'd think twelve cats were being slaughtered, dismembered, and baked in my oven the way Perry screeches and protests. It's a cat massacre gone horribly wrong—much worse than the leash—but it gets even more awful when Olivia looks at me and slams my ego with a few well-placed words.

"Stop being such a coward and get over here!"

I approach her cautiously. "I have no idea what you want me to do," I say. "I'm not a big fan of cats, especially not this one." It's the wrong thing to say, and she shoots me a look. And then she shoots me with the spray nozzle, and now my shirt is wet. Holy crap, she's hostile. I swear I see smoke coming out both ears and maybe even her mouth.

Her mouth. If I leaned a little closer, I could take her lower lip between my teeth.

I squash that thought before I can make a move. I might be a coward, but I'm not stupid.

Reaching for the shampoo, I dump a mound of it on Perry's back, making circles with my left hand while keeping my right hand out of the way.

"Am I doing it right?" It's a sincere question, but Olivia rolls her eyes.

"You're barely doing anything." She swats my hand away and begins scrubbing the animal back and forth with a vigor that makes me wince. "And next time, before you take my cat to your work and dump mud all over his back, maybe you'll remember this moment. Because next time I'll make you bathe him by yourself."

And with those words, all I can think is . . .

I like forceful Olivia.

I like passionate Olivia.

But I don't like what I'm beginning to suspect. Olivia knows I did this on purpose. Olivia is slowly learning me. Pretty soon Olivia is going to have me dissected and figured out. If this keeps up, she might know things about me I don't even know myself.

———

Twenty minutes later Perry is wrapped in a towel and blissfully silent, and the fallout of the bath debacle is minimal. I have one scratch across my forearm and a couple of teeth marks on my left shoulder, but nothing that should affect my game. My ego, however, all but shattered the moment Olivia saw me squeal and jump back to avoid Perry's wrath. Even though Olivia bore the brunt of it and is now covered in scratches on her neck, shoulder, and forearm, she hasn't stopped laughing since, and I haven't stopped resenting the sound.

"For the love of God, knock it off." I reach for a bag of coffee and begin scooping some into the filter. I have no idea if she drinks the stuff this late at night, but I add a couple extra scoops just in case and glance at her. "You need a Band-Aid. You need a dozen, actually."

She shrugs. "I'm fine, and I can't help it. Turns out the big, strong baseball player is a teenage girl in disguise. I haven't heard a sound like that since a seventh-grade slumber party, and even that wasn't as dramatic as the sound you made."

She laughs louder at the same time my mind conjures up images of a young Olivia engaged in a pillow fight while wearing nothing but a T-shirt. Feathers and bouncing cleavage may also be involved. Unable to help myself, I glance back at her in time to catch sight of her rubbing Perry's back with the towel, leaning down to plant a kiss on his nose. A slight wetness is suspended in both corners of her eyes. I'm not sure if it's from the bath or from crying, but I find myself wanting to kiss them off to see if I taste salt. I turn away and continue the task in front of me, though my mind stays back there on Olivia.

Something about that sight stays with me. Olivia, loving. Olivia, caring. Olivia, mothering that cat with a gentleness I haven't seen from her before. It unnerves me and has me thinking all sorts of uncomfortable things.

I'm shuffling around the kitchen, filling the pot with water, returning the coffee canister to its spot in the cabinet, when I realize Olivia has gone silent.

Just as I turn to find out the reason, she hits me with a question.

"Will, what are these?"

She's holding a stack of photos in her hand. Photos I meant to hide before she came over. When she looks up at me, there's a question in her eyes. A dozen questions, even. Ones I'm not prepared to answer.

Olivia just discovered a side of Will Vandergriff I work hard to keep hidden from the rest of the world. I'm not happy about it.

Chapter 23

Olivia

Something inside me cracks at the sight of the photos lying on the kitchen table, and I know things won't be the same. I can't believe what I'm seeing, because it doesn't make sense. What I'm looking at goes against everything I thought I knew about Will. Absolutely everything.

"When did you take these?" I flip through them slowly, a deck of cards tucked one behind another. I count twelve Polaroids and then stop, figuring there are probably twenty in all, maybe more. All of them of Perry—most of him alone, a few of him and Will together, taken selfie-style in this apartment, at the ball field, in the grass just beyond the parking lot. For all his protests, I just discovered Will's very soft side for four-legged creatures. Namely mine.

He shrugs as though my rapidly beating heart isn't resting in his hands. He shrugs as if I didn't just discover that we have something very personal in common . . . as if it doesn't make me like him even more.

"This weekend while we were out. He was a cool companion. It's no big deal."

No big deal. It's no big deal that he just displayed more interest in Perry than anyone else ever has—more than my mom, my dad, my brother, anyone. I know he's just a cat, but he's been my one constant companion in a world that often finds me without one, due to choice or circumstance or old-fashioned yet all-too-common loss. "There might be more pictures over on the dining room table if you want to check," he says.

I feel my eyes widen. More? Unable to help myself, I wander over and pick up another five or six photos left sprawled out on the mahogany, all similar to the others. Except in one, Perry is wearing a Rangers cap and sitting on what appears to be the pitching mound. It's adorable and I'm taking it home with me. I set the photos down—save for that one—and give myself a moment to think. Will has hit some kind of emotional nerve inside me that sits way below the ones concerned about appearances and what other people believe. This one is raw and deep—in a place where feelings reside and pulses trip and hearts wait to break. But the feeling isn't unpleasant or uncomfortable. It doesn't leave me wanting to flee like I once thought it might. The opposite happens, and suddenly I want to stay in this apartment awhile longer instead of scooping Perry up and heading for the Sonic drive-through like I had originally planned.

I pretend to be thinking about something, then push my eyebrows together and look at him.

"Do I smell steak?"

Will rubs his hands together and glances toward his oven as though just now remembering he stored steaks there. His eyes light up, and my stomach growls. It's been hours since I've eaten, but that isn't the point. The point is that Will heard the sound and glances at my midsection. Normally this would embarrass me; this time I'm pretty sure my stomach's timing couldn't have been better.

"Steak, potatoes, bacon-wrapped green beans, and rolls. I made them earlier," he says. "Want to stay for dinner?"

"You made all that just for you?"

He grins. "Well, I mean, a guy's got to eat."

"He says to the girl who normally grabs takeout."

"That's crap food. So do you want to stay?"

I make him wait a moment, then make myself pause a moment longer. In a halfhearted tug-of-war, l tell myself to say no, that I love Sonic chicken strips with honey-mustard sauce and that they sound much better than red meat prepared by a guy who has probably cooked three meals in his life, because what professional athlete has time to hone that particular skill? I tell myself to bite down on those words and force them out, to grab Perry and head for the door.

Of course I don't listen to me. I never do.

"Sure, since it sounds like you made enough for the whole building," I say instead. "Is there anything I can do to help you get it ready?"

The next thing I know I'm reaching for plates and setting them side by side on the kitchen table. Weighing the wisdom of that decision, I change my mind and move the plates across from each other—less intimate, less . . . *close*. It isn't until we're halfway through dinner that I wish I'd left them where they were.

Because now I'm too far away.

———

In the middle of dinner Will decided he wanted pie, so now we're making one. Apple with a cream cheese middle and caramel oatmeal streusel something on top. I'm checking the recipe while I search for ingredients. Locating the oatmeal, I measure a half cup and pour it into a mixing bowl with melted butter while watching Will out of the corner of my eye. He's like Julia Child in male form, complete with the bottle of red wine sitting to his right. He pours a little into a glass, takes a sip, then reaches into his own mixing bowl and begins to knead stuff together. The girl inside of me can't believe he actually knows how to make a pie crust—with shortening and flour and salt—and that he's doing everything I remember seeing my grandmother do. It's surprising and more than a little charming to watch. And I could watch, for hours even.

Except the neat freak in me is too on edge about the ungodly mess he's making.

"You have more flour on the floor than you do in that bowl."

He glances over his shoulder and nods at something behind me. "If it bothers you so much, there's a mop in that closet over there. Why don't you grab it and get to work?"

My mouth falls open. "What do I look like, your maid? You grab it."

"I'm not the one complaining."

"I'm not complaining. I'm saying that your floor is a mess and—"

Before I can get my sentence out, he scoops up a handful of sticky flour and flings it at me. It lands on my shoulder, and I just stare at it in shock. No one has ever thrown food at me before, probably because they know I hate messes. Plus . . . germs. But Will. Will just did. And I don't know what happens, but something comes over me then. I think of Snow White's stepmother morphing into the evil witch.

"You know, for a pitcher, your aim could use work." I fist some oatmeal and toss it at his head. It lands smack against his forehead. I'm not sure which one of us is more surprised, but I can't stop my smile.

"My aim is fine." This time a shower of dry flour hits me in the face. I close my eyes just in time to avoid a whole lot of burning, then open them to glare at him. Mostly what I see is powder falling off my lashes like snow. "See?" he says. "Bull's-eye."

That's it. No one makes a mess out of me without consequences. I stare at the hunk of cream cheese in a nearby bowl. It's covered with milk, but I don't care. Squishing it between my fingers, I take aim and hit him in the neck, then use my hands to rub it in good.

Before we're finished, Will has dumped his entire bowl of dough over my head and I'm wishing I'd never brought up the minuscule bit of flour that was on the floor. With the stupid mop I refused to get, that mess would have taken two seconds to clean up. Now Perry isn't the only one requiring a bath tonight. I'm in worse shape than he was.

———

Will

I can't remember when I've had more fun. And I can't remember seeing a woman more beautiful. We're sitting on my kitchen floor, surrounded by mounds of dried white grossness because we're too dirty to sit anywhere else. Despite the mess, we did manage to make an apple pie, minus the oatmeal, because Olivia threw the entire canister at me, literally, after she showered me with the contents. It's been nearly two hours since I instigated turning this room into a mass of white, but it's been the best two hours in recent memory.

"Black," she says.

I've just asked her to name her favorite color, and I don't agree with her answer. What happened to blue? At the very least, Olivia looks like a pink or a purple or, God help me, a siren red, but not this.

"Black isn't a color. Black is nothingness."

She gives me a look. "Black is absolutely a color. Add it to any other color and it gives everything more depth. Whether it creates shadows or is just used for layering, every color becomes richer when you add a little black."

The profoundness of her statement hits me in the chest. It's almost like adding a little Olivia; bring her into my day and the dark moments somehow get brighter. Just as I start to say something along those lines, a blob of pie crust dough falls from her hair and lands on her shoulder, effectively saving me from saying something stupid.

"Favorite food?" I laugh when she rolls her eyes and brushes the dough onto the floor.

"*Not* pie crust. Not anymore." My heart does a little flip when she smiles. "Probably guacamole. Tied with pizza."

"Favorite movie?"

"*As Good As It Gets.*"

I snicker. A movie about OCD. "Figures."

Probably a mistake to laugh. "What's that supposed to mean?" she says with a scowl.

"Not a thing. Favorite game?"

"Scrabble."

I pause at this one and give her a look. "Wrong answer. You should have said baseball."

She scratches her chin. "Except I thought you wanted truthful answers, and we both know that would be a lie."

"Sometimes your words are like knives that cut me right in the heart." I grab my chest and pretend to look wounded. She doesn't pretend to care, instead she flicks more bits of dried dough out of her hair and drops them to the floor.

"How about you start listing some of your favorite things instead of just giving me the third degree?"

I take a drink and set the cup on the floor in front of me. "Hit me."

"Don't tempt me." She smirks, then forks a bite of apple. "Favorite pastime?" she says around a mouthful.

"Sleeping."

"I guess I can understand that. Favorite song?"

"'Hallelujah.'"

"As in the chorus?"

I smile, because it's a cute guess. Of course Olivia would think this. "As in the one written by Leonard Cohen."

She nods, but she has no idea what song I'm talking about. I can almost picture her making a mental note to look it up when she gets home. She takes a sip of water.

"Favorite game?"

I slow down my chewing. This is where I should say it, but Olivia just pointed out that we're supposed to be truthful. And since that's the object of the game . . .

"Football."

She raises an eyebrow. "Not baseball?"

I use a napkin to wipe at my mouth. "I love baseball, but it's my job. If I'm looking for an escape, I'll always choose football."

She thinks on that for a moment. "Makes sense. If someone asked me to read books out loud to a group of kids in my free time, I would turn them down flat." She rubs her hands together and inspects her fingernails, grimacing when she finds them caked with brittle dough. She drops her hands and looks at me. "What's your favorite memory about the game?"

The question surprises me, but not because it requires more than a one-word answer. It surprises me because her eyes are locked on mine and she looks sincere—like it's something she really wants to know. So I take a breath and launch into the story. It's a short one.

"It was eight years ago this month—Fourth of July—and the first time I started in a big-league game. We were playing the Cubs, and I even got my first hit—and that's saying something coming from a pitcher. I was more nervous than I'd ever been before, worried I wouldn't be able to perform. But I played well, and we wound up winning the game. When it was over, I cried."

Olivia is quiet. When I look up at her she is staring straight ahead, lost in a memory. Hers? Mine? It's hard to tell. I think about asking her, but she surprises me by standing up and carrying her dishes to the sink.

"I should probably get going. It's later than I thought . . ." Her voice trails off. Her change in demeanor is confusing.

I want to ask her what happened, what about my story bothered her. But a small part of me is worried about what she'll say. Instead, I help her retrieve a sleeping Perry and walk her to the door. I think about leaning down to kiss her cheek, and then I stop thinking and just do it. Her face is rough with dried flour, but my lips hum from the sweetness.

"Bye," she says. "Thank you for taking care of my cat."

"I'll do it again, anytime you need."

And there it is again, that faraway, almost troubled look in her eye. I wish I knew what it meant. I wish I was brave enough to ask.

But I don't. I just stand there and watch as she lets herself in the apartment next door, leaving me alone in an apartment that suddenly feels too quiet and dark and cold.

And empty.

Chapter 24

Olivia

Will has been gone three days, and I keep trying to tell myself it doesn't matter. That I don't miss him. That I don't keep looking out the front window in hopes of seeing his car magically sitting in his parking spot, that instead I'm checking the weather, even though I know he still has one game to play in Houston and four to play in Chicago before he heads home. With travel, that's six days. Six days that might as well be six months for as long as they're taking. I keep telling myself that I like the quiet coming from the apartment next door—so much nicer than the rap and occasional grunge music that normally pounds its way through my walls. I hate that music almost as much as I hate his profession.

Though I seem to be softening even on that.

I keep trying to tell myself that I hate baseball as much as ever. The sport is the cause of all of my childhood disappointments, and it fills the interior of my very overstuffed adult baggage. But then my mother called yesterday and tugged that theory up by the roots.

"What do you mean, they released him? I thought he was in for another year. You never told me there was a possibility of him getting out now."

"Well he did," she gasped. "As of today, he's out on parole and living with me. I want you to come here and see him, Olivia. Promise me you'll be here by Labor Day."

I pinched the space between my eyebrows, overcome with a pounding headache I hadn't had only seconds before.

"I can't promise that, Mom. There's too much history there. Too much—"

"Olivia," she barked. "I don't know what it is you think your brother did to you, but it's time you forgave him."

A little understanding. Just a little understanding was all I'd ever asked for, but it was never even remotely what I received. And because of that, all the frustration I'd held onto for years came bursting out of me like a cannon heading straight up to nowhere.

"He stole my family because of that stupid sport!" I yelled. "You dragged me to game after game after game and for what? So that I could be ignored? So that I could be told to shut up and let him shine? So that he could work and work and work while I did nothing but sit in the dirt by myself? I couldn't even take dance lessons because there was no time to fit it around Bradley's schedule. And then finally—finally— when he made the big leagues, which was the only thing you and dad ever wanted, he starts taking drugs, selling drugs, getting arrested for selling them, and then winds up in prison for five years!" By then I was on too much of a roll to stop. "And oh, oh! The real kicker is that after everything, my parents get divorced and I haven't seen or heard from my father in over three years. And you. All you ever call to talk about is Bradley. 'Olivia, Bradley wants to see you. Olivia, your brother is hurting. Olivia, it's his birthday.' His his his. Well, what about me? All I ever hear about is that stupid game. That stupid game that you forced me to live through even though I hated it!"

Silence. Nothing but silence on the other end of the line. That and the sound of my mother's labored breathing. It might've broken my heart a little if I hadn't been so angry.

"Olivia, your brother made a mistake. One he's paying dearly for. Don't hold a grudge against him for that; people make mistakes all the time. And as for his involvement in baseball, he never even liked the game. He was forced into it by your father and wound up being good at it. Eventually it was the only thing he was good at because his grades suffered, his social life suffered, his mental health suffered—all because your father pushed him too hard."

I heard her take a deep, shuddering breath. I was taking them as well, because everything I had just heard was news to me.

"I'm convinced he got mixed up with drugs to have a way out, to get even with your dad. The day he signed with the Cardinals, he cried. What should have been the happiest day of his life was one of the worst, because now he was stuck. You have every right to be angry about your childhood; I didn't do enough to stop it. And as for your father . . . all he wanted to be was the dad of a baseball player. When he wasn't anymore, he felt he had no reason to be a father at all. Don't blame Bradley for your father's poor decisions."

I'd been sucker punched, the wind knocked out of me. I slowly backed up toward my bed and lowered myself onto it, breathing in and out, in and out. A panic attack threatened to rise up and overwhelm me, but I kept breathing until it slowly subsided.

It's been twenty-four hours since that phone call, and I still don't know what to think about anything.

The day he signed with the Cardinals, he cried. My mind keeps replaying that sentence.

When it was over, I cried. It keeps replaying the words Will spoke to me as well.

Two very similar reactions to the same game; one born out of hate and the other, love.

My brother hated the game. Will loves it. And I've been punishing one for the sins of the other. Turns out even that sin was secondhand, delivered in the form of pressure from a very overbearing father. A father whose worth was tied up in a game, and who cut ties as soon as two kids who loved him no longer held any value.

My phone buzzes from the table, and I blink up at my bedroom ceiling. I don't remember lying down and I'm unsure how long I've been here, but Perry is on my stomach and he's twenty pounds of dead-weight. I sit up and move him to the comforter, stopping a moment to right myself when I'm overcome with a wave of black spots. Stress, worry—I've dealt with this before, but it's been a while. I take a series of deep breaths and slowly my vision clears, though the aftermath brings with it a dull headache. My phone buzzes again. A text message, then another. My heart feels heavy and my head full as I shuffle toward the phone. My heart takes off like a million fireflies when I see his name on the screen. My head remains the same.

Will: Hey stranger.

Ignoring the pounding, I smile to myself and count to twelve before answering. No need to appear too eager.

Hey yourself. What's up?

There is a long pause. Too long, if you ask me. Either he's playing it cool or he's forgotten we're talking. Both options are unacceptable because I didn't initiate this conversation. My heart is beating wildly, a mix of anger, anticipation, and fear, when the phone finally buzzes again.

Will: Getting ready to play. Just wanted to say hi before I head out. Can I text

```
you after the game is over if it's not
too late?
```

```
It won't be too late. I'll be awake. You
winning?
```

I want to kick myself for agreeing so quickly but figure there's no point in pretending. I'll be awake. I'll be awake until sunrise for the chance to talk to him.

```
Will: Miraculously, yes. But that doesn't
get you out of next week's games. How's
the furball?
```

I roll my eyes.

```
I'll be there. But Perry hates you and
always will. Go play your game, and text
me when it's over.
```

I picture him laughing.
I hear myself laughing.
It's strange how one conversation can turn a day around.

Will

We've spent the past two nights texting, and now it's become somewhat of a habit. It's a habit I'm not sure I should keep up, but one I'm not willing to break. At least not yet. Maybe when the season is over. That's what I keep telling myself.

I reach for my phone and check for a reply from Olivia. Still nothing. It rings in my hand instead. My nerves flare when I see Jerry's name light up the screen.

"Hello?"

I wander over to the bathroom sink and fill a glass with water, then take a long drink. I feel more bad news coming, and my throat is dry with dread.

"She's not going to sue. Her lawyer told me that five minutes ago."

Not what I expected. "Then why put me through all that?"

"I think she was after the attention and wanted to see how far she could take it. Now that the press has died down, I guess she figured it was no longer worth it. Bottom line, you're off the hook. And since we're winning now, the pressure should ease up too." I hear him sniff. "Even Olivia can go away if you want her to. Now would probably be the best time. Don't want her to get the wrong idea."

Despite the red that fills my vision, I look at the wall above the mirror and concentrate on the positive side of his words. He's right. Now might be the best time to cut ties with her. As far as my reputation is concerned, having a steady date is no longer necessary. Though there is the issue of my winning streak . . .

Even that might not be a factor. We've won every game on the road so far, and Olivia hasn't been here to make it happen.

"True," I say quickly. Jerry doesn't know the other reason I keep Olivia around. "Let me think on that and I'll get back to you. No sense in making a quick decision on that yet."

There's a pause. "Sounds like you might not want to make that decision at all. Good thing I like Olivia. Just don't let her mess with your game."

Unwilling to point out that she's already messed with it in the best way possible, I assure him I won't, hang up, and set the phone on the counter, then stare at the blank screen. I could pick up the phone right now and text Olivia. Tell her everything is good now, that it's all over, that we no longer have to pretend. I could give her an out, give her the chance to finally avoid the game she so fiercely hates. For a minute I toy with my conscience, trying to convince myself to do right by her and let her decide for herself. It's the nice thing to do. The honorable thing to do.

Something tells me I know what she'll decide.

With a sigh, I pick up the phone. It's been twenty minutes since she last texted me.

```
You doing okay?

Olivia: Sorry, my phone rang. I'm great.
Okay, what were we talking about?
```

We spend the next hour texting back and forth about nothing and everything.

Chapter 25

Olivia

Will picked me up as soon as he got back into town and brought me to Six Flags. It's the first time I've been here, but I was so happy to see him that I would have agreed to almost anything. So glad he was back that I might have even agreed to a roller coaster or two. It wasn't until later that my excitement bothered me.

Just like it bothers me that they won every game on the road.

Just like it bothers me that he might decide he no longer needs me to show up to any of the games.

He just won me a giant stuffed hippopotamus in a dart-throwing game, even though of course he won it because Will knows how to throw things and makes a ridiculous amount of money because of it. This stuffed animal bothers me too. But not enough to give it away or to quit thinking about sleeping with it tonight, curled around it full-body like it's a substitute for—

I stop that thought before it has a chance to materialize and think of a way to redirect my mind.

"You haven't ridden the Batman yet." It's a stupid thing to say, because of course he's going to follow it up with—

"I'm not riding it without you."

I clutch the hippo to my chest. "I can't ride it and hang on to this thing. You go without me. I'll stand here and watch."

"Nice try, but you're not standing anywhere." He moves into the line and takes the stuffed animal from my hands. I watch while he asks the ride attendant to store it for him, then I look up and swallow. The Batman is a twisting, winding, terrifying-looking yellow roller coaster known as the scariest one in Texas. I inwardly curse myself for bringing it up.

"Way to go, Olivia," I mutter to myself. "Now the only reason you have not to ride is your stupid fear."

"What fear?"

I look up to see Will staring at me, a concerned frown on his face. I force myself out of my fog of memories and run a hand through my hair.

"No fear. There's no fear."

Wow. Lie much?

I duck my head and focus on the ground.

"You look pale. Like you might faint."

Someone dropped a wad of pink bubble gum three inches from my feet. If I hadn't looked down I would have stepped on it, and that makes me mad.

"I'm not a big fan of roller coasters." This is true, if *not a big fan* means that I haven't ridden on one since I was five and hung upside down for sixty-two seconds and am deathly afraid of history repeating itself right now with Will sitting next to me to witness my meltdown. "Haven't been since I was a little girl."

"Bad experience?" He props a hand on the sidewalk railing and leans into it.

I look ahead. "A bit of one. Not something I like to revisit often."
Or ever.

"Tell you what," he says. "If I promise to hold your hand and not
make fun of you when you throw up, will you try it this one time?"

I level my gaze at him. "I'm not going to throw up."

"I don't think you will either."

Tension sits in my throat and chest. "I don't know . . ."

"I'll buy you a funnel cake when it's over."

"That's not fair. Funnel cake is my favorite."

"Then I'll buy you two."

I roll my eyes. There's no winning this one. I stare at a child in front
of me and let resignation sink in. "Two and a smoothie. Strawberry.
With whipped cream on top."

"Where do you put it, all the food you eat?" His gaze drifts down
my body, a funny look on his face.

"I run, remember? And I guess I have a decent metabolism." I try
not to blush at his scrutiny. "Fine, I'll go on the ride. But one word
about my screaming or crying . . ."

"Or throwing up." He holds out both hands. "Scout's honor."

I take a deep breath. It does nothing to calm my erratic nerves. "I'm
not going to throw up."

"I still don't think you will."

———

Will

"Are you okay?"

"Just go get the funnel cakes. And don't forget the smoothie."

"I already have the smoothie. Do you want me to bring it in now?"

"Into the women's restroom? Probably not a good idea." Her voice
is muffled, anguished, and for the hundredth time I want to rewind

time and shove my own size-eleven shoe in my mouth. Why did I pressure her into riding that thing? "Do you feel okay?" she asks. It makes me feel worse. Here she's the one feeling awful, but she's asking about my well-being.

"I'm fine. I didn't even see anything happen." It's a lie. I saw everything; Olivia's white knuckles, Olivia's face as it turned green and then white and then yellow and then—

It wasn't a pleasant sight, but at least I wasn't unlucky enough to be the poor guy sitting behind her. I'm not sure he'll ever recover. After he yelled a few choice words into the air and then subsequently at Olivia's face, he stomped off in disgust. Can't say that I blame the guy, although his suffering didn't stop me from hurling a few choice words of my own in his direction. He might have been covered in a mess, but it was hardly Olivia's fault.

I mean, it was her fault. But it was also mine. A little more hers, but I'll keep that thought to myself and wait here against the wall.

Finally she walks out of the restroom. She's still a little pale, but I think she's turned a corner. A slight corner from the looks of it; I'm praying to God that there won't be any detours or speed bumps on this very perilous road in the near future. Dear God, anything but that.

She grabs the smoothie out of my hand and takes a long gulp. "Let's go get a funnel cake."

I study her. "Are you sure you—"

"A funnel cake, Will. You owe me two, and I will have them both eaten before we leave here."

"Okay, I just—"

"Funnel cakes, Will." She points one finger ahead and takes off walking, sucking on that straw like it contains her dignity and self-respect. Knowing Olivia, she's mentally lacking in both right now, even though she's putting up a brave front. I admire her for it. She turns to look at me. "And then I want you to win me a stuffed pig to go along with this hippo here. Can't head home with just one zoo animal. What would the neighbors think?"

"The neighbors would think you're crazy, that's what they would think."

"One of them already does."

When she winks, I'm not going to lie, my knees go a little weak. The hair, the smile, the eyes . . . Olivia doesn't even know she possesses such a killer combination. We walk to the funnel cake stand in silence. I make it until we're second in line, and then I can't take it anymore. Bravery can hit a person at the strangest times. Like when you're at an amusement park with a girl you're fake dating and you realize maybe you don't want things to be so fake anymore. Or when someone asks you what you want to order and all you can think is that what you would really like is a lean platinum blonde with a killer smile on the side and you start to wonder what her skin feels like.

So you reach for her hand just so you'll finally know.

And you link your fingers through hers because you feel a little possessive and a whole lot proud.

And she looks down at your hands joined together and then back up at you, scanning your face to find out what it all means.

And she smiles. And you have trouble remembering that this is supposed to be pretend.

And you swallow.

And try to command your racing heart to slow down.

But it doesn't.

So just to lighten the moment a little—just to make it feel a bit less tense and important—you make a joke. Because sometimes humor is the only way you know to mask your true feelings.

"I still can't believe you threw up on that ride. That poor man behind us . . ."

"Shut up, Will. And I'll take three funnel cakes," she says to the man behind the counter just to stick it to you because there's no way she can eat them.

And now you're both joking, both working overtime to lighten the mood.

But you can't help but notice that your grip . . . her grip . . . they both get a little tighter.

And that, for the rest of the night, neither of you lets go.

Chapter 26

Olivia

I've snapped more than a dozen pictures on my phone before I realize what I'm doing. Lowering the phone to my lap, I stare at the last one—the one I took of Will on the pitcher's mound just as he was winding up to throw. His right leg is in the air, elbow up, bottom lip tucked into his teeth in concentration, hat slightly off-center like he accidently knocked it askew. It's a clear shot with the sun setting on the horizon behind him, adding a slight shadow to his form. It is reminiscent of a movie poster or a magazine cover, like many I've seen before. My hands burn with the desire to flip through the others, to memorize them, to compare and contrast Will in motion, Will in flight, Will on his game.

The game I keep forgetting to hate.

It's the bottom of the seventh inning and a saunalike heat is hovering in the stands. The headache I developed a few days ago has ebbed and flowed since, and right now it's pounding at the forefront of my temple. Chalking it up to the oppressive heat, I pull my shirt away from my skin, cringing at the feel of sweat on my stomach and back. No matter how long I live here, I will never get used to a Dallas summer.

"It's so hot tonight. I don't know how they play in this heat." Fanning my face, I press the off button on my phone just after Kimberly leans into me.

"I think I've lost three pounds just sitting here. Wait, what was that?" She nods to my phone. "Can I see?" She reaches for my phone before I can toss it into my purse. Of course I wasn't fast enough. Story of my life.

With a quiet sigh, I push a button and watch the screen light up, dread sitting like a barbed ball in my stomach. It doesn't help that my heart is pounding with the strength of a bass drum inside my chest at the mere thought of viewing those pictures again. How in the world will I be when this game is over and I'm once again able to view him up close?

"Sure. Take a look." I hand the phone to her, and she begins to scroll. I stare straight ahead until I can't take it anymore, then lean in to watch her progress. Will is inside the dugout anyway; there's nothing else for me to look at besides shelled peanuts, hot dog wrappers, and overturned beer cans.

"Olivia, these are really good," she says. "Have you ever taken photography classes?"

I shake my head. "No, it's just something I've always liked to do. When my brother played I—" I stop talking because this is something I never discuss with anyone. I hadn't spoken about it in years before I accidentally mentioned it to Will. I'm not sure why I felt so free to speak this time, and it bothers me.

"Your brother played baseball?"

I take a minute to think, but I've already opened the door to this conversation and there's no way to shut it gracefully.

"Yes, he played in high school and college. Could have had a career in the major leagues but he gave it up." I leave out the Cardinals part because what's the point? His career there didn't last long, and he did in fact give it up. Technically. "I used to sit on the sidelines and snap his picture with an old Polaroid of my mother's. I took hundreds, maybe thousands, over the years." There's a drawer in my old bedroom overstuffed with those photos. Pictures of Bradley taken from a four-year-old's perspective, a seven-year-old's perspective, a ten-year-old's perspective. His shoes in the dirt, his bat tilted heavenward on the upswing, his hat propped on his head, the red-billed underside showing. As far as I know, no one has ever looked through them. As far as I know, no one knows they're there.

"Must have been tough having to sit through that as a kid," she says, surprising me. "It's hard enough as a wife. All the time it takes, the separations you live through, the pressure you're under even though no one ever thinks about what wives deal with . . ." Her voice trails off. I wonder if I can hear regret or sadness between the syllables but then recognize the emotion for what it is: loneliness. Deep, profound loneliness that I know all about because I share it. I've always shared it. That's what comes from living in someone else's very large shadow for far too long. You become so soaked in gray that your own light is significantly dimmed.

I have to ask the question.

"Do you regret it? Marrying a ballplayer, I mean?"

I'm not sure what I expect. Maybe a frown, maybe a sigh, maybe just a wringing of the hands. What she gives is a smile. A slow, broadening smile that reaches her eyes. I'm jealous of it.

"Honestly, at times, yes. It's a tough life, living on your own most of the time, especially when your friends get to greet their husbands at the end of every day. But Blake isn't accountant material, and he never would have made it as a businessman. He isn't wired that way. He loves the game, and really—overall—it's been good to us."

"How?" I hear what she's saying, but this sport has been nothing but bad for me. I'm drenched in neglect and abandonment because of it, and every daddy issue in my psyche is a direct result of the sport.

Kimberly reaches for her soda and takes a sip, her bracelets clinking together around her wrist. "We've gotten to travel and see things we never got to see growing up. We have a nice home and good friends. We're happy." She shrugs. "Plus, the money doesn't hurt."

She laughs, and I try to return it even though my head feels a bit worse. I've seen her home; it's ridiculous, every girl's dream. And definitely not something one could ever afford on a teacher's salary. But I know the truth. She would have married Blake without the sizeable bank account.

Around us, a roar travels through the crowd. A ball sails into the outfield and over the fence. Bottom of the sixth inning and we're ahead by three. Will is never going to let me out of this arrangement, an idea I've grown more and more comfortable with.

"That boy is on fire," Kimberly says. "And hey, you should show him those pictures after the game." She nods to my phone. "They really show how much you care about him. Most people don't put as much thought into photos as you put into these. If the ones you took of your brother are as good as these, I think you could have had a career in photography." She glances at me and frowns. "You feeling okay? Your face looks a little pale."

"I'm okay," I say quickly, wanting the topic off my health. "And I'll think about showing him." There's no way he will see them, ever. My reasons are my own. We sit in relative silence for the rest of the game. I won't let myself reach for my phone or even admit it to myself, but there are dozens of opportunities to snap more pictures. Will plays a beautiful, nearly flawless game.

I spend the rest of the game alternately feeling nauseated, rubbing my temple, and sitting on my hands.

Will

It happened right after the game ended. I was standing on the mound, shaking hands with my teammates, when I glanced up at the stands to search out Olivia's face. Whether she likes to admit it or not, she's the reason I'm playing well and, in turn, she's the reason I'm winning. Might sound dumb, but that's just the way of it.

I found her, and my face and heart were just starting to fill with a smile when I saw her fall.

Her head hit a seat back.

Hard.

She landed at a weird angle, her body slumped over a seat.

And that's when Kimberly began to scream.

I didn't need to see it happen to hear the commotion that followed, which is the exact reason Blake took off running, me trailing right behind him. He recognized the sound of his wife's voice from midfield, something I quickly envied despite my panicked state. What might it be like to have that kind of connection?

We reached the stands and flew over the gate in only a few seconds, taking the steps in twos and threes—whatever might get us there faster. Blake tossed his glove on the way up. My hat now lies on a seat somewhere unless a fan ran off with it.

That was ten minutes ago. Olivia came to right after we reached her, and she hasn't stopped complaining since.

"Would you please humor me and be still?" I roll my eyes. I'm sitting on a concrete step with her head in my lap, and I'm trying real hard to be patient, but I swear the woman is driving me nuts. There's a giant knot above her left eyebrow and a tiny cut over her ear, but you'd think she'd just received a mosquito bite the way she insists on trying to sit up. Our team doctor is examining her, and he throws me another look. What does he expect me to do?

I rub circles on the back of her hand and try to calm us both down.

Dr. Mike slips his lens into his pocket and stands up. "I don't see anything wrong with your vision, and if you're telling me the headaches are new . . ."

"They are," Olivia says, nodding her head on my lap. I shoot her a glare and brace her head with my fingers. I'm rewarded with an eye roll. Typical, but I don't care; she can deal with it. "They started a few days ago and just come and go. I'm sure it's nothing to worry about."

Mike crosses his arms. "For now I'll agree with you. My guess is it's caused by stress. But to be safe, I want you to stay awake for the next four hours, understand?" He sends me a pointed look. "She tries to fall asleep or complains about feeling nauseated anymore, you call me."

This time I nod. "I will." Olivia tries to lean forward; I gently push her back down. I don't miss the way Mike holds back a grin.

"She's okay to get up now. But be careful about it." This time he addresses her. "I mean it, Olivia. No sudden moves, and I want you to take it slow." He descends the steps. "Will, keep her awake and call me if you need anything."

"I will," I say after him. As soon as he hits the bottom step, Olivia sits up and scoots away.

"You didn't have to baby me." With a disgusted sound, she stands, completely ignoring the protests of Blake and Kimberly and Jerry to *Stop moving so fast! Slow down, Olivia! What do you think you're doing? You're not going anywhere.*

That last one was from me. And I meant every word.

Olivia sways, catching herself on a seat back. Instead of sitting down like a person with common sense, she starts walking toward the exit without even glancing back. I dart over three seats and up two steps to stand in front of her, blocking her path.

"You're not leaving," I say.

"Will, get out of my way. I'm tired and I'm going home."

"You're not leaving unless I come with you." This time I put a little more force behind my words. But that's the thing about Olivia—she's not impressed by my fame or clout or attempts to intimidate.

"Whatever. Now move."

Man, this chick is stubborn. Then again, so am I. "So do you want to go to a movie or a bar or just for a walk? It's your lucky day because you get to choose. It's not something I offer to all the ladies."

"Oh for the love of—you should try out that line on someone who might actually be impressed. I, for one, am not. It's eleven o'clock at night, I'm tired and not about to stay awake for another four hours, and the only place I want to go is home."

I wink at Kimberly, who is standing over Olivia's shoulder. "Home it is."

Without giving myself time to think about it, I scoop Olivia up in my arms and head up the stairs. "Blake, grab my hat and the rest of my crap, please," I yell over my shoulder, smiling when he responds, "Got you covered."

As for Olivia, she yells like I'm trying to kill her—after this, maybe I will—but I don't set her down until we reach my car. I deposit her inside and shut the door, then walk around the front of the car and slide in. Olivia's car can stay put for the night. She won't be needing it anyway.

"Don't you have a team meeting or something to go to?" She shoves against me and backs herself against the passenger door, sending a glare across the seat that might burn a hole through a lesser man. But me . . . I'm just trying not to laugh and tick her off even more.

"As a matter of fact, I do. One that's taking place between you and me until at least three a.m." I shove the gearshift in reverse. "Now since we probably shouldn't go mountain climbing or bowling, considering the size of that knot on your head—"

"I hate bowling."

"I'll pretend I didn't hear that even though my opinion of you just took a nosedive."

"As if it were ever that high in the first place."

I ignore that remark. "So since we'll be spending the next four hours together, tell me, Olivia, your place or mine?"

When the only response I get is a bunch of hostile sighs, I decide for myself.

Olivia's place it is.

Chapter 27

Olivia

"Validify isn't a word." This is so elementary it's absurd. Why does everyone get the most basic words wrong?

"Yes, it is. As in, 'Please validify that information for me.' Everyone uses it, so it counts."

"No, it doesn't. The correct term in that situation would be *verify* or *validate*, not validify. I win."

"Oh no you don't," he says, snatching up his tiles and placing them back on the holder. He studies them for a long moment, his frown deepening a bit more for every second he knows he's been beaten. We're sitting cross-legged on my living room floor, facing each other, and I'm trying not to smile. This is why I love Scrabble, because the rules are strict and there's always someone dumber than me playing along. Not that Will is dumb, but I'm a teacher and therefore much better at grammar. I could have bent the rules for validify, except it would have garnered him fifty-two points, and I'm not about to let him win. He might be the gamer in this relationship, but I'm just as competitive. Not that we're in a relationship. Even though we are—a fake one. I blush at my train of thought and focus on Will.

With a scowl, he grabs one tile and places it on the board in front of us. I bite the inside of my cheek.

"*Hi*? That's the word you came up with?" I can't help the laugh. He adds another four points to his losing total and gives me a look.

"I didn't have enough tiles for *suck it, Olivia,* which would have been my first choice."

"You're a sore loser," I say, smiling around a yawn. "I would think an athlete like yourself could handle a loss better than that by now."

"You might think, but you haven't yet seen my temper in a game. That"—he gestures toward the board—"was nothing."

"Sorry I've missed it."

Folding the board in half, I slide all the tiles into the box, replace the lid, and carry the game to a closet across the hall. Behind me, Will stands and makes his way to the sofa, then lowers himself with a sigh. He looks as tired as I feel, and I didn't have to play four hours of baseball earlier tonight.

It's two a.m. and we've been at this for three hours now. One more to go, and I'm home free. But that means Will won't have a reason to stay here any longer, a fact that has me praying for time to slow down over the next hour. I walk toward the sofa and sit down, making sure to leave plenty of room between us.

"What now?" He says it in such a way that I think I hear regret. Or boredom. Or a mix of both. Either way, I feel bad for being an imposition.

"Will, you don't have to stay here. I'm sure three hours is long enough and I'm so tired and—"

"I'm staying. Now, what do you want to do? Sleeping is out of the question."

"Will," I don't mean to say his name like a curse, but . . . "so far we've made brownies, played Monopoly, and you've painted my

222

toenails—nice color, by the way." I wiggle my toes in front of me. Orange. It isn't something that I would normally wear, but he found it at the bottom of my nail-care bag, a color my mother gave me forever ago that I deposited in the bathroom and promptly forgot about. I nearly came undone with embarrassment at the thought of his touching my feet, but by the second toe I decided the pampering was worth it, leaned my head back in my chair, and let him do his work. Turns out orange toenails are now very much my thing.

"You really don't have to entertain me anymore."

He sits forward and places his hands on his knees. "Name something, Olivia, or I'll start naming things myself."

I yawn. "I don't know . . . maybe . . ." My mind is a blank slate of tiredness.

"We make out right here, right now, on the sofa."

My gaze snaps to his. "What are you—?"

"I could use a shower. You? Because your shower is huge, and we could save money on the water bill if—"

Now I'm awake. Every part of me. "You have no idea how big my shower is!"

He shrugs. "Same size as mine, I assume." He scratches his chin. "Since we're both fans of games, we could play a quick round of strip—"

"A movie!" I blurt, mortified but trying not to laugh. "Let's watch a movie." My skin is on fire, and not just my face. He's ridiculous and knows how to humiliate me, but darn if I'm not burning up in all the wrong places just thinking about his suggestions. And the fact that he suggested doing all of them with me makes me more than a little happy. It's not something I'm proud of.

Okay, maybe a little proud.

"A movie it is," he says under his breath. "But it doesn't sound like nearly as much fun as the ideas I came up with." He eyes the DVDs in front of us and stands up.

"That's a matter of opinion," I quip.

It was the wrong thing to say. Will stops in the middle of the living room floor and turns around. He deliberately walks toward me and leans forward, bracing both hands on the sofa on either side of my shoulders. My heart takes off inside my chest; our faces are inches apart. My breath hitches and my stomach clenches when his gaze drops to my lips. Everything aches and I want so badly to kiss him. For him to kiss me. I'll take either.

"Let's get something straight, Olivia," he says slowly. "If I ever decide to kiss you, or make out with you, or—heaven forbid—*shower* with you, it won't be a matter of opinion." His eyes fall to my chin, my neck, my chest in a long linger, and I notice his lungs are suddenly pulling in air with as much effort as mine. His eyes meet mine again. "It'll be the best day of your life." He doesn't move away and I don't know what he's doing, but my eyes grow heavy with anticipation. So heavy they almost close. I move forward and let my eyes fall and . . .

"So, what are we going to watch?" he says.

I touch nothing but air.

My eyes fly open and he's standing straight up, looking down at me with a triumphant gaze that deserves to be slapped right off his face. What kind of man does that? Gets a woman worked up and then acts like it's no big deal? I'm mad and embarrassed and wishing for a redo, and—dang it—my lips are tingling.

I can't believe I allowed myself to go there.

I can't believe how much I wanted him to kiss me.

I really wanted him to kiss me, and now he's across the room thumbing through DVDs. With disappointment rolling through me, I sink into the sofa and reach for a blanket, watching with no small amount of resentment while he pops in a movie and walks back over to join me. While I try to rein in my emotions, he tugs on my blanket.

"Get your own blanket." The words come out on a bite, but I don't care.

Will stands to retrieve one from the chair next to us and sits back down, but I see the way he smiles. I see it. It's all I can do to swallow a growl.

"Someone's awfully tense," he says. "You know, they say one of the best ways to relieve tension is—"

"Shut up, Will. Just shut up."

When he laughs, I bury my mouth underneath the blanket. It's the only way I can think of to hide my smile.

Will

What the heck is going on?

I hear myself cursing and I feel myself touching something and I catch myself in the middle of a panicked state, but I can't remember why I'm panicked or who I'm touching or why I'm cursing. I'm in a box, or a cloud, or a haze. And none of it adds up because I'm just so tired.

My eyes fly open. I'm under a blanket with a ball cap covering half my face. Not in a box, not in a haze. Under a blanket on a sofa I don't recognize, and Olivia is lying on top of me. I grab the cap and throw it on the floor.

Olivia.

She's asleep.

She's not supposed to be asleep.

And I just found the reason for my panic.

"Olivia, wake up!" I try to sit up, but she's deadweight and won't budge. My pulse trips in my neck, and I shake her shoulders. "Olivia. Olivia! Wake up, wake up, wake up! Good lord, will you wake up!"

Finally I feel her body move, and I lie back with a relieved sigh. I didn't know I was clutching her hair until I release it from my fist. "Are you awake?"

She moans from on top of me, one hand instinctively reaching for her head. It hurts. I saw the way she fell, the way she hit. It has to hurt. Keeping one arm protectively around her shoulder, I brush her hair out of her eyes and gingerly touch the spot with my free hand.

"It hurts, Will." Her voice is drugged, groggy.

"Does it hurt when I touch it?"

She nods on top of me. "Yes, but in a good way. Keep doing it."

I smile at her soft command and trace circles on her forehead with my fingertips, listening as her breathing gradually grows steady and even. She's asleep again. This time it's fine.

I wasn't lying earlier.

If I had kissed Olivia earlier it would have been the best day of her life. If I'm being honest, it might have been the best day of mine too. It's all I've thought about since I saw her fall at the stadium. The way her head slammed against the seat . . . the way she bounced and fell . . . it would have reduced many people to tears. But Olivia . . . she has strength. Guts. An ability to pick herself up and shake things off. To take care of herself and keep moving ahead. That trait definitely has appeal, especially for someone who travels as much as I do, and something tells me self-preservation is Olivia's way of life.

It makes me wonder if anyone has ever taken care of her.

I move my hand to her cheek, run my thumb over her jaw, slide my fingertips down her neck. She shifts when I reach her shoulder and I hold my breath, but then she settles again and I let the air go, careful not to wake her up. I gently massage a spot right above her collarbone. Her skin is soft to the touch, softer than I imagined it would be. Maybe it takes a soft shell to protect a strong woman. Either way, I like the way her skin feels underneath my palm—like butter or satin—smooth to the touch with a little give, a little take.

My hands find her hair—the hair that's driven me crazy since the first day—and I allow myself to touch it. To feel it. To thread my fingers through it like I've wanted to every day since I met her. The strands glide through my hands, and it's the softest hair I've ever felt, as rich as I imagined it would be. It smells like honey, warm and liquid. I continue to run my fingers through the strands. This might be my only chance, and I don't want to miss it.

Don't ask me how I know, but all at once I'm certain she's awake. It might be the way her breathing is no longer steady or the way her heart is pounding against my own or the way her thumb is tracing the tiniest of circles just above my rib cage, but Olivia is awake. I'm certain of it. I feel it everywhere.

"I guess I should go." I force myself to say the quiet words, even though I don't want to end the night by leaving. I want to prolong it, let it stretch until morning to see how the story unfolds.

"I guess you should." She doesn't sound convinced. She also doesn't move.

I don't move either.

"Can I ask you a question?" Olivia's voice is so soft I almost don't hear it.

"Yes," I whisper. My hands stay on her because she hasn't yet told me to move them.

"Why do you like my hair so much?"

The question is so unexpected I'm not sure I heard it right. I've never mentioned my fascination with her hair, or any part of her appearance really. All along, I've thought I was good at covering my thoughts; as far as emotions go, the expert at camouflage. I guess I'm not.

"Because it's beautiful. At first I thought it was odd; a woman like you being blessed with a head full of incredible hair that she always hid inside a knot or ponytail. The first time I saw it down around your shoulders, I was stunned at how different you looked. I've always thought you were beautiful, even when you try not to be. But with that hair . . ."

I let my words trail off to a place where she can find and translate the meaning. I'm not sure how she'll take what I just said. Olivia is hardly her hair; she would be just as beautiful without it. Without it she would be like a queen without a crown. Still regal, still powerful, still a sight to look at. But the crown makes it official. Olivia with her hair . . . it's hard to tear my eyes away.

I run my hand back down her shoulder and wait for her to speak. When her head comes up to look at me, there's a sheen of moisture in her eyes.

"No one's ever said anything that nice to me before." Her voice breaks a bit on the last word, and that's when I know.

No one has ever taken care of Olivia. Not in the way she deserves to be taken care of.

Maybe I shouldn't, and maybe my idea of taking care of someone isn't the same as what she has in mind, but I pull myself up and bring her with me. We're half sitting, half lying down, but all of me is focused on this moment. She looks at me with wide eyes as my hand traces her cheek, but she doesn't look away. My hand moves to her hair and the back of her neck and then my mouth is on hers, like I couldn't wait another minute or take one more breath without her. Maybe I couldn't. She gasps into my mouth and fists my shirt, and then we fall into each other like we're afraid to let go.

It's been a while since I've kissed someone.

Something tells me that for Olivia, it's been a lot longer.

She's hesitant when I'm bold, slow when I want to speed up, pulling back when I'm pushing forward. It's almost like she doesn't know what to do, so I break away to ask her.

"Is this okay? Are you alright with me . . . with this? Because I can go . . ."

She shakes her head quickly and then turns it into a nod. I smile and lean back in, forcing myself to take it slow. If Olivia needs time . . . if she needs patience . . . if she needs someone to guide her . . . I'll be that person. And I won't be a jerk about it.

I feel her lips part beneath mine and take that as permission, and the second my tongue grazes hers I'm struck. She's a feeling of awareness. She's mesmerizing. She's too much. Not enough. Soft in all the right places. Warm in the better ones. I'm in trouble and I don't even care.

I press in harder, closer, chest to chest, skin on skin . . . until she whimpers next to me.

Olivia is innocent.

Olivia is smart.

Olivia is everything.

And I need to slow down so I don't mess it up.

Even though it physically hurts, I unlace my fingers from her bare back and carefully lower the shirt I don't remember raising, keeping my mouth on hers. I might be slowing it down, but that doesn't mean I have to stop it completely. My hands are on her face again. Her hands are on my neck. Her touch feels like fire. I'm glad she keeps going, because it turns out I love getting burned.

When she breaks away to kiss the side of my neck, that's when I exhale a pent-up breath. The last thing I want to do is leave, the only thing I want to do is stay, but I force myself to sit up and face her. My forehead presses against hers. I'm not able to speak yet, so I just breathe. In and out, in and out, listening as she does the same.

"You should probably go." Her words are raspy, and it makes me smile. I like the way my kiss has affected her voice, like it got lost somewhere down my throat. Nice to know I'm not alone.

"You're probably right." I slowly stand on shaking legs and bring her with me. It isn't fair to have to leave, but it wouldn't be fair to her if I stayed. I know exactly where I would try to take things, and Olivia deserves more than that.

From me, I mean. Definitely from me. No way some other guy is coming anywhere near her now. So long, fake boyfriend. Adios, sucker.

Linking her fingers through mine, I lead us to the door. As soon as we reach it, I turn around and pull her to me. Her head rests on my chest; my chin settles on her forehead.

"How's your head?" I ask, genuinely concerned. "You might want to take something for it before you go back to sleep."

She nods into me. "I will." Her voice is small, sad.

"Hey." I tilt her chin to look at me. "I'll see you tomorrow, okay? Call me when you wake up."

That earns a smile, one unlike any I've seen before. Olivia's smile can light up a room, but this one lights up her eyes from the inside out. As soon as it disappears, I kiss her again. Her mouth is as soft as I remember from a few seconds ago, and it takes everything in me to pull away.

But I do.

And she closes the door behind me.

And I let myself in my own apartment.

And slide against the closed entryway door, all the way to the floor.

Like I said earlier . . .

I'm in trouble.

Chapter 28

Olivia

"You heading out?"

The voice behind me makes me jumpier than I've been all morning, and that's saying quite a bit. I haven't slept in two days, and I haven't seen Will in the same amount of time. *Call me tomorrow*, he said. Well, I did, and the only thing he said was, *Don't come to the game*. He wouldn't let me go to it or the one last night because of my slight black eye and large goose egg of a forehead, and, to make matters worse, they won both of them. Those facts have jumbled together in my mind over the last two days, playing all sorts of games with my imagination.

I'm tired, and my mind can't settle down.

They're winning, and I'm no longer necessary.

Will kissed me, and I haven't seen him since.

Which can only mean one thing. I'm a terrible kisser. Twenty-nine years old, and I can't even do that right. I close the trunk of my car and walk around to the driver's side, stopping just before I open the door.

"Yes, I have to go visit my mother," I say with as much enthusiasm as I can muster. Which is zero, because making an effort to see my mother—and consequently my brother—has taken the joy out of this day and all the days I have in front of me. Dramatic maybe, but that's just the way it is. I cross my arms and stare at Will, fresh from an early morning jog, as damp as he might be if he'd just hopped out of the shower, and looking as hot as ever. My skin hums with anticipation just looking at him.

Even though there's clearly nothing to anticipate.

"Your mother? Where does she live?"

He leans against a neighboring car and crosses his arms and—my gosh, those muscles. I look away so my eyes won't give away just how much the last two days have hurt me.

"Oklahoma City."

He frowns. "How long is the drive?"

"Three hours."

My side of the conversation is short, clipped. But I can't help it. You don't just kiss a girl and then not see her, demanding career or not. This is a very basic concept, one that most men can't seem to grasp. At least that's what I assume, based on my very limited experience. And seeing isn't even necessary. There's texting. Texting is quick and simple and can do wonders to mask all evidence of a shaky voice or lying mouth.

Men and their lying mouths.

"Are you staying the night?" he asks.

A bird lands on the roof of the car three rows down. I stare at it.

"No, but I'll be back late."

Will shifts in place. I try really hard not to notice.

"Olivia, are you mad at me?"

"No." I say it too quickly. I'm pretty sure my fist just clenched and my jaw just flexed.

So maybe I'm the liar.

"Then do you mind if I come with you?"

That gets my attention, and my gaze snaps toward him.

"Why would you want to come with me? That would require you hanging out with me all day, and that's obviously not something you want to do." Wow, I sound bitter. I hate bitter and all the emotions that come with it, but I'm mad. Mad and hurt and trying not to cry and he smells bad. "Plus, you need a shower because you stink."

He takes a step toward me, and I try to pull back but I can't. This car is in my way and I already have that fairy-flying feeling in my stomach. Unfortunate, since butterflies are safer and much easier to slap away.

"You think I stink?" he says.

He's such a jerk. Moving this close to me makes him even more of one, and I scowl at him. "Worse than that dumpster over there."

"How about now?" His hands are on my shoulders and I'm looking at everything but him.

"Worse than all the dumpsters combined." Dang it, I think my mouth just twitched.

"And now?" His arms come around my back and I'm settling into his chest and since he can't see my face in this position, I allow a small smile. But only a small one.

"Why haven't you even tried to see me since the other night?"

His chin comes to rest on my head.

"Because I've been working."

"You're always working." My voice is muffled, soft.

"Yes, but not as much as I have the last two days."

"Why the last two days?" I hate how fragile I sound. Like at any moment I'm expecting my heart to break. This is why I don't do relationships. This and because, when it comes to men, I've never been all that confident.

"Well, it's not because I kissed you, if that's what you're thinking." I hate that he can read my mind. I love that he can read my mind. "Because two days ago I went home and slept until it was time to be at the field, and when that game was over I figured you were already asleep and it was too late to call. And last night's game went fourteen innings."

"Fourteen innings?" Suddenly I'm glad I wasn't required to be there.

His arms pull me closer. "Yep. Game didn't end until one in the morning."

"But you won." Again with the monotone voice.

"We won. But that doesn't get you out of tomorrow night's game. It hasn't been the same without you there, so show up, headache or not."

I nod into his chest. "My head's fine," I say, finally pulling back to look at him. He said everything I needed to hear in order to feel better, which makes me feel worse, because when did I turn into a needy teenage girl?

I look up at him and he gives me a slow smile, his gaze settling on my mouth. "Good to hear." And then he leans in and all is right in my world, because my world just became reduced to the size of Will's lips.

What great lips they are.

What a beautiful world we live in.

He pulls back to look at me. "Now, can I go with you or not?"

"Don't you have practice or something?"

He shakes his head and runs both hands up and down my arms. "It's Monday."

Monday, an off day. I want to say no because I haven't seen my mother in a year and my brother in even longer, but I won't tell him no and he knows it. There's not a lot of time to spend with Will outside of his job, so I'll take what I can get when he's willing to offer it.

"Sure, you can come. But Will?"

"What?"

"Please hurry up and shower. You really do stink."

He pushes away from me and jogs to his front door. "I'll be ready to go in five," he calls.

I can hear his laughter until the door closes behind him.

———

Will

It all makes sense.

Olivia is fiercely independent and somewhat neurotic.

Olivia doesn't like to speak about her family.

Olivia hates baseball.

At one time I thought Olivia might have hated me.

And then there's that conversation we never finished up in the locker room, the one that Olivia didn't seem too eager to continue. *Why did your brother quit, Olivia?* She went mute. Changed the subject. Looked visibly relieved when we were interrupted by the two coaches who came stomping in, mad at me and my bad temper.

And now I know why.

But that isn't even the worst of it.

And now that I know the worst of it, I can't say that I blame her for any of it.

"So you played for the Cardinals?" I casually ask her brother, though it's hardly a casual question. It's a question disguised as small talk and nothing more because I already know the answer—I've known the answer since we walked inside this house. But I'm busy staring at a picture sitting on the oak mantel above the fireplace and the evidence is inside it, and I'm having trouble dealing with the idea that reality does indeed bite.

It bites hard.

"Yeah, I played with them for a season," he says, flipping through channels with the remote. He's wearing sweatpants and an old white tee and an entitled attitude—probably not the greatest combination for a guy who just got out of jail. Then again, you can always spot a guy who was raised to believe he's the center of someone's very small universe. They never outgrow it, even as the world continues to spin and enlarge around them.

"Not for a whole season," his mother chimes in, completely unnecessarily, if you ask me. The woman has inserted her take on things all afternoon, and practically every word comes out steeped in bitterness. Other than in looks, Olivia is nothing like her mother. She is soft where her mother is hard, timid where her mother is bold, gracious where her mother is blunt. But they look exactly alike. If the woman's hair weren't cut to her shoulders, and if there weren't a few vaguely noticeable lines around her eyes and mouth, I might think they were twins.

Except Olivia smiles more. Thank God Olivia smiles more.

She's in the bathroom right now, trying to get over a particularly harsh assessment her mother made about her absence this past year, namely that she was *selfish and unthoughtful, but then again you've only ever thought of yourself.* I might have gotten a couple of words wrong in the retelling, but that hardly matters. From the bits and pieces I've managed to gather since our arrival a few hours ago, Olivia is the one most overlooked in this house.

Of the nearly thirty pictures scattered all over the fireplace mantel, Olivia is in only three. The rest are framed photos of her brother—mostly in uniform. Based on appearances, Olivia is not much of a second or third or fourth thought.

"Why only a season?"

I ask the question to be polite; I'm pretty sure I already know the answer. I've seen it happen before. Guy makes the big leagues and can't handle the pressure. Guy declines an initial offer of "help," but then when fear becomes overwhelming, he begins to compromise himself. Just once, he thinks, because the brain is very convincing when it's trying to calm itself down. But once turns into twice and twice turns into a habit they can't kick. Some men live with it and keep playing the game. They become dependent, drugs turn into a crutch, their game actually becomes better, their bodies become stronger. It's an easy lie to believe when the cheering swells louder and the bank account grows bigger and the ego increases to a monumental size.

But occasionally you'll find a guy who can't handle it.

Or one who gets so wrapped up in himself that he becomes careless and self-destructive, starts believing he's superhuman and can do no wrong. In Bradley's case, the no-wrong lie turned into selling drugs. And for what? For the rush of adrenaline that came with every transaction. Because, for some people, the rush of twenty thousand people calling their name just isn't enough. Especially when they've been plagued with self-doubt their whole lives. Sometimes insecurity is a harder habit to kick than drugs. And always . . . *always* . . . an oversize ego is wrapped in an even bigger amount of insecurity.

"I got arrested," he finally answers from his spot on the sofa. "For dealing."

I nod, admiring his honesty. It's surprising, considering the circumstances. He looks every bit the athlete-in-training, and if you didn't know better you might think he just came off the field after losing a game; there is a look of defeat about him. But I do know better. The dark circles under his eyes are from lack of sleep. The lack of sleep is from the time it's taking to get acclimated to the outside world. The time spent in jail is from a few years of bad decisions. But I've also learned that bad decisions don't make a bad man. Everyone has a past full of mistakes they would like to undo, and everyone has a future full of errors ready and waiting for them.

"You're not the first person, man," I say. "Not the best decision, though. Especially in light of the opportunity that was handed to you."

"Tell me about it. Cost me everything."

"Cost all of us everything, you mean," Olivia's mother mutters as she rearranges magazines with one hand and sips coffee with the other. "You had a two-million-dollar contract and flushed it away. It's been nothing but hard times since." She sets the mug down and turns to take in the room, a hand perched on her hip.

Bradley sighs the sigh of a man used to being beaten down. I bristle and bite back the desire to say something to shut her up.

Instead, I knead the back of my neck and look for an escape.

"Olivia's taking a while. I think I'll go check on her."

"Yeah, tell her to come back out here. I could use help with dinner."

My eyes. I don't think they've rolled this much all year and it's actually starting to hurt.

I find Olivia inside the last bedroom on the right. The room is purple and orange—purple on the walls, orange on the bed—with white beads hanging from the windows and a yellow-flowered ceiling fan that rotates just enough to circulate the smallest amount of air. A thin layer of dust has settled against the top of the ivory-colored dresser. Pictures of high-school dances and old family pets line the mirror. I see two golden retrievers and a kitten. A white kitten. And what do you know? Perry hasn't always been a fat sphere of fur.

I pluck that picture off the mirror and bring it to my face.

"Is this Perry?"

Olivia looks up at me from her spot on the floor and nods. "That was taken the day I found him. He was under a bush in the front yard, and he was starving. I begged my parents to let me keep him. For two days they said no, but they finally relented as long as I promised to be the one who took care of him." She shrugs. "So I did."

"Where did you come up with his name?"

She shrugs. "I was a big Journey fan."

I smile. Steve Perry. I should have known. I return the picture to the mirror and focus on her.

I see the two trails of smeared mascara underneath her eyes, but I pretend not to notice. She's sitting in front of an open drawer filled with old photos. Color photos, faded photos, all taken with a Polaroid camera. There are hundreds of them, maybe more, and something tells me she took them all. I sit down across from her in the middle of what still looks like a teenage girl's room, but all I can feel is very palpable adult-sized rejection. I attempt what might be a pathetic way to change the mood.

"And from all appearances, you did a good job. You might have fed him a little too much, let him be entirely too lazy, but other than that . . ."

She laughs the kind of watery laugh that has me giving myself an internal high five. Maybe it didn't change much, but at least I got her to laugh. Laughter is something. Everyone needs more of it.

"He's not fat," she says, slowly flipping through photos. Now she's not looking at me.

"You're right. He's obese."

I'm rewarded with a shove on the arm. Reaching inside the drawer, I pull out a stack of pictures and flip through them.

"Did you take all these?"

She nods. A new tear spills down her cheek and lands on her lap. I wish I could catch them for her, but Olivia is dealing with things I know nothing about. The best thing I can do is sit here and let her. I wait in silence, the only sound in the room the whooshing slide of paper against paper.

Minutes go by.

More and more minutes.

And then I speak up. There's a fine balance between caring about someone's life and inserting yourself into a situation where you don't belong. I tread carefully, not wanting to land on the wrong side.

"So your brother was a pitcher. And now I know his number was thirteen."

Everything stops, noticeably Olivia's breathing. "He told you?"

I shake my head and return the photos to the drawer. "No. I saw the pictures above the fireplace."

Her bottom lip quivers. "Of course you did. They're everywhere." Her voice cracks on the last word. And then I crack. My heart, my emotions, my reserve. I reach for the photos in her hand and return them to the drawer, then quietly shut it for what I hope is the last time.

"Those photos aren't you, you know. You're not still the little girl being dragged to her brother's games, forced to sit in the shadows. You're not the little girl whose parents overlooked you while you watched from the sidelines. You're not the little girl told to be quiet, listen up, let your brother shine, stop being a nuisance."

She looks straight at me, her lips moving like she doesn't know what to say.

"How do you know—"

"I have a family too. I know how it works. Except in my case I'm your brother and my older brother was you. Everyone sacrifices something in this game, but it has to suck to be the one expected to do most of it."

She drops her head, trying not to let me see her cry.

"As for my number, there's not much I can do about it, but now I understand why you've hated the game so much. There seem to be a lot of parallels between your brother and me, and I—"

"You're nothing like him." She shakes her head, and something about that statement makes my heart swell a few sizes. "And it's not just your number. True, I'm not a fan. But there are other reasons too."

"And maybe one day you'll share with me what those reasons are." The last thing I want her to feel is pushed, especially when she's surrounded by people who are constantly pulling.

"My dad left on the thirteenth. Did anyone tell you that? November thirteenth. This November it will be four years since anyone has seen him. All because my brother blew his contract, landed in jail, and locked my father's self-worth up with him."

"That's not true. A man doesn't abandon his kids because his dreams for the future didn't go the way he planned. A man abandons his kids either because he's entirely self-absorbed, or because he never cared about them in the first place."

She looks at me with sad eyes. "Is that supposed to make me feel better?"

I shake my head. "Not better, because that means you had a dead-beat for a dad. But it also means you weren't responsible." I reach for her hand and wait until she looks at me. "Your dad had problems, and they had nothing to do with a beautiful girl who cared about him."

For the longest time we just sit. She's numb. Processing. But that's what the heart does when it's wounded; it bleeds, it ebbs, it stops. But still it's in pain. And heart pain almost always subsides, though it never goes away entirely.

"Do you want to stay in here for a while longer?" I finally ask. "Or do you want to go out there and make the best of it for an hour? But when an hour's up, I swear we're leaving. I don't care where we go, just point me in the right direction and I'll drive."

Surprising me, she smiles. Then she stands and pulls me up with her. "We'll stay. But you're on a timer." She laces her arms around my neck. "One hour, that's it."

I study her face. It's transformed from a few minutes ago, a small amount of happy soaking up the sad. I like thinking my words caused some of it.

"Thank you," she says.

When she stretches up to kiss me, I really really like it.

We break away and I kiss the tip of her nose.

"You can attack me later. But right now, your mom told me to tell you she needs help with dinner."

She smirks. "I'd rather attack you. But alright, I'll help."

She turns to lead the way out of the room, giving me a nice chance to stare at her butt.

One hour. Clock starts now.

Chapter 29

Olivia

"What's that smile for?"

Kelly enters my classroom with three reams of printer paper balanced in her arms in front of her, a mug filled with orange juice balanced precariously on top. I do not understand how she does this without making a mess. None of us understand it, but she hasn't had an accident to date. She bends forward and slides the pile on my desk, snatches up her mug, and turns to look at me.

"What smile?" I pick up a dull pencil and stick it in the electric sharpener, hopeful the loud buzzing will deter her line of questioning. Of course it doesn't.

She sips her juice and grins at me over the rim. "The smile that's still plastered on your face. Things look like they're going well with that Will guy. When am I going to meet him?"

Will and I are dating. I can't believe we're dating. He met my family and he didn't run. Even *I* wanted to run. But in the month since we returned from that visit to hell that accomplished nothing more than finally seeing my brother face-to-face and consequently satisfying my mother, Will hasn't left.

I drop the smile and curse myself for being so transparent, then reach for another pencil. "They're going well. And soon, I hope." Although if I'm being honest, I'm not sure that's an entirely true statement. There's something nice about keeping our relationship private—as private as one can keep it at a major-league ball field—and maybe it's the superstitious side of me, but I don't want to do anything to jinx it. "Maybe when the season is over. It won't be too much longer."

And it won't. I'd be lying if I said I'm not excited about the idea of his being available for four straight months this fall and winter. Not long ago I discovered that Will is originally from San Diego and normally spends the time off there with his family. This year he has decided to stay here. The idea that he made that decision for me does more to assuage my insecurities than anything else he could have done.

"I'll hold you to that," she says, leaning against the edge of my desk. "I did a little more digging on him, just so you know." When my eyes go wide, she holds up her hands in self-defense. "What? I know what you've told me, but I wanted to find out more about the guy my friend is dating. Besides," she says with a shrug, "it isn't every day that someone around here dates a celebrity, and I wanted to see pictures."

"He's not a celebrity." It's a stupid thing to say, because of course he is. But that isn't how I view him. Will could work a minimum-wage job and I wouldn't think less of him. In fact, I'd probably prefer it.

Kelly sets her cup on my desk and smirks. "He's a celebrity, and a pretty high-profile one at that. But he's hot as heck and seems like a decent guy. He has had a string of famous girlfriends that—"

"Do you have a point?" I say as a pencil falls from my hand. It isn't like I haven't spent time wondering what Will sees in me when he could be with almost any other more interesting woman out there. Pick a state—any state—and I'm certain a few hundred from various counties would step up in fishnets and stilettos. Why would he want to be with me? I have no idea, but here Kelly stands, echoing my own private fears.

She gives me a look. "My point is, be careful. I don't want you to get hurt. No matter how wonderful he is, I'll break both of his arms if he hurts you. And then he can kiss good-bye any hopes of continuing his career."

At that I smile. Kelly could do it. Even though she stands five foot two and has the wide-eyed innocence of an American Girl doll, she's tough. I like having friends who want to defend me. There's something nice about knowing someone would maim another individual for you. That's real friendship.

"I'll remember that. Woe to any man who crosses you."

She snatches up her mug and walks toward the door. "Tell me about it. I've made tougher men than that baseball player of yours cry." She winks. "But they all like me. What can I say?"

I roll my eyes. "Go get your room ready and stop bothering me."

She pats the doorway. "I'll be back in an hour. Want to get lunch when we're done?"

"Yes. Come get me when you're ready."

I gather up a pile of sharpened pencils and deposit them into a bin above the filing cabinet. School starts in less than two weeks, and there's still so much to do to get the classroom ready. I can feel the anxiety crawling up my insides with its sharp claws, ready to grip me by the neck. Bits of paper all over the floor. Marker streaks on the dry-erase board that I wasn't successful at completely eliminating before the break. A couple of last year's backpacks still hanging on hooks by the doorway. It isn't like me to just leave them so forlorn all summer; they should have been placed in lost and found weeks ago. So much work to do, and time is quickly running out.

I'm finding it a bit hard to breathe when I hear the soft ding of my phone from inside my purse. I pull it out, Will's name lighting up the screen in the same way his message lights up my insides.

Will: Hey beautiful. What are you doing?

My smile is ridiculous. I don't need a mirror to confirm it.

Just getting my classroom ready. It's a mess. So much to do.

Will: I was there last month and from what I know, you haven't been there since.

True, but if you could see what I see . . .

Will: Don't stress too hard. It can't be that bad. Something tells me the kids won't even notice. But hey, I've got to go. Game in three hours and we have batting practice. I'll text after.

Okay. Talk soon.

I'm still smiling, because I know he will. Text me, I mean. It's a routine that has become familiar, something I've come to depend on. It worries me a little, but not enough to stop. Will is a magnet and I am a nail. With everything in me, I find myself hoping he doesn't wind up latching onto me, flipping me around, pointing the sharp end toward my heart, and plunging it forward.

I set my phone down and sigh. It's what I do—mentally sabotage any flicker of personal happiness that comes my way. Not this time, I tell myself. This time is different. This time I'm going to overthink my circumstances less and enjoy the present more.

Besides, I'm suddenly hungry. Kelly offered lunch and I'm going to take her up on it now. I walk over to my desk and grab my purse. Just before walking out of the room I reach for the light switch and take in the room.

I think about Will's words, and for the first time, I find myself agreeing with him on this.

The room isn't that bad, and I need to stop stressing about it. It's funny how sometimes it takes just the right set of eyes to begin to see things a bit differently.

———

Will

"What's wrong?" I say to Jerry as he walks down the hotel hallway with a familiar scowl on his face. Lately it seems to be a permanent expression, something he might want to have surgically added just to make things simpler. Mouth turned down, nose crinkled, eyebrows pushed together—I'm so tired of him looking at me like this.

I jam the key card into my door and open it. All I want to do is rip off these clothes, text Olivia, and go to sleep. I'm tired and cranky despite the punishing win we delivered to the Dodgers. I've been gone three days already and it's three days too long where Olivia's concerned. I've never been one for relationships, but somehow I fell headfirst into this one and I don't even mind the concussion. I welcome it, even. Pass the Tylenol and hit me harder. Olivia is worth the pain.

"This is what's wrong." He shoves a paper at me, and I hold it to my chest for a second, wondering what I did to make him so angry. Seriously, I'm not that complicated or dramatic. As far as parties go, I'm not big on them. Take last night's, for example. Except for two minutes on the dance floor, I spent the night brooding in a corner, nursing a scotch, and cursing myself for agreeing to show. But it was for charity—children's cancer research or something along those lines—and to say no would have appeared heartless.

You can call me a lot of things, but I'm not heartless. With a sigh of exhaustion, I look at the paper in my hands.

Stupid. You can definitely call me stupid.

"What is this?" I look at Jerry and something slips. Maybe it's my pride. Maybe it's my confidence.

Maybe it's my relationship with Olivia, gone before it had much of a chance to start.

Jerry squares his shoulders. "About an hour ago I got an email. Another client telling me to get online and google your image. So I did." He scratches his nose. "This is what I found. Three pages' worth of photos just like this. Want to explain it?"

I don't. Not at all.

Last night's fund-raiser was held at the Chateau Marmont, an old Hollywood hotel located on Sunset Boulevard. The wealthy dine there. The even wealthier sleep there. The wealthiest of the wealthy are invited to fund-raisers because they have deep pockets and almost always say yes, especially when childhood cancer is involved and photographers with big connections might be there.

Photographers with big connections were there.

Lots of money was there.

Famous actors and actresses were there.

And here I am, dancing with one of the most famous in Hollywood, a girl known as much for her hookups as for her roles in blockbuster movies. Scratch that. We're not dancing. Grinding is more like it. She is facing me, my hands are on her hips, her hands are on my chest, my leg is between her thighs, expressions on both our faces like we're going at it upright, unashamed, right there in the middle of the dance floor.

The picture doesn't show that I stayed out there two minutes.

The picture doesn't show that I was just going through the motions.

The picture doesn't show that when she asked for my number, I politely declined and walked off the dance floor, then halfheartedly engaged Blake in a conversation while simultaneously cursing myself for not just sending a check instead of myself.

The picture doesn't show everything Olivia won't see.

I look like a womanizer. A guy wanting a one-night stand. A player.

And therein lies the problem, especially with her.

I am a player, and she won't be able to look past it. Not when it comes to this.

"Three pages?"

"And counting." Jerry sears me with a look. "Three months ago I wouldn't have cared. Three months ago I probably would have given you a pat on the back and told you to go after this chick. All publicity is good publicity, as they say." He props one hand against the wall and points at me with the other one. "But I like Olivia. We all like Olivia. If you're playing with her like you play with all the others, then break it off. Don't do this to her."

I scrub a hand over my face. "We were just dancing, and I didn't even finish the song before I walked off the floor." I stare at the picture again, sick at what I see. Sicker knowing what Olivia will think. "Who took this?"

"It looks professional, not like someone shot it with a cell phone. But it doesn't matter. Any idiot can tell it's you."

Any idiot is right. Me being the biggest one.

"I'll talk to Olivia. Hopefully she'll believe me."

Jerry pushes away from the wall and takes a few steps backward. "It's your relationship, but I'd hate to see you screw up a good thing. You do know you have a good thing with her, right?"

I nod and ball up the paper. The only thing I can do is nod. I have a great thing.

As long as I haven't ruined it.

Four hours later, I'm pretty certain I have my answer.

I've sent her more than twenty texts and all have gone unanswered. And we still have a game to play.

The next thirty-six hours are the longest of my life.

Chapter 30

Olivia

I pick up my phone and study it through red-rimmed eyes and even redder vision, then begin to count. One, two, seven, ten, sixteen. Eighteen texts, all sent over the last twenty minutes like he has nothing better to do than hold a phone in his hand. And those don't even count the dozens I've already deleted over the past two days, as though bombarding me with messages means I'll pay attention to anything he has to say. Truthfully, I'm barely reading them. Pretty soon I'm going to delete all of our texts—the good ones, the great ones, the sweet ones, all the messages we've exchanged in the past month—most in the middle of the night, which really are the best kind. The middle of the night is when a person's guard is down. The middle of the night is when you say things you really mean because your filter has fallen right along with your heavy eyelids. The middle of the night is when I fell for so many lies.

It's over . . . it's over . . . it's over . . .

It doesn't matter how many times I've repeated those words to myself, I'm still having trouble believing them. But I'm having no trouble believing this: she can have him, that actress he's practically mauling on the dance floor in that photo. I've seen her movies; she's not even that great a performer. Clearly her skills lie elsewhere, and Will is completely mesmerized by them.

I slam my computer closed, then begin to pace the floor. I'm surprised my living room carpet doesn't have permanent track marks with all the back and forth I've been doing from my desk to the refrigerator. Plus it's nearly dinnertime and I still haven't showered and I'm still wearing a bathrobe, completely unlike me. The last time this happened was—

I remember the weekend Perry spent with him.

I remember the tiptoeing and hiding and spying.

I'm so tired of Will Vandergriff messing up my life and rearranging my ordered existence.

With a new determination, I open a drawer in my bathroom and begin to throw things away. An old tube of lipstick that should have been tossed weeks ago. An eyeliner sharpened down to a nub. An emery board too dull to be effective. Why do I still have these things? When did I let my life get so out of control?

Four drawers and one trash bag later, I've finished this room and am contemplating beginning on another when an idea hits me. It's crazy. It goes against all the organized brain cells that make me . . . me. But in a rush of adrenaline, I decide not to care. I reach for a towel and head for the shower, determined to get the feel of Will off my skin. I spend the next twenty minutes getting dressed, making phone calls, and packing a bag. There is a week left of summer vacation, and Will comes home tonight.

I'm not going to be around when he shows up.

Before I walk out my apartment door, I turn down the air conditioner, grab Perry, and try not to worry as I look around the area one more time. Even though my kitchen cabinets are disorganized and one door is hanging open—I really should shut that; who leaves a door open for no reason?—I force myself to look away and close the apartment door. We'll only be gone a week; I can fix things later. It feels weird to be this hasty; it's something I've never done.

Yet another aspect of my personality that Will has managed to affect.

A black cloud lifts when we pull out of the parking lot. A tiny light begins to shine when I pull onto the interstate. The wind begins to blow through my cracked window when we exit Dallas. I feel free when we hit Houston. By the time my feet are in the Gulf of Mexico and I'm watching Perry play in the sand, I've almost forgotten that ballplayer I thought I was falling for.

Maybe change isn't so bad after all.

———

Will

Olivia is gone. My mouth tastes like Styrofoam.

She's been gone three days and she won't return my texts. Even worse, she sends my calls straight to voice mail. I check social media and she hasn't posted. I check my phone and there's nothing from her. I've even taken to checking the mail, hoping someone with old-fashioned values like Olivia might think to send me a letter. It's a waste of time. Something tells me she's not even sending me a thought.

This is what I get for falling into old ways. A pretty girl asks me to dance and I take her up on it. Sure, I was swayed by her fame. Absolutely by her looks. If I'm being honest, even by her body. But it took only seconds to know my heart wasn't in it. Not even the slightest spark of interest lit my insides, so I walked off the floor and left her dancing alone.

The pictures don't show that, despite what I've done to refute them. *Are you and Alicia dating, Will? No, we're not. Did you and Alicia hook up, Will? No, we didn't.* It doesn't help that for every *no* I utter, the chick in the photo exclaims a loud *yes*. If Olivia is following any of this on television or online, I'm certain she's finished with me. The fact that she won't answer my calls proves it.

I grab my keys and head to the field.

For the first time in my life, I'm even mad that we keep winning. We don't even have a losing streak I can fall back on to convince Olivia I need her to come home.

Chapter 31

Olivia

I'd like to say that I spent the week relaxing by the shore, reading a good book, and working on a tan, while a cabana boy oiled my back, brought me drinks, and fanned me as I drifted off on pleasant dreams, Perry stretched out comfortably at my feet. I'd like to say that.

What I can say is that I sat by the shore so long that I got a first-degree burn, two layers of which are currently peeling off my skin—my nose and forehead bearing a frightening resemblance to a shedding snake. I did lie by the pool until what felt like hurricane-force winds blasted through South Texas and knocked all the lawn chairs to the bottom of the deep end, my worn copy of *Jane Eyre* going in right along with them. As for Perry, the storm frightened him so much that he clawed his way to the top of my head and stayed there for a solid two minutes. And twenty pounds of cat on your head for that long results in a decent-sized bruise and several visible scratches running from cheek to collarbone. Stupid cat. I'm starting to see Will's point.

Which makes the week even worse. No matter how hard I've tried to forget the past couple of months, reminders of Will's statements . . . Will's thoughts . . . Will's humor . . . Will's eyes . . . keep coming up. In two men sitting one table over from me at a restaurant, engaged in a conversation about the Cardinals and the Cubs and how neither stand a chance against the Rangers next week. In the Polaroid of Perry that fell out of my purse when I was searching for my wallet to pay for aloe at a convenience store across the street.

I even saw reminders of him in the ocean—his eyes are a perfect match to the bluest part of it, the part by the sandbar where dolphins jumped every morning while I sipped coffee and watched resentfully from my patio.

Several times this week I wanted to swim out to them and drown myself.

Instead, I endured the reminders for five days, then slipped on a pair of sunglasses, perched Perry in the passenger seat of my car, and started driving. I'm now halfway home and wondering how in the world to avoid pulling into my parking space. I'm not ready to go back. I'm not ready to face Will. I am ready to be back in school for the distraction, but even that requires getting through the weekend. And because the devil is having a grand time making sure everything crashes together to wreak all sorts of havoc, Will's next eight games are at home. Glory hallelujah, everything about my life is going to hell.

I exit for a gas station just as my phone buzzes. I swear, the man won't leave me alone. I stopped counting when his texts hit the hundred mark, and I've done my best to ignore all subsequent ones. For some reason I check this time. I immediately wish I hadn't. It's David Nichols, the nice man I met on that ridiculous night out with Kelly. Another time, the sight of his name might cause a swarm of butterflies to take off in my stomach. Right now, the feeling resembles something more like gnats.

No one likes gnats.

They're a pain to deal with and almost impossible to swat.

```
Him: How are you?

Peachy. Yourself?

Him: Pretty good. Wondered if you wanted
to go out this weekend. Maybe catch a
movie, get drinks, see where the night
leads us . . .
```

It's the ellipsis that kills it. Every girl knows what an ellipsis means, even girls who barely date and then find themselves somehow attached to someone everyone knows is one of the world's most notorious players. It doesn't matter that Will has refuted the story, that he denies dating Alicia what's-her-name, whose movies break box-office records because the citizens of America have bad taste in entertainment. He's denied things before. The ink had barely dried on the lawsuit-that-wasn't before this new issue cropped up. And to think I fell for him and all his lies.

Hook.

Line.

And sinker.

But as for David, thoughts of him need to be tied to an anchor and dropped to the murky bottom of a river. As of now, I'm through with men. Done. Every other red-blooded, tight-skirted American woman who believes a man is what it takes to achieve a happily-ever-after can have them with my blessing.

Hopefully, in time, my heart and brain will catch up and start believing that lie. I reach for my phone and type a short reply to David.

```
Can't. Busy this weekend.
```

That's all he deserves. No man should give me three dots and expect I'll respond positively. I'm better than that. Worth more than that. Like I said, I'm done with men. At least the kind who treat me badly.

Before I make it home, my phone buzzes twelve more times. Eleven texts from Will and one from my brother. I don't bother reading any of them. Instead, I stretch my arm over the passenger seat and drop my phone to the floor. It clangs against the door and settles into obscurity. Maybe it's cracked. Maybe it's ruined. Maybe I don't care.

Like I said, I'm done with men who treat me badly. I just wish they would be done with me.

It isn't until I'm home three hours later that I see a thirteenth text. It's from Kimberly. She's asking for a favor.

She has got to be kidding me.

I type a quick reply to her question, but all I can think is . . .

Just like always, thirteen is a bad number.

Will

This is the dumbest idea anyone has ever had, but here I am agreeing to it because it's what I do—offer myself up for the absurd. I'm the bearded lady in a traveling circus sideshow. Cat sitting. Deal making. Crazy-woman dating. We might as well add one more thing to the ever-growing list of ridiculous things I keep signing up for.

"You're telling me that, in all of Dallas, there are no other available men to do this?"

"Will, it's for charity and it's you and forty others." Kimberly stands in my bedroom and straightens my tie, then pats me on the chest while Blake sits on my bed and grins like an idiot behind her. Of course he's grinning. He's married and he doesn't have to stoop to this humiliating level. Isn't there a better way to help fight leukemia? Like a raffle or paying money to shove a pie in someone's face? "Stop whining and step up to the plate," she adds.

If I had a chocolate one topped with whipped cream that I could smash on Kimberly's head right now . . .

"You can't think of a better cliché than that? And what are you smiling at?" I growl at Blake. "If I have to do this, you should too. And don't use the 'I'm married' excuse because no one cares."

"I care," Kimberly protests.

Blake's hands go up. "Dude, I *am* married. What would that look like?"

"It would look typical. You could just join the club of all the skanky athletes with women on the side."

"Hey!" Kimberly slaps my arm and scowls. "Not everyone is like that. Not even most. You're just mad because we won't let you stay home and mope all night. It's time to get over it and move on. Who knows, maybe you'll meet your soul mate tonight."

I try not to roll my eyes. "On the other side of a speed-dating table? I doubt it. That'd be kind of like meeting my soul mate on a street corner on Hollywood Boulevard."

"It happened in *Pretty Woman*," Kimberly says, examining her fingernails.

"Except I'm not Richard Gere, and I'd rather not fall for a hooker."

"Wouldn't be the worst thing you've done," she mutters. "Great attitude, by the way. You're doing this for kids' cancer." She looks over her shoulder. "Alright, Blake, he's all yours."

Okay, well now I feel a little bad. But only a little.

"Lucky me," Blake says. They both sound as enthusiastic as if they'd just been handed a wiggling, screaming newborn to deal with all evening. Well, I'm not screaming and I'm certainly not fidgeting, but how in the heck I got talked into speed dating, I'll never understand. *These women paid a lot of money,* Kimberly said when she asked me. *It's for the children. Children with leukemia,* she added, emphasizing that last word in four very strong syllables to make me feel extra guilty. It worked. Of course it worked. And now, just because a bunch of chicks I don't even know paid one thousand dollars each for the chance to go on a date with me and thirty-nine other single ballplayers in the great state of Texas, I'm stuck.

It's only been two weeks since I've seen Olivia. I'm not ready to go on another date, especially not a fake one.

Why does it seem like fake dating is all I do lately? It's practically become a second career, with no financial benefits.

"Let's go help the kids," I say to no one in particular. My feet are literally dragging as we walk out of my bedroom. "Where is this place?"

"It's at the Hilton Hollywood Boulevard," Kimberly says, giggling into her hand. Of course it is. "What a coincidence," she says. "Though I'm pretty sure I've told you this at least a dozen times already."

I reach for the doorknob and look at Blake. "Dude, control your wife. She's being awfully condescending tonight."

He laughs as they both follow me out the front door. "Wouldn't have it any other way."

Chapter 32

Olivia

"No, schoolteachers aren't poor. Depending on the district, we actually do quite well." I'm lying a little, but seriously. What kind of question is that? It's an insult to teachers everywhere, and not all of them are as nice as me.

"Have you ever thought about trying a different career? Maybe something like interior decorating or web design?" he asks.

I swing my leg a little and try to unclench my fists. "I didn't get a college degree for that. Do you have a thing for designers or something?"

"No, it's just that a couple of my buddies have dated women in the design field and they seemed cool. Sexy for sure."

"And schoolteachers can't be sexy?" I don't mean for it to sound like a question, but how have the tables turned here? "Besides, I thought I was the one who's supposed to be asking the questions."

He shrugs. "Ask me a question."

And here's a problem: I don't exactly have one ready. Because I still don't want to be here, but I was forced against my will. I look over my shoulder. Where is Kimberly anyway?

"Um . . . I'm sorry." *Think of something, Olivia.* "What position do you play?" Not exactly a stroke of genius, but it's all I can think of under pressure.

"I don't. I'm the mascot for the Mavericks."

I scratch my arm and try not to point out the shortcomings of this revelation. "And I'm sure that's a very respectable career. So why don't we just agree that both our careers are something to be proud of and move on from here."

He shrugs. "If you say so. It's just . . . schoolteachers aren't my thing. In my experience, they're kind of mean."

I fist the paper in my hand and stand. "It was nice to meet you. Maybe the next woman will be more what you're looking for."

He opens his mouth to say something, but I don't give him the chance before I walk away and set my sights on Kimberly. She's next to the bar, holding the Coke she offered to get me before this started. I snatch it out of her hand and take a sip.

"I may never speak to you again after this. A pity, since we've only spent a grand total of twelve days together, and I actually found myself enjoying them."

"Oh, would you stop whining?" she says, then mutters something else under her breath. If I didn't know better, I might think she just said something about Will. As it stands and if she did, I don't want to know about it.

This place is fancy, not exactly my dream location for meeting Mr. Right or Wrong or Anyone-Who-Isn't-Will-Vandergriff, especially considering I'm a schoolteacher who spends half her day worried about some child giving me lice or worse. Anyone but Will, that's pretty much my only criterion. Though at one thousand dollars—which Kimberly paid before she asked if I would come, giving me no choice in the matter—I guess Will wouldn't be so bad. I wish he'd paid the money. I wish I could at least have the satisfaction of knowing I could go on a very expensive date with him and not feel bad about it. As it stands, he's not even here.

I stir the ice with my straw and take another sip, then crunch on an ice cube. It's loud and obnoxious and a couple of heads turn, but I'm a schoolteacher. Everyone knows they aren't classy.

"I'm not whining."

"Stop chewing on ice; it's bad for your teeth. And, yes, you are whining. There's a lot of that going around tonight," she mutters.

"From who?"

She goes still. "From who what?"

There's something about her expression. It's frozen, caught. I don't like it and find myself scanning the room. "Who else is whining?"

She flutters away my question with her hand. "Everyone here. Now, how many men do you have left to go through? Found anyone you like yet?" In a very quick change of subject, she peers over my shoulder at the paper in my hand and studies the names. I watch her for a moment longer and then give up. I've never been that great at analyzing people anyway.

"That guy was a jerk," I say, nodding my head to the left. "Number four wasn't awful, but I'm not sure how he felt about me." Barry is a little on the short side, with a receding hairline, but he's an assistant coach for the Dallas Mavericks—a step up from the mascot—is built nicely, of course, and has a very charming smile. His voice is slightly nasal, probably from some sort of allergy, because doesn't everyone have them this time of year? But even if this is his natural voice, a girl can't have everything, I suppose. People can't always help the way they sound.

"And then number nine was okay. Divorced three times, but—"

"No," she says, snatching the paper out of my hand. "He's probably paying alimony and child support all over the place. What about number seven? He's pretty good looking, and Blake has met him before. He plays for the Astros, so what's not to like?"

He's a baseball player, for one thing, but I can't say that. Besides, she sure is pushy tonight. For someone who's supposed to be good friends with Will, she's practically thrusting me with both hands into the arms of someone else. Or at least trying to. Maybe Will is an even bigger jerk than I thought. Sad, since I was starting to believe his statements that the pictures weren't telling the whole truth . . . that maybe he really didn't do anything with Alicia what's-her-name, and what kind of name is Alicia? It's gratey and whiny and hardly respectable. Ask any female with brains and she would probably tell you the same thing.

"His name is Kevin," I say, as if that explains my bad mood, the drizzly weather, and the fact that the Texas mosquito population is at an all-time high. Kimberly just looks at me.

"What's wrong with the name Kevin?"

"I just don't like it."

Really, I just don't like this and I don't like the fact that Will isn't here. Why isn't he here? My arms become fidgety, and my fingers begin to scratch at things, and I really hoped he would be here.

Kimberly sighs. "Well, you were matched up with fifteen men, so you still have four more to go." She hands me back my paper. "And since that lady finally stopped talking and stood up, that guy's free. Not bad looking either. Plus, his name is John. Any issues with that name?" I give my head a shake, and she gives me a little shove. "Then go get him."

I take a couple steps away and then turn to look at her. "Don't you know most of these men already? You should just tell me which one to choose and make my life easier."

She looks to the left, then the right, then finally at me. That expression. Those fluttering hands. Both are making me nervous for some reason I can't pinpoint. "Of course I don't know them. It's not like all I do is hang out with athletes." She plants a hand on her hip and gives a nervous laugh. "Some of them play basketball, Olivia."

Half the men here play for the Rangers, she and Blake have no kids, and Kimberly works part-time only when the season is over. During the season, she travels with Blake. All Kimberly does is hang out with athletes. My suspicions double while I'm standing there.

When she says nothing else, I walk over to guy number twelve. My heart isn't in this anyway. He could be the most charming, wonderful, charismatic man I've ever met, but when the night is over, I'll wind up telling him to find someone else. Thanks but no thanks. I'm not your girl. There's a thousand dollars well spent.

Ten minutes later I find out I was right. The guy asked for my phone number. Right before he asked how I felt about open relationships. He has two girlfriends—two!—one based in Atlanta and another who lives in Boston, but he told me he's looking for someone closer to home. Closer to home, as if convenience would be the primary factor for me. As if I would feel like a golden chosen girl because I live only ten miles from the stadium. After a rather loud *no thank you* to the man, I snatched up my paper and stalked off. Now I'm back at Kimberly's side, thinking how lucky she is to already be married and finished with these kinds of humiliating situations.

"Okay, I'm done. Thank you for trying, and I swear I'll pay you back all the money you spent. But I can't take it anymore. Most of these men are nice, but none are for me. Now where do I go to get my bag?"

Kimberly's eyes go wide as she latches onto my arm. "You can't go yet. You only have three more to get through. Give them five minutes, that's all."

"I don't think I can take another five minutes of anyone. If you knew what some of them are asking me—"

"And you can tell me after this is over." She pulls the paper from my hand again. "Now, table thirteen is just around the corner. Go over there and see what that guy is like."

"Kimberly, I—"

"For me, Olivia? If he's as bad as the rest, I'll grab Blake and we'll go get takeout. You can pick the place, I swear. Just one more."

I give her a look, take a long pull on my soda, and hand her the glass. "Stay here. I'll be back in two minutes. Three, tops." With a long-suffering sigh, I force my feet forward and around the corner to guy number thirteen.

I should have known she was up to something.

Will

I should have known they were up to something. As soon as she rounds the corner I see it in her face, the same stunned expression I can feel on my own. But stunned gives way to impatience and then anger. At the situation. At the setup. At me. She stops in front of the table and raises her chin a notch, then another. She doesn't even attempt to sit down.

"Of course you're table thirteen. I'm an idiot for not figuring it out sooner."

"So am I, and I'm sorry. If I'd known you were coming here I would have—"

"You would have what? Brought a date? Made sure to have some bombshell on your arm so that you could really humiliate me?"

I stand quickly and reach for her hand. My chair scrapes against the tile floor. "Olivia, I wasn't trying to humiliate you. That dance, that party, it wasn't what it looked like. I didn't leave with her. We didn't hook up. It was one dance. Not even one dance. Like, half a dance." My voice has risen and people are turning to look, but I don't care. Out of the corner of my eye, I see Kimberly standing with her hands clasped, taking in the scene. She's a cross between worried about us and irritated with me. Join the freaking club.

Olivia rips her hand away and runs it across her middle as though trying to erase the feel of my skin. "So you keep saying. The problem is, I don't believe you. Our entire relationship is based on lies. You only wanted me around to clean up your reputation. What's to say you're not lying right now?" She's doing a good job of putting up an angry front, but I see it. Even if no one else can see it, I do. Olivia is hurt, and I'm the cause.

I flick a glance at Kimberly. There's no mistaking her expression now. Now she's just mad.

"Because I'm not lying. Please believe me. Please give me another chance."

It hits me then—she's going to leave, and I'm going to lose her. Will Vandergriff—the man who never begs a woman to stay—finally got caught by a woman who is making it her mission to shake him off. I can see it in her eyes. Olivia's grown cold; she's not buying any of what I'm saying. She picks up her paper and folds it in half.

"Sorry, Will. I'm done playing games. I'm done with your indecision, I'm done being just another woman on your arm, I'm done with tonight, and I'm done with baseball." She smiles. There's not a trace of amusement on her face. "Thirteen. Will there ever be a day when that number doesn't haunt me?"

It's a rhetorical question, one that doesn't require an answer.

Even if it did, I wouldn't be able to respond.

Because Olivia just walked out and took my brain, my ability to speak, and my heart with her.

Chapter 33

Olivia

School has started, and it's been a nice distraction. We've been in class eleven days now, not counting weekends, and I've been so busy that I barely even remember what happened this summer. I remember spending a lot of time outdoors, I remember being sweaty, I remember making new friends. I remember loud music . . .

Really, there's not much to recall.

The kids this year are just a joy. Pure love and light that add so much richness to my day. Take Landon for instance. He's smart and inquisitive and funny and has a real knack for soccer. He stands out on our school's intramural league, even if he is only in fourth grade. Among most of the spectators on the field on Saturday mornings—myself included, because Perry loves to be outside, especially in mud puddles, a new thing for him and an irritation for me—there's already talk of him being a standout in high school. Landon reminds me so much of my brother that—

Anyway, Landon's a good kid.

As is Avery, whom I continue to see a few times a week when I drop off packages for his family. They're all doing a bit better—the boys now have their younger sister living with them, and his father has a single full-time job that pays enough to keep food on the table. Now my drop-offs often consist of things like new shirts, new shoes, and the occasional package of socks. But it works. They seem much healthier. Definitely happier.

I can't help but remember the one thing that would have made Avery really happy. More than happy. And my only regret is that I'll never be able to fulfill it . . . that second condition on my requirement list with—

Enough thinking about regrets. I don't believe in them.

As for Perry, we never did get around to those Mommy and Me cat day-camp classes, since I was distracted doing . . . other things. So we enrolled for fall classes. We've only been twice so far, but he loves them. There's a jungle gym for him to climb and catnip toys for him to play with. There's a calico named Tasha that he hates, but I just chalk that up to the animal being typically female. I don't normally have such a sexist attitude, but in this case the parents need to train their cat better. I am the only cat parent who stays for the class, which I find disturbing. Cats need attention just as much as toddlers, and what kind of parent would drop a toddler off at camp? But no matter. I stay. It's only an hour, and Perry thrives on the attention. With pets—as I'm sure is true with children—it's all about staying consistent. And present. Some people just haven't learned this yet, I suppose.

Life with a cat is just awesome.

Oh, and I enrolled in a photography class at the community college. We meet on Tuesday nights at seven, and my teacher says I'm a natural. I've learned so much about focus and angles and resolution and megapixels, and I just love it. It's a nice way to better myself. To deepen my interest in a lifelong hobby. I have no idea why I didn't think to pursue it until now. I probably should have decided to do it the moment we were at my mother's house, looking through that drawer of old photos in my bedroom and—

You know, life in general is just awesome.

I did take David up on his request for a date. I called him up after I got home from the speed-dating thing that I've managed to completely block from my memory and told him I'd misunderstood his first inquiry. I didn't mention the ellipsis. It didn't seem appropriate and, really, I figured he didn't mean it quite as harshly as I took it. Plus, some people don't enjoy being the subject of impromptu English lessons.

But an ellipsis can mean many things. Like, the night could lead us to a movie . . . to ice cream . . . to a scenic drive through the city. We never wound up doing any of those things, but we have been out twice since then, and he really is as lovely as I remembered from the night we met. His manners are impeccable, and he's a pharmacist. Did I mention that he's a pharmacist? There's a lot that goes into becoming a pharmacist. So many drugs to memorize and so many medical terms to keep straight. And the measurements. The measurements alone can be exhausting, really grating on a person's nerves by the end of the day.

David is just lovely.

I've never seen him without a tie and dress slacks. I'm not sure he owns a sweatshirt. I can't imagine him in sneakers. Definitely not in a ball cap. He doesn't strike me as the type to play sports or even wear sports attire.

There are so many advantages to dating a pharmacist.

I have kept in contact with Kimberly. She tells me the play-offs are next week, though why she thinks I would be interested in that information is anyone's guess. In the past two weeks we've gone to dinner a time or two. She's kept me posted on her life, and I have to admit it sounds exciting. I might be jealous of her if I were into that sort of thing. You know, sports and other things sports-related. She's kept me posted on a few other things as well . . . things I haven't even had to ask her about. Kimberly has some very strong opinions. Mainly about my choices. About my attitude. My attitude is fine.

It really is nice dating a pharmacist. Have I mentioned that?

———

Will

Life sucks and I hate it. And maybe that's an awful attitude, but I'm not exactly asking for opinions here. It's been over two weeks since I've seen or heard from Olivia, unless you count the times I've pressed my face against my living room window to get a glimpse of her, on the off chance we're home at the same time, which has been only once. And even though we only dated for a month—real dated; I'm not talking about the fake-date thing because that puts us at more like three months and she would never let me count it—I've had more than enough of her absence. The woman managed to get under my skin, and women never get under my skin. It's a personal life rule. One, put socks on left and then right. Two, show up on time to meetings, practice, and games. Three, own up to my mistakes. Eventually. And four, steer clear of commitment.

Right now, commitment is the only thing I want.

I miss the days of thinking she was crazy.

For that reason and that reason alone I decided to throw another party tomorrow night after the game. If Olivia refuses to see me, she'll have to listen to me. If she refuses to return my calls and texts, she can accept her fate of dealing with a bunch of loud music.

Olivia likes her sleep. That's one thing I learned about her.

Too bad tomorrow night she's not going to get any.

Suddenly feeling in an upbeat mood that might have a little to do with annoying the chick who refuses to get out of my head, I fist my car keys and head for the door.

I'm out of soda, and I need to buy some.

And while I'm at it, I think I'll pick up some new speakers. Ones that get really loud. Like, a million decibels that will reverberate through the walls.

Straight through my living room to Olivia's bedroom.

Good luck sleeping, lady.

Chapter 34

Olivia

I barely make it into bed before it starts. Music. The worst kind of music—the kind that vibrates against the floor, pounds through the walls, rattles across the ceiling, and shakes my bedroom fan, then ricochets into my head. It takes two seconds for me to have a headache. It takes three seconds for me to be blazing mad. He's hosted exactly two parties since I met him, and it's no coincidence that he's having one now.

I throw back my blankets and launch myself out of bed. Stupid nonexistent property owner rules. Will must have paid the fine up front, and now nothing will be done to stop him. Except me. I'll stop him. I reach for a T-shirt and tug it over my head, then pace the bedroom floor, recalling Kimberly's latest words and trying to decide what to do.

He really does care about you, you know. You might find it hard to believe, considering his reputation, but Will was happy with you. He smiled when he was around you. Will doesn't smile around women unless he's trying to put on a show. Unless he's trying to bide his time until the night is over. Will always smiled with you. Will smiled just talking about you. I saw his face when you walked out of the fund-raiser. He was devastated, Olivia. I've never seen him look like that.

She said more. Much more. Each word like a nail being driven into the fence posts around my heart: one strike, two strikes, three, until they were in danger of toppling over. And as I've done every day since hearing those words, I find myself wondering if I was wrong. What if he was telling the truth about that actress? Worse, what if the last few weeks have found him moved on and dating other women? Worse still, and this thought jolts me to a stop in the middle of my bedroom floor—what if he's not hosting a party after all, and he's actually in his apartment with another woman right now?

That last thought makes me mad and gets my feet moving. How dare he forget about me that fast. I haven't forgotten about him.

I don't even like pharmacists.

Within seconds I formulate a plan, one that I should probably think through a bit more before implementing. But I forgo a plan and go with my instinct. Four months ago, I didn't know I possessed much of an instinct, or if I did, there wasn't time to consider it around the schedules and organizations and charts and graphs I lived by. Tonight, it's time for spontaneous. Tonight, I'm grasping instinct and tugging it by the hand.

I catch a glimpse of myself in my bedroom mirror and roll my eyes.

No one said spontaneous had to be pretty.

I grab my cat and head to the kitchen, then yank open the closest drawer.

And then, hammer in hand, I march out the front door.

Will

The first song isn't over before it starts. Maybe she's kicking with both feet, or maybe she's pounding with two angry fists; either way, she's taking out her aggression on my front door, and I find it amusing. I should probably stop her before serious damage is done to the finish, but I'm having fun listening to her temper tantrum and imagining her wild-eyed anger, that blonde hair falling in her face and swinging in all directions.

I force myself to stop thinking about the hair and instead focus on Olivia getting giant purple bruises on her hands. That's much easier.

Maybe unfair, but Olivia brought this on herself.

If she had only believed me, she wouldn't be out there hurting unknown body parts while I stand inside and smile about it. I lean against the wall and take in the scene all around me. This party has sucked. This whole night has sucked. The past two weeks have sucked, and judging by the sound of Olivia's fists, the suckage isn't going to end anytime soon.

"What is that sound?" Ricky asks, walking over with a beer in his hand and a swagger in his step.

I shrug. "It's Olivia. She's mad because of the music, but I'm letting her sweat a little. Frankly, I'm enjoying it." I smile. I've smiled a lot in the past few minutes. Not as much in the last couple of weeks, but it's nice to feel it return.

Ricky takes a slow sip of beer and swallows. "It sounds like someone is destroying your front door, dude."

At that, my eyes go wide and I push off the wall. Olivia is angry. Olivia is angry at me. Though that might be enough to make a fair amount of the female population do crazy things—threaten a lawsuit, claim a fake affair—I have no idea what it might do to Olivia. She's . . . well . . . crazy. At least she used to be. Maybe she still is. Maybe she's insane and ripping apart my expensive mahogany door with a screw-driver and—

The door is open and we're face-to-face.

Yep, she's mad.

"What are you doing and why is the music so loud?" She doesn't even try to be civil. She's holding a hammer in one hand and Perry in the other. One glance at the front door tells me she was kicking it. No real damage to be seen except a white scuff mark at the bottom—no wood splinters or holes in the panels. With a quiet sigh of thanksgiving, I look at her and try not to notice the way my heart thuds. Wild-eyed and disheveled, she glares up at me while I force my face to harden and take in her appearance. Her T-shirt is inside out and she's wearing familiar blue flannel pants. Her hair tumbles over her forehead and slides down her shoulders just like I imagined. Her curls are wild and tangled and messy. She looks like she just rolled out of bed.

My mouth goes dry.

I've never seen her look so beautiful.

I scrub a hand over my face, because it's just so typically Olivia, then peer at her through the slits in my fingers.

"I'm having a party. Want to come in?"

I don't expect her to nod. I don't expect her to move past me and into my living room. When she reaches the middle of the floor, she turns to face me. If she's aware of how out of place she looks, she doesn't seem to care. My lips itch with a desire to kiss her. The way she stands out among this gathering . . . it turns me on.

She sets Perry down and palms the hammer. "Where are your speakers?"

"What do you mean, where are my speakers? Are you going to smash them?"

She sighs dramatically. "Yes, I'm going to smash them. Unless you end this party right now and tell everyone to get out, that's exactly what I'm going to do."

I take a couple steps toward her, facing an opponent. It's nothing I haven't done before. "You sound crazy. You can't just come in here and threaten to ruin my property. Get out."

"I've been called worse, even by you. Now make everyone leave or I'm going to start swinging. What's it going to be, Will? What's it going to be?"

She's serious. When I see her scan the room and lock her sights on the new speakers I dropped a lot of money on just last night for the sole intent of annoying her—what do you know, it worked—I know she's serious. With a growl that can't be heard over the noise, I walk over and turn off the stereo, then make an announcement that everyone should go home. Everyone turns to look at me like I've lost my mind, and maybe I have. After all, it's common knowledge that you eventually take on the personalities of the people you hang around most. For me and Olivia, that pretty much adds up to a two-person gathering of the insane.

Five minutes later, we're alone.

The apartment is a mess, and I remember why I hate parties, and Perry is licking pizza grease off a paper plate that's lying in the middle of the carpet, and any minute now I fully expect Olivia to start screaming about it.

But we're alone.

Olivia drops the hammer. "I'm sorry."

At first I don't think I hear her right, and I tilt my head. "For what?"

She looks at me with sad eyes—basset hound eyes, though I probably shouldn't say that out loud—and sighs. "For everything. For not believing you. For thinking you would go on the road and get together with some other girl so quickly."

Quickly is the wrong term. I take a step toward her. "Time has nothing to do with it. I wouldn't get with another girl at all. Not after you, Olivia. There isn't a single woman on the planet who compares to you."

Her mouth twitches. I swallow a smile when I see it. What do you know, this girl likes compliments. "Darn right there isn't. After you've had crazy, who wants normal?"

I move a little closer still. Something tells me thoughts of that hammer and smashing things are over. I'm pretty sure my head and body are safe. "Not me. Certainly not me."

Olivia glances at the floor and makes a face at her cat. His whiskers are dripping with spilled soda, and there's a tiny speck of crushed potato chip on his back. But at least she doesn't scream, just gives him a long look before locking eyes with me. "You're going to have to help bathe him, you know."

When her arms reach around my neck, in that moment I know I'll do anything she wants. "We'll bathe him later. Just give me a minute." I lean in to kiss her, but she moves her head back and frowns up at me. I'm not going to lie; it's more than a little disappointing.

"What?" I say.

"You called me crazy."

I grin. "For a minute there, you were acting like it."

She shrugs and leans in. "Fair enough."

And when Olivia kisses me . . .

Man, when Olivia kisses me . . .

I'll admit it.

In that single second, I officially lose my mind.

Chapter 35

Will

"I can't believe this was your second requirement."

"That's because you were thinking in complicated terms. It's what I wanted all along."

"You realize I would have done this at the beginning, right? I knew a few people back then. I could have pulled a few strings a lot earlier than today."

She smiles. "I know you could have. But where would the fun in that have been? Without my last requirement, you might have lost interest a long time ago."

This woman. When is she ever going to get it? I know we've only officially dated for two months, and that's if you don't count the two weeks when we sort of broke up, but I don't plan to ever lose interest. I'm getting more interested every day. This time next year, I plan to be fully interested. And fully invested.

Speaking of, engagement rings cost a fortune. A small investment in themselves.

Anyway, what were we talking about?

"I wouldn't have lost interest. But this is a little easier now that the season is over."

And yes, the season is over. We made it to the American League Championship Series before losing to the Mariners in game five. The Mariners. The loss hurts even more because the Mariners haven't made it that far in years, and they have never made it to the World Series at all. It's an easier pill to swallow when you at least lose to a team that stands a chance.

"Then get to it, Thirteen. Go out there and give him a chance to see what it feels like."

Thirteen. This is my new nickname. Olivia christened me with it the night we made up last month. And in case you're wondering, the nickname has nothing to do with my number. It has everything to do with our little speed-dating night and her thirteenth chance to make a match.

Lucky for me, I was the guy given that number.

"Fine. You coming with us or staying here in the stands?"

She answers me by sitting down and stretching her feet across the seat in front of her. She smiles up at me. Even though it's nighttime, the whole world just got a little brighter.

"I think I'll stay here and watch."

I smile. "Okay. You ready, kiddo?"

"I'm ready," Avery says, swallowing. The kid is nervous. It's his first time in a ballpark, though according to Olivia he loves the game. Apparently he's never actually been to a game because his father can't afford it. Good thing I have connections. I already have passes set aside to give them for next season.

I walk with Avery to home plate and hand him a catcher's mitt. Before we arrived, I asked him what position he wanted to play tonight. He said catcher, so I ran into the locker room and grabbed a glove. The chest protector and face mask are way too big for his small frame, but I won't throw too hard. He won't get hurt.

Once he's situated, I walk toward the pitcher's mound. On my way there, I look up into the stands for another glimpse of Olivia. She isn't there. I grow alarmed for a second, but then I look around and spot her.

With a grin, I shake my head. She's come a long way. Longer than she even knows.

The last thing I see before getting into position is Olivia. She's across the field and circling a mud puddle. It hasn't rained in days, but somehow she managed to find one. I give her five minutes before she's walking through the middle of it. Like mother, like . . . cat, I guess.

With a laugh to myself, I set my sights on Avery.

Aim.

Wind up.

And throw.

ACKNOWLEDGMENTS

First, I want to thank my readers. You've come with me on a journey of "What the heck is she going to write next?" and I appreciate you for sticking with me. I know my stories vary from book to book—some silly, some lighthearted, some pretty serious—but hopefully they've been entertaining and marginally well written. I owe you my career and will forever be grateful to each one of you.

And now I'd like to thank everyone who had a hand in this book— my close friends, family, beta readers, and those who help to keep my life together.

To Vance Wilson, my neighbor and friend. If I didn't know you, this book would not exist. When I told my editor, "I think I'll write a book about baseball because I have a neighbor who played professionally and now he manages, so it shouldn't be that hard . . ." I didn't realize what a stupid statement I was making. This book was hard. Really hard. I got next to zero baseball details right in the first draft, but because of your help, guidance, kindness, and willingness to temporarily turn in your man card and read a romance, it was finally in publishable shape. You're a good soul, and I appreciate you more than you'll ever know— even though I still don't see why a pitcher can't play every single game in a season. Wouldn't that be easier? Plus they wouldn't have to pay as many people. Someone should totally change that rule. Thanks for everything, dude. I enjoyed the process. Any mistakes still in existence belong solely to me.

To Nicole Deese, my soul sister and friend. Thanks for reading my awful early drafts, for telling me what worked and what needed to be fixed, for sending me songs and texts, for being willing to talk on the phone after midnight, for making me laugh and cry (in a good way). But most of all, thanks for being you and for your ability to understand and relate to my weird mind and heart. Your friendship means everything.

To Jessica Kirkland, my fantastic agent. You make my life easier to manage and much saner to live through. Thanks for taking a chance on me four years ago. I couldn't do one minute of this without you and your friendship, and I wouldn't ever want to.

To Tami Kirkpatrick for being a consistent friend through all my changes in career, ups and downs in life, and mood swings caused by both. Thanks for not getting mad when I named a villain in my last book after you. Also thanks for the walks and talks and for lending an ear, even though you probably get tired of hearing my constant whining. But life is hard. And book writing is hard. And raising kids is hard. And cooking dinner is hard. And . . . thanks, friend. Love you much. Let's go for a walk in the rain.

To Stacy Henagan for the leash idea. I'm not sure I've ever laughed as hard as I did the night you mentioned it, but I am pretty sure I still have a bruise on my elbow from falling off the bed. Love you always, sweet friend.

To Joy Francoeur. Even though you didn't help on this book, you've helped on all my others and I'll need you for more in the future. Thanks for your never-ending encouragement. I appreciate you.

To Rel Mollet once again. Thanks for your encouragement, help, and kind words. Someday I'm going to visit you in Australia. Partly to see where you live, but mainly because I want you to take me to an Australian coffee shop so a cute barista with a cool accent can call me "love." Wouldn't that be fun?

To my editors Amy Hosford, Erin Calligan Mooney, Faith Black Ross, and Amanda Gibson for signing me, for cleaning up the original mess I made of this manuscript, and for understanding and supporting my vision for the book. Working with such a talented group of women has been a great experience, one I'll never forget.

To my publishers at Waterfall Press. I can't thank you enough for welcoming me onto your team and for the support you have given me. From inception to cover to publication, it's all been rewarding and fun. Thanks for bringing me along for the ride.

And finally to my parents, sisters, husband, and kids. Family is everything, and I'm so glad that you're mine. I love you all.

ABOUT THE AUTHOR

Photo © Kathy Mahue

Amy Matayo is the award-winning author of *The Wedding Game, Love Gone Wild, Sway, In Tune with Love, A Painted Summer,* and *The End of the World.* She graduated, with barely passing grades, from John Brown University, earning a degree in journalism. But don't feel sorry for her—she's superproud of that degree and all the ways she hasn't put it to good use.

Matayo laughs often, cries easily, feels deeply, and loves hard. She lives in Arkansas with her husband and four kids and is working on her next novel. Visit her website at www.amymatayo.com to find out more.

Made in the USA
Lexington, KY
15 November 2016